SURVIVING THE WILD

SUNNY
THE SHARK

BY REMY LAI

HENRY HOLT AND COMPANY
NEW YORK

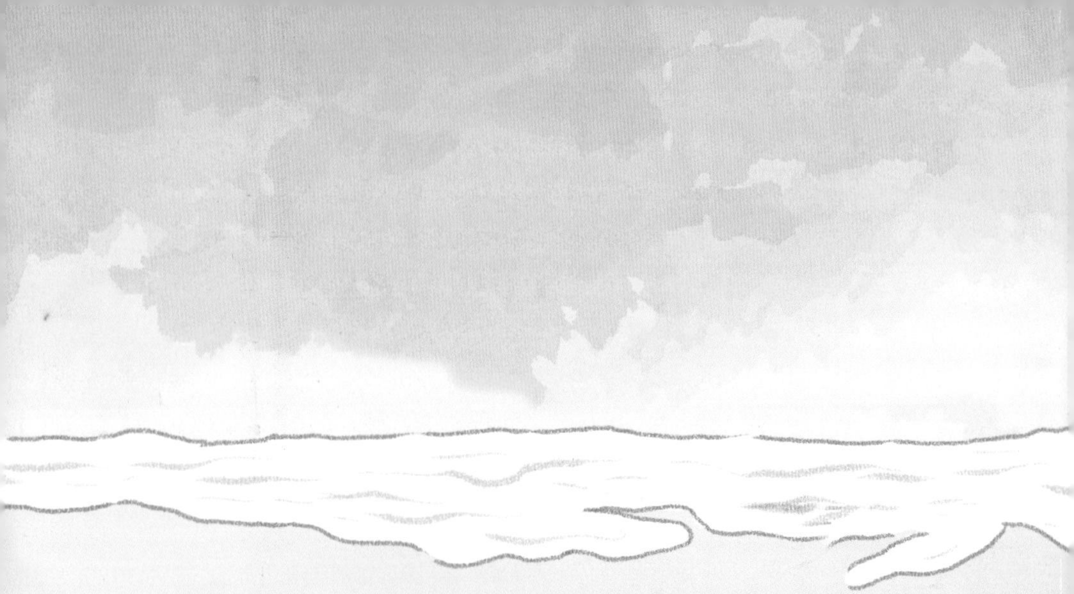

I ACKNOWLEDGE THAT THIS BOOK WAS
WRITTEN AND ILLUSTRATED IN BRISBANE, AUSTRALIA,
ON WHICH THE TURRBAL AND JAGERA PEOPLES ARE THE
TRADITIONAL CUSTODIANS OF THEIR RESPECTIVE LAND.
I PAY MY RESPECT TO THEIR ELDERS,
PAST, PRESENT, AND EMERGING.

HENRY HOLT AND COMPANY, PUBLISHERS SINCE 1866
HENRY HOLT® IS A REGISTERED TRADEMARK OF MACMILLAN PUBLISHING GROUP, LLC
120 BROADWAY, NEW YORK, NY 10271
MACKIDS.COM

OUR BOOKS MAY BE PURCHASED IN BULK FOR PROMOTIONAL, EDUCATIONAL, OR BUSINESS USE.
PLEASE CONTACT YOUR LOCAL BOOKSELLER OR THE MACMILLAN CORPORATE AND
PREMIUM SALES DEPARTMENT AT (800) 221-7945 EXT. 5442
OR BY EMAIL AT MACMILLANSPECIALMARKETS@MACMILLAN.COM.

LIBRARY OF CONGRESS CATALOGING-IN-PUBLICATION DATA IS AVAILABLE.

FIRST EDITION, 2022
DESIGNED BY LISA VEGA
PRINTED IN CHINA BY RR DONNELLEY ASIA PRINTING SOLUTIONS LTD., DONGGUAN CITY, GUANGDONG PROVINCE

ISBN 978-1-250-78545-9 (HARDCOVER)
1 3 5 7 9 10 8 6 4 2

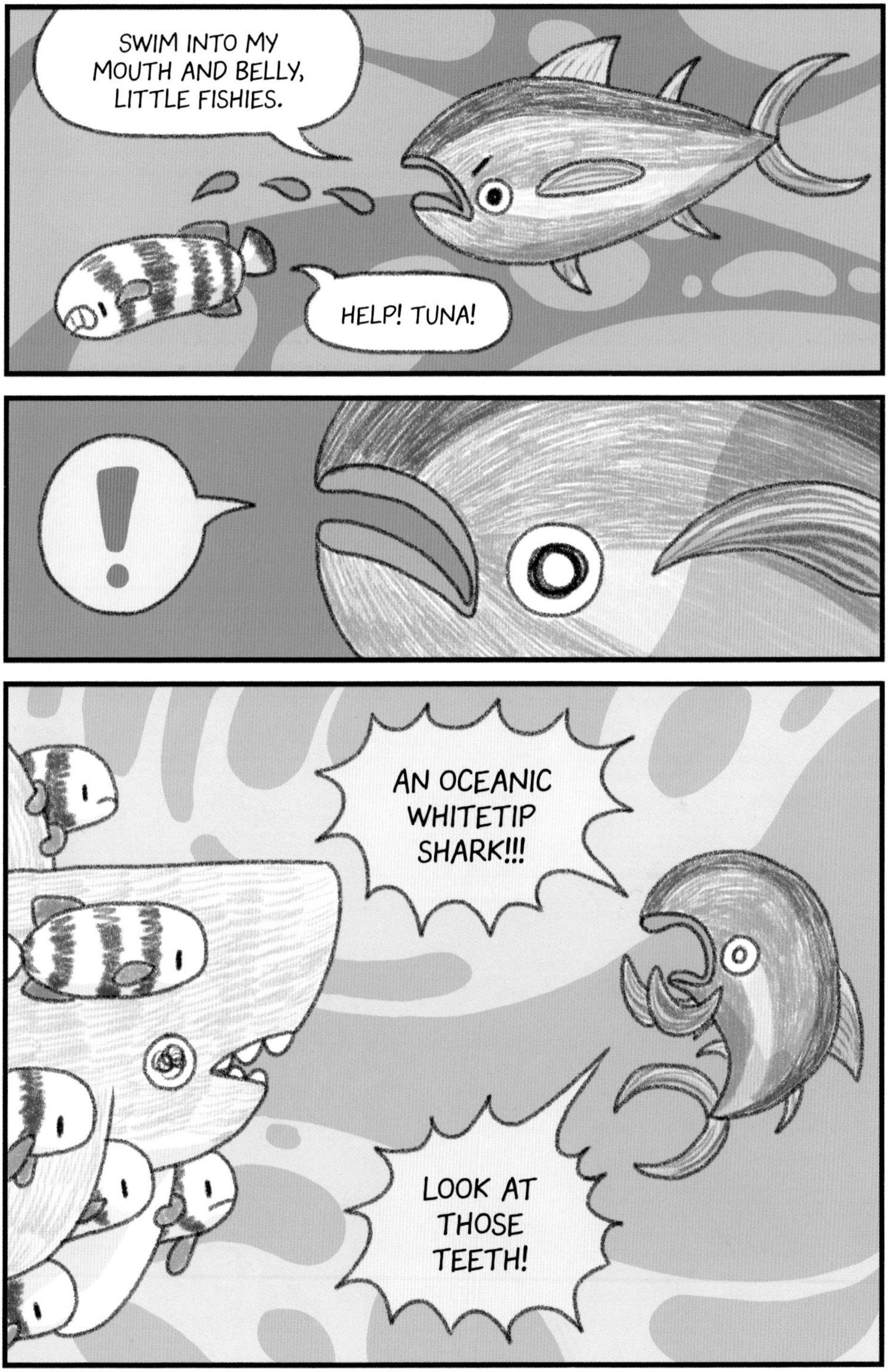
SWIM INTO MY MOUTH AND BELLY, LITTLE FISHIES.
HELP! TUNA!
!
AN OCEANIC WHITETIP SHARK!!!
LOOK AT THOSE TEETH!

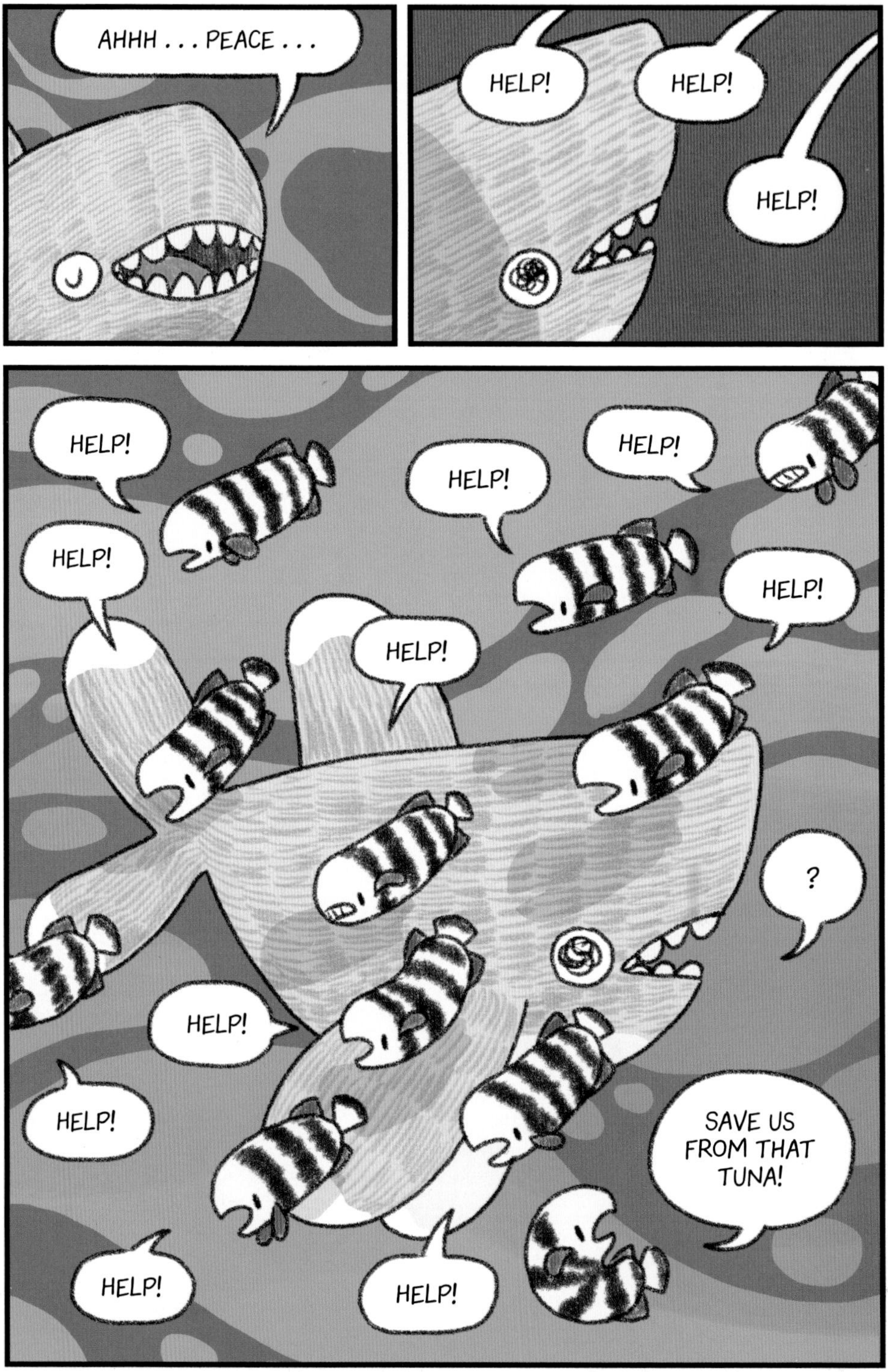
AHHH . . . PEACE . . .
HELP!
HELP!
HELP!
HELP!
HELP!
HELP!
HELP!
HELP!
HELP!
?
HELP!
HELP!
SAVE US FROM THAT TUNA!
HELP!
HELP!

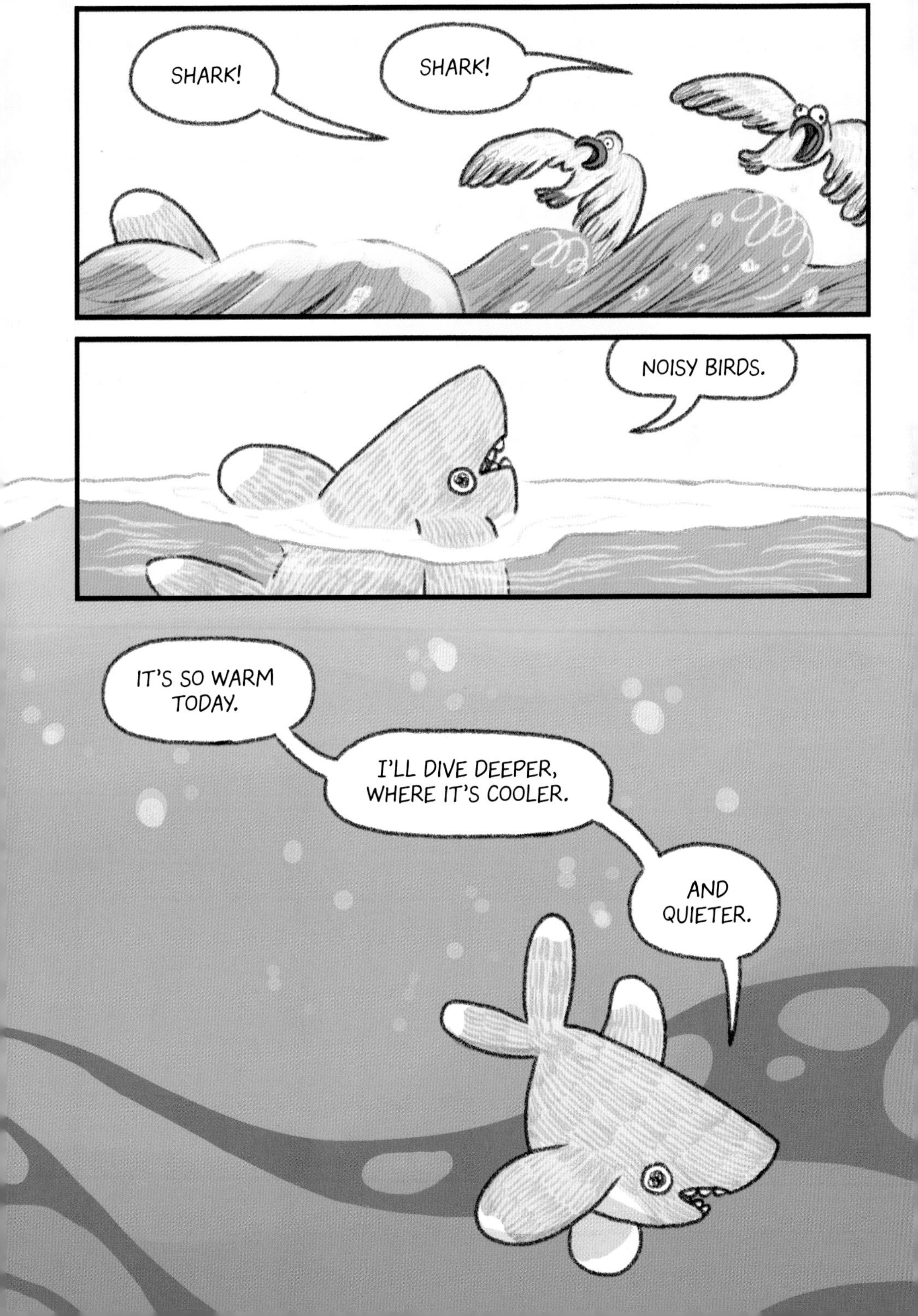
SHARK!
SHARK!
NOISY BIRDS.
IT'S SO WARM TODAY.
I'LL DIVE DEEPER, WHERE IT'S COOLER.
AND QUIETER.

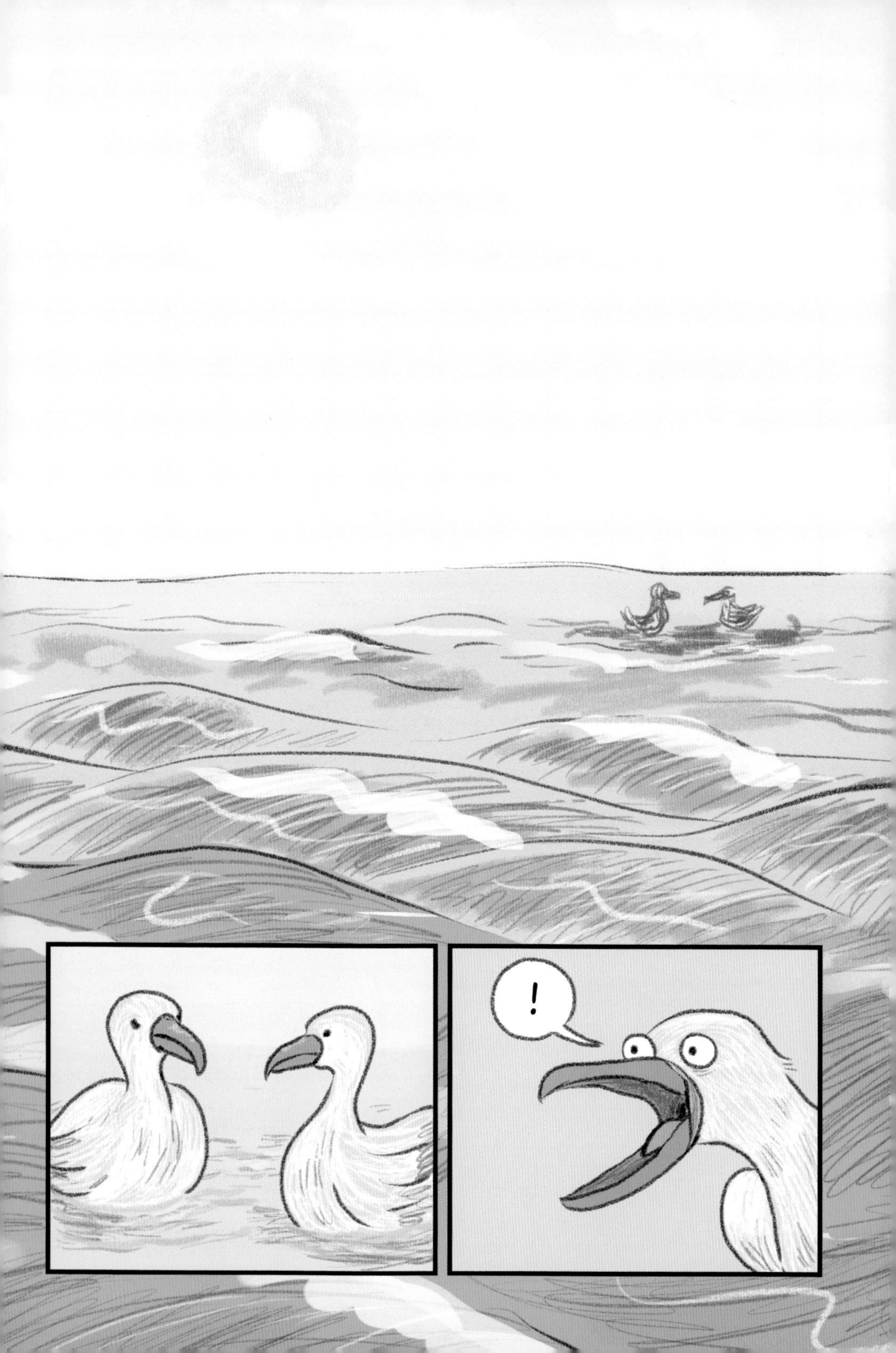
!

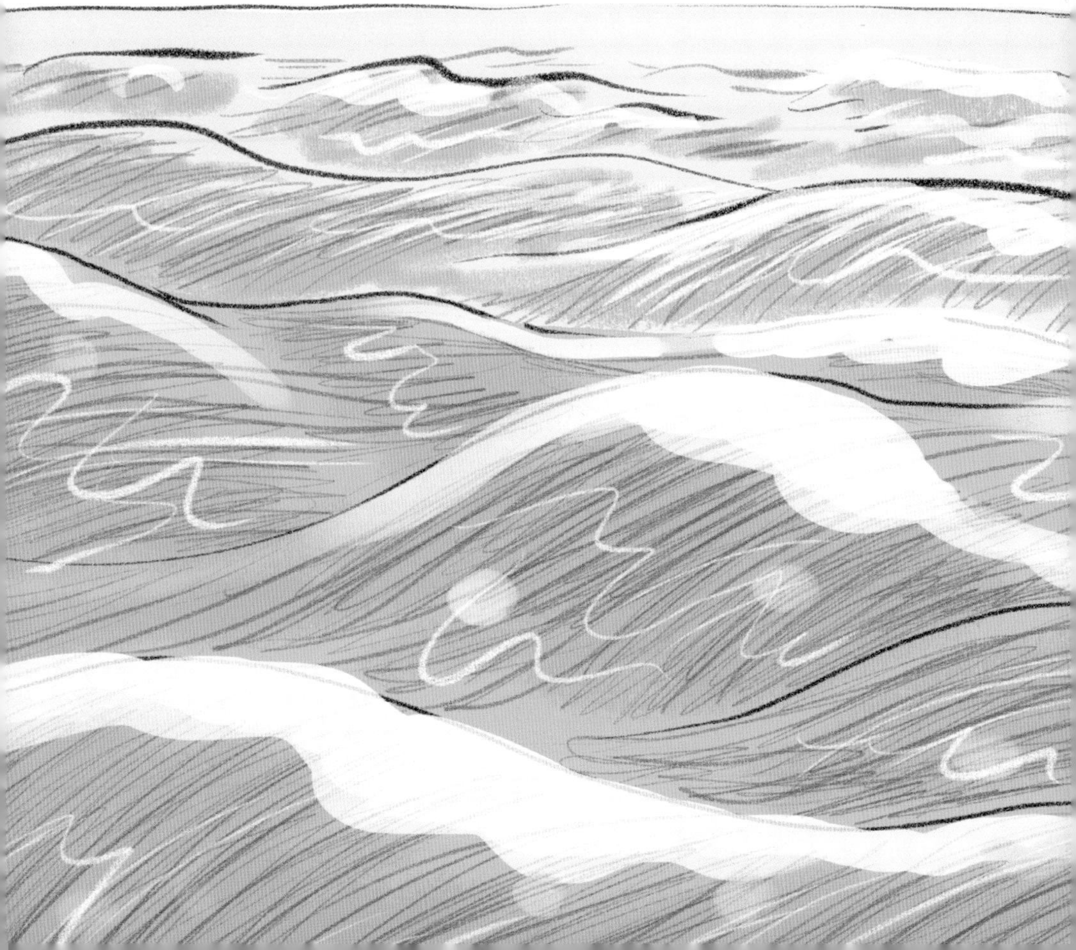

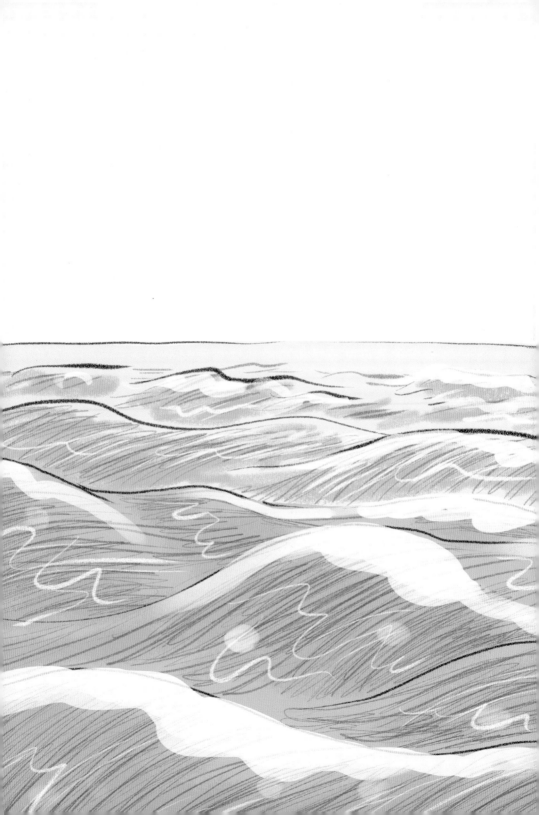

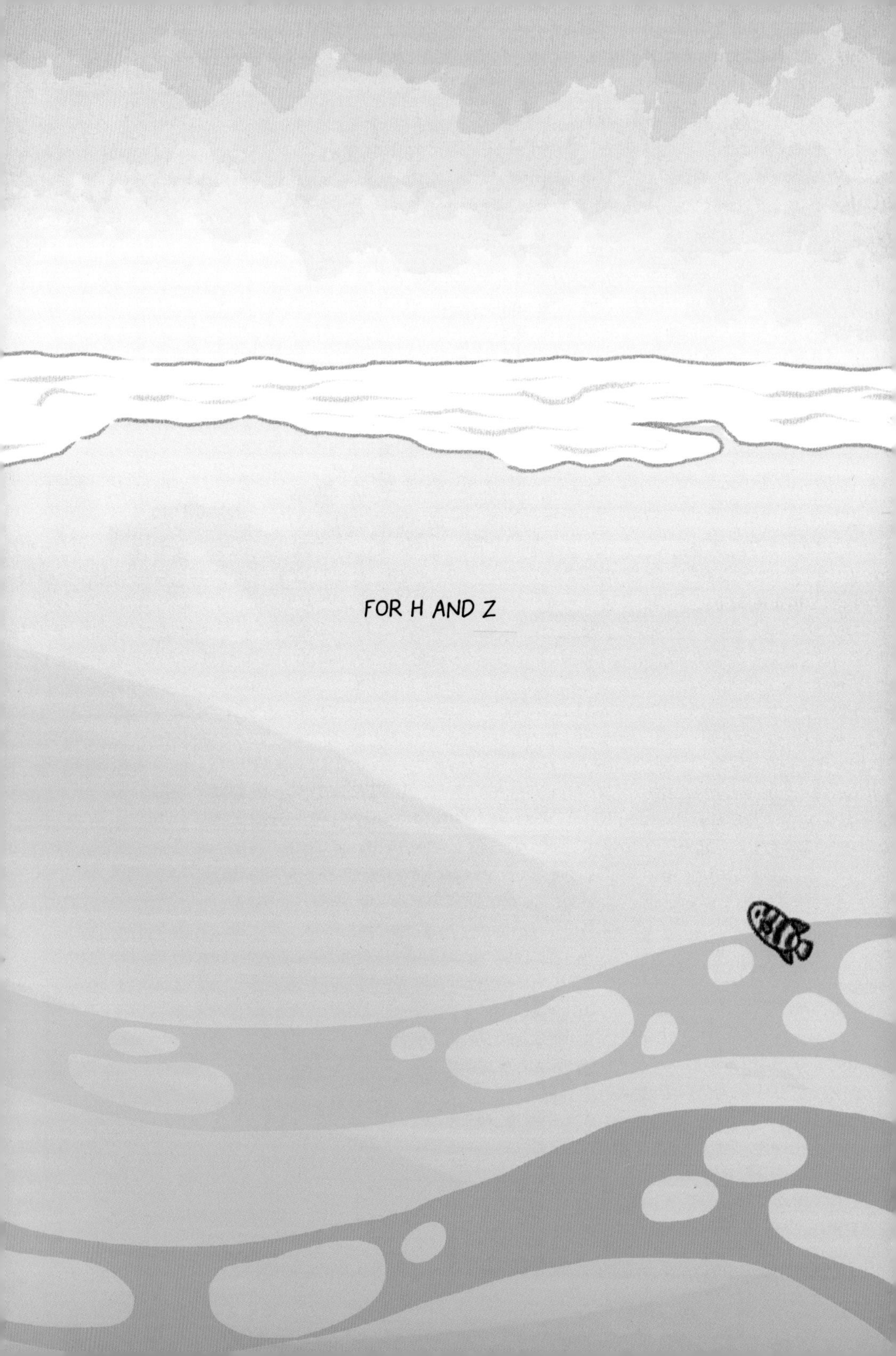

FOR H AND Z

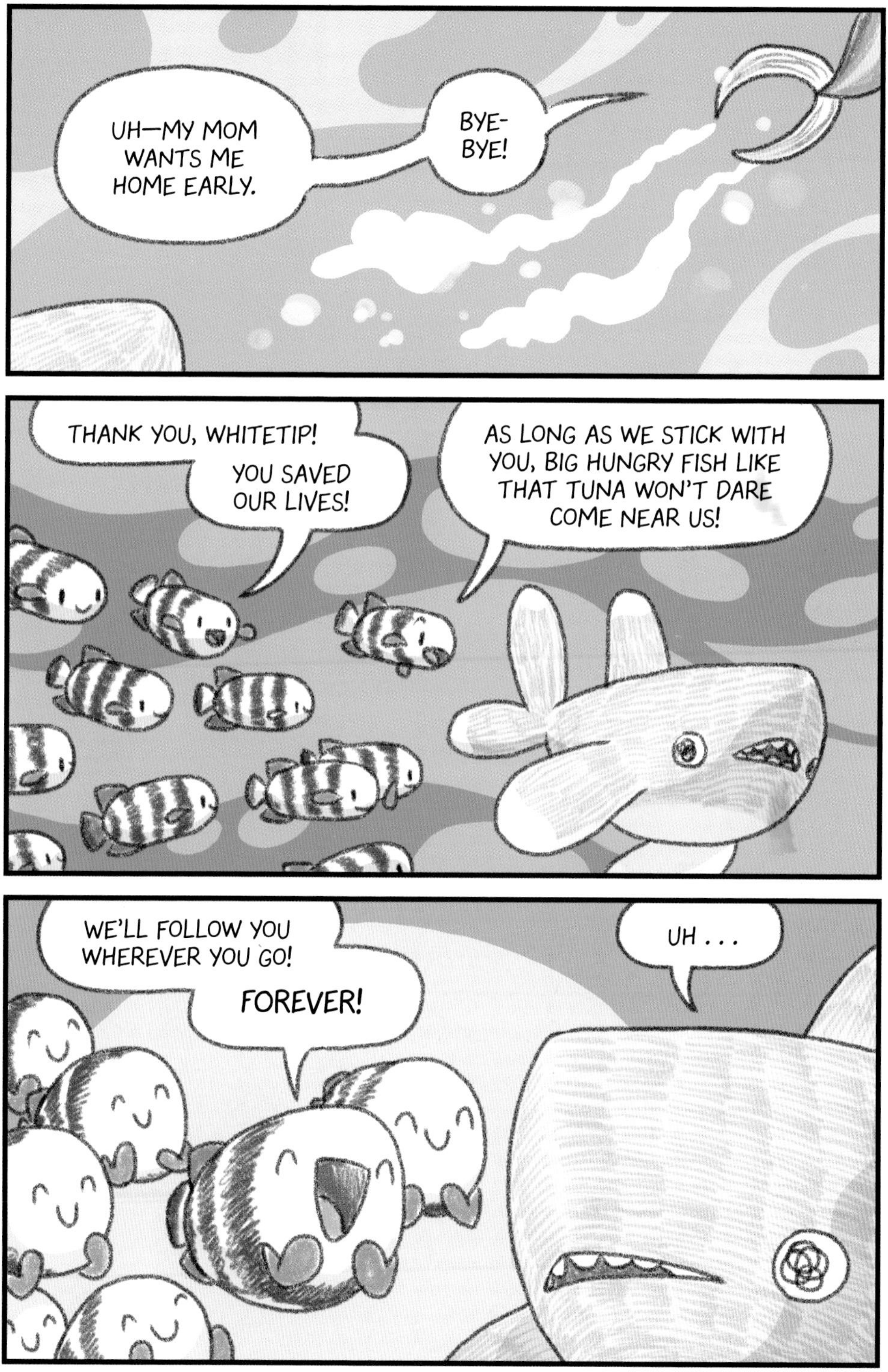
UH—MY MOM WANTS ME HOME EARLY.
BYE-BYE!
THANK YOU, WHITETIP!
YOU SAVED OUR LIVES!
AS LONG AS WE STICK WITH YOU, BIG HUNGRY FISH LIKE THAT TUNA WON'T DARE COME NEAR US!
WE'LL FOLLOW YOU WHEREVER YOU GO!
FOREVER!
UH . . .

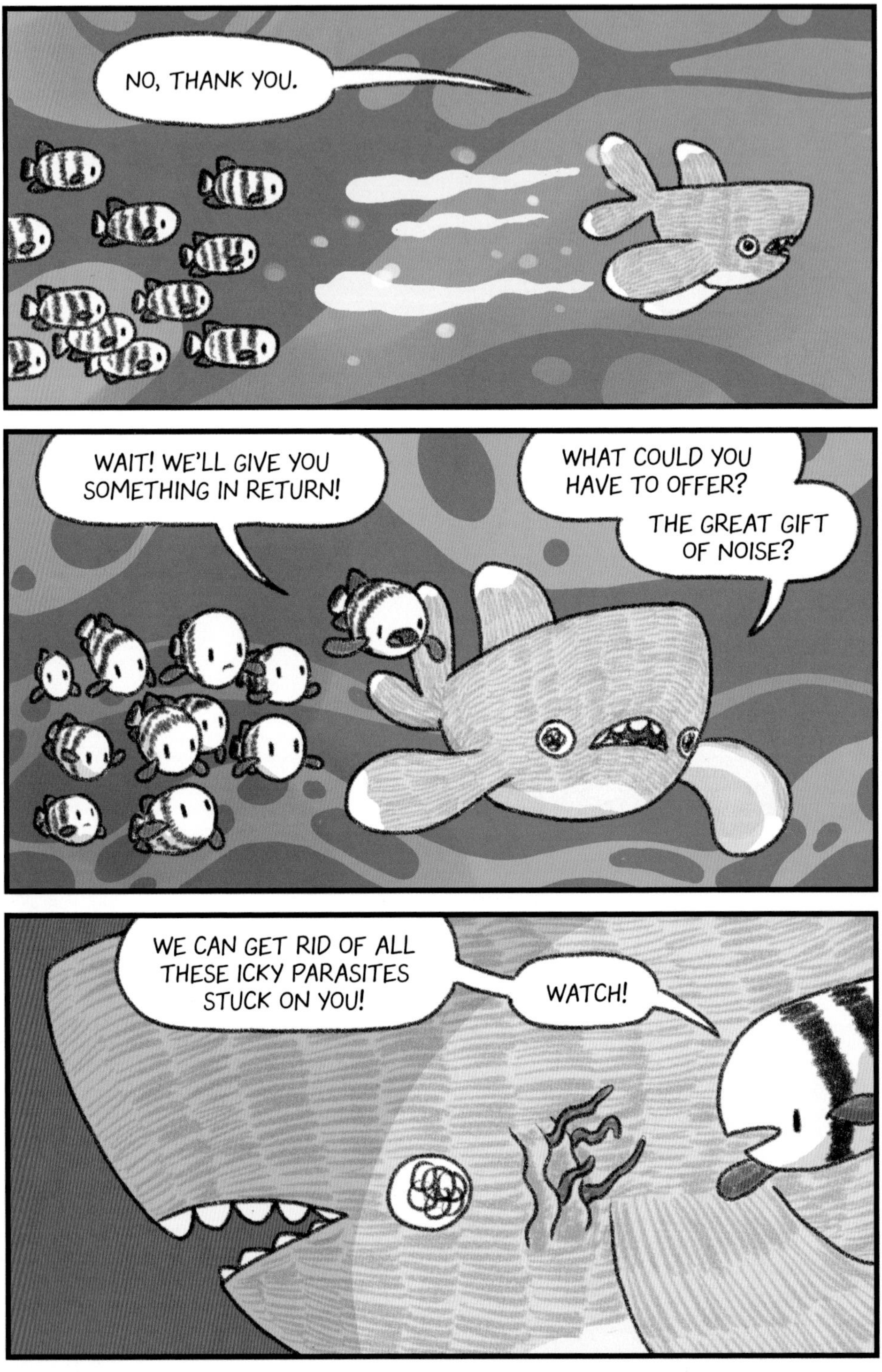
NO, THANK YOU.
WAIT! WE'LL GIVE YOU SOMETHING IN RETURN!
WHAT COULD YOU HAVE TO OFFER?
THE GREAT GIFT OF NOISE?
WE CAN GET RID OF ALL THESE ICKY PARASITES STUCK ON YOU!
WATCH!

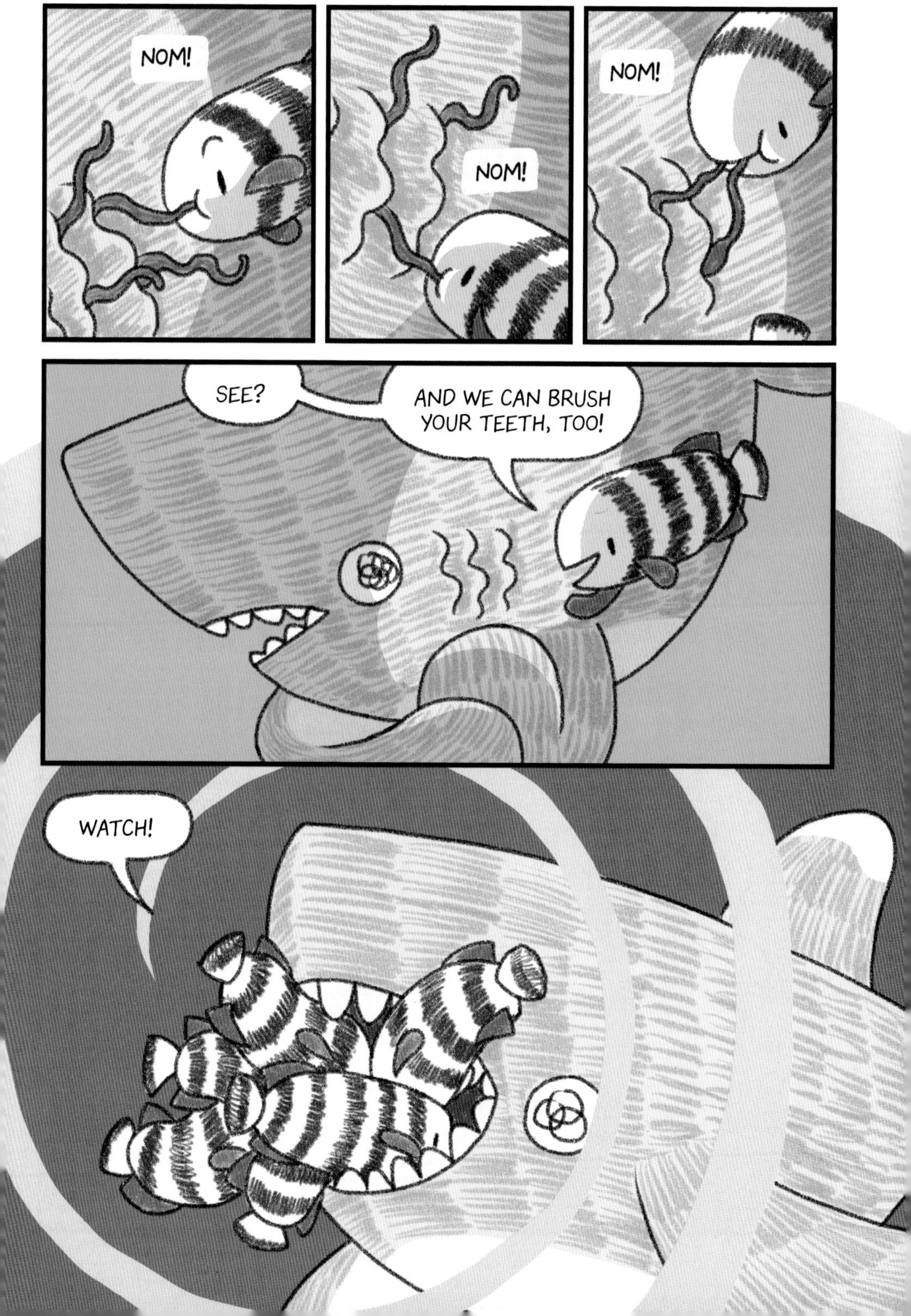
NOM!
NOM!
NOM!
SEE?
AND WE CAN BRUSH YOUR TEETH, TOO!
WATCH!

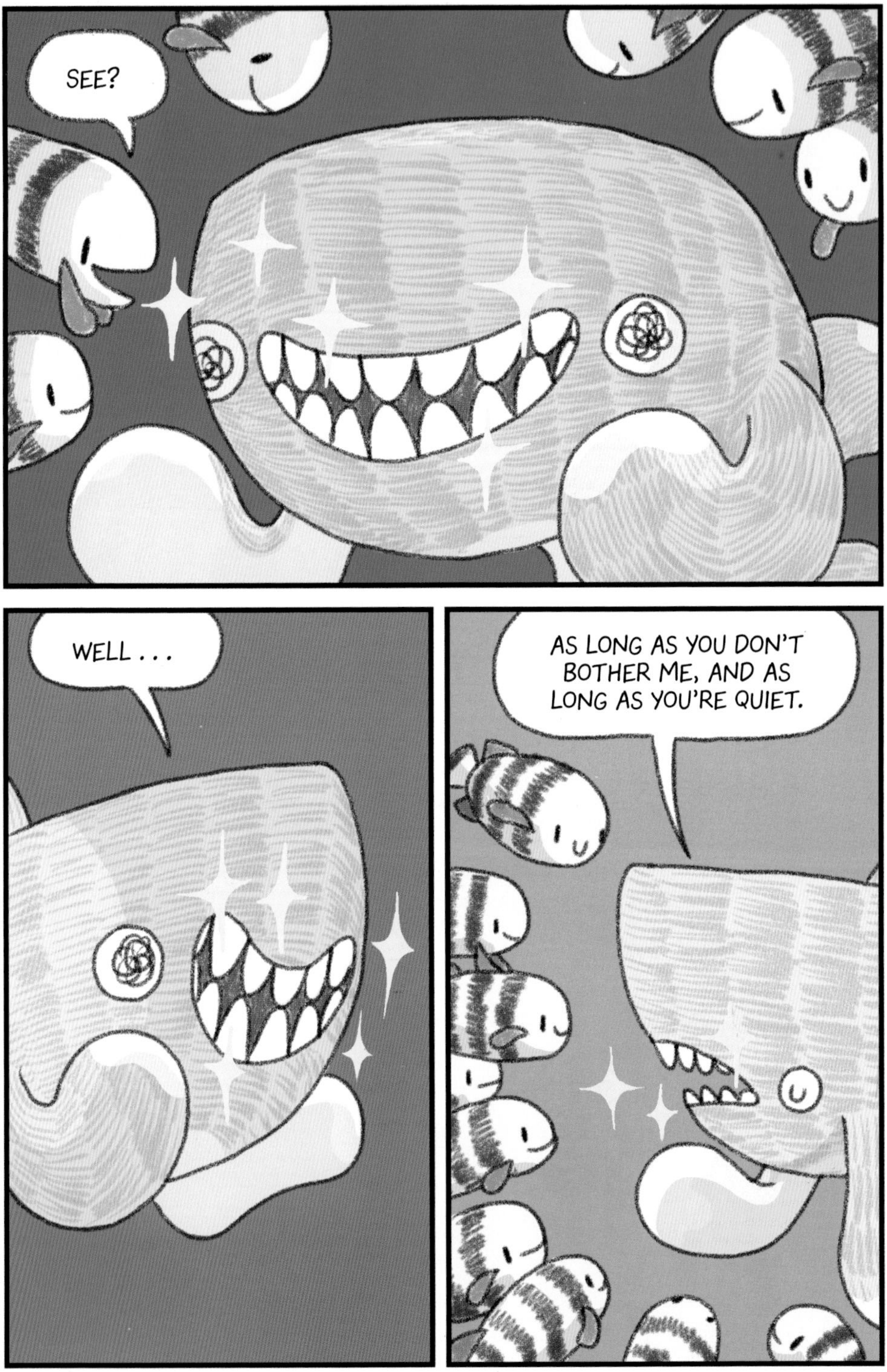
SEE?
WELL . . .
AS LONG AS YOU DON'T BOTHER ME, AND AS LONG AS YOU'RE QUIET.

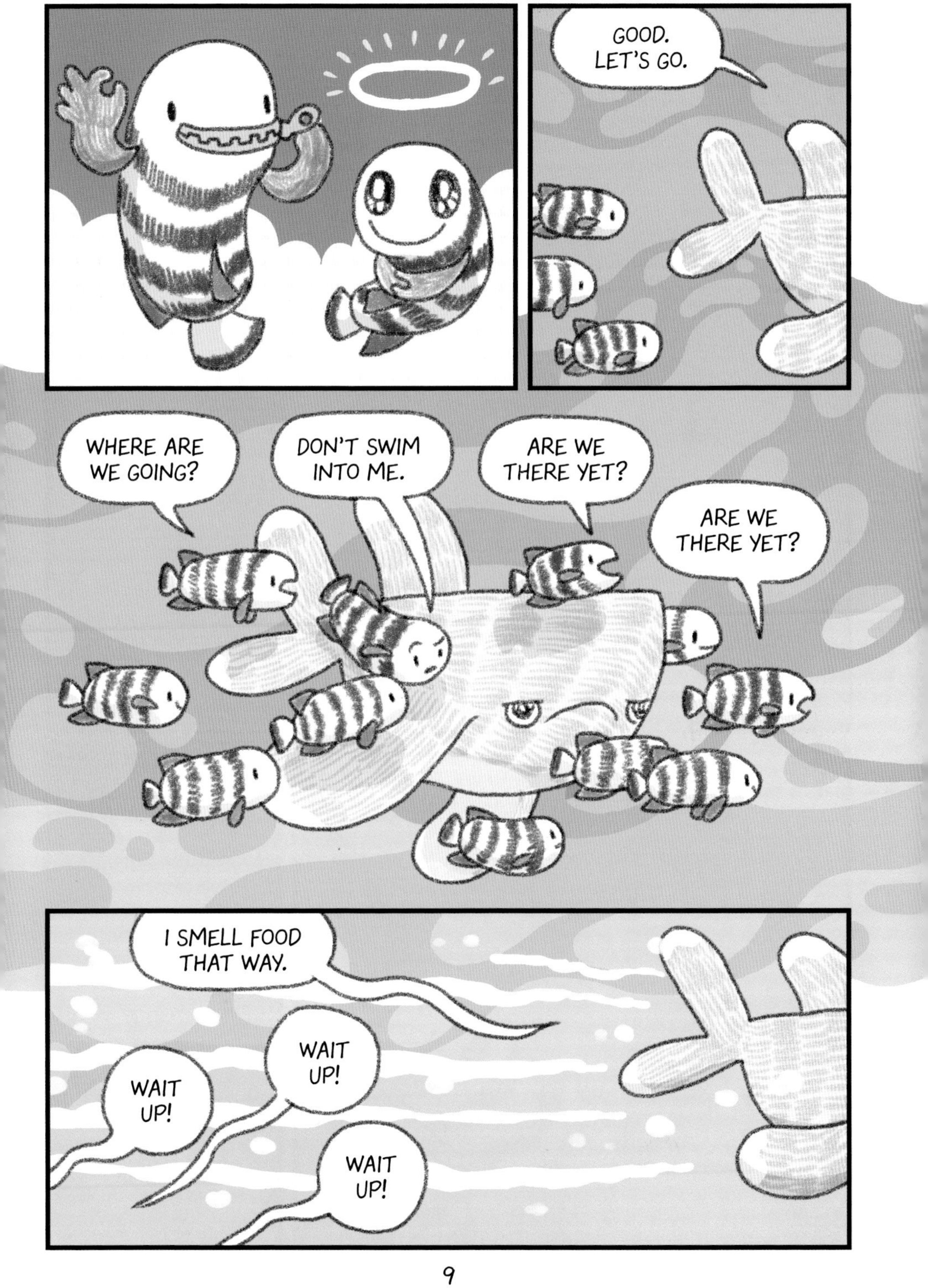
GOOD.
LET'S GO.
WHERE ARE WE GOING?
DON'T SWIM INTO ME.
ARE WE THERE YET?
ARE WE THERE YET?
I SMELL FOOD THAT WAY.
WAIT UP!
WAIT UP!
WAIT UP!

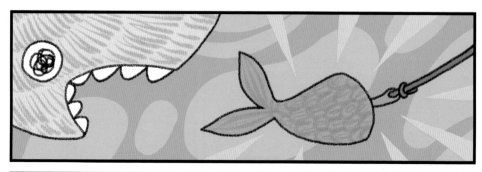

CHOMP!

CRUMBS!

AS LONG AS WE FOLLOW OUR SHARK, WE'LL NEVER GO HUNGRY!

CRUMBS!

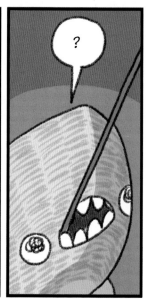

?

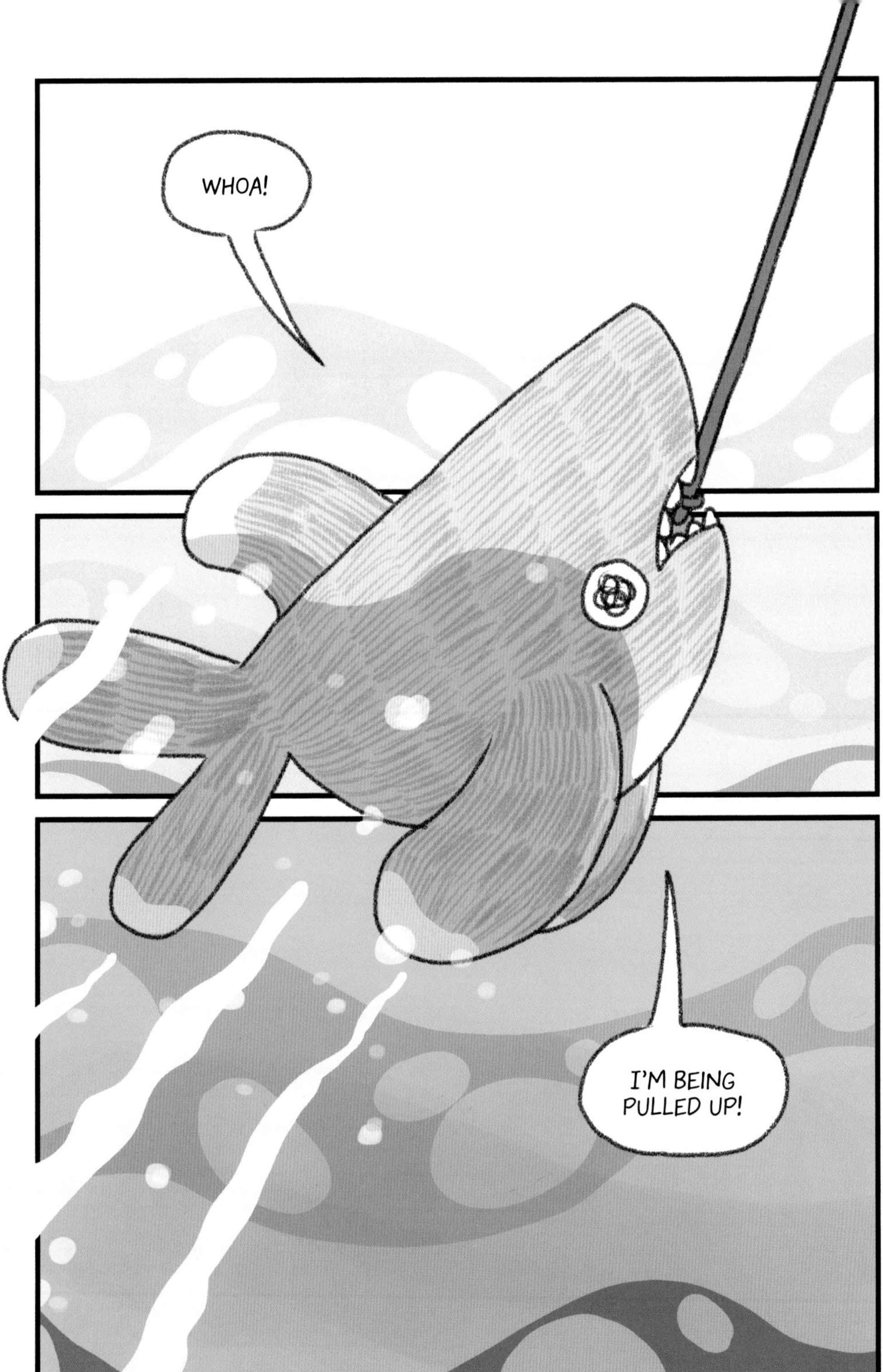
WHOA!
I'M BEING PULLED UP!

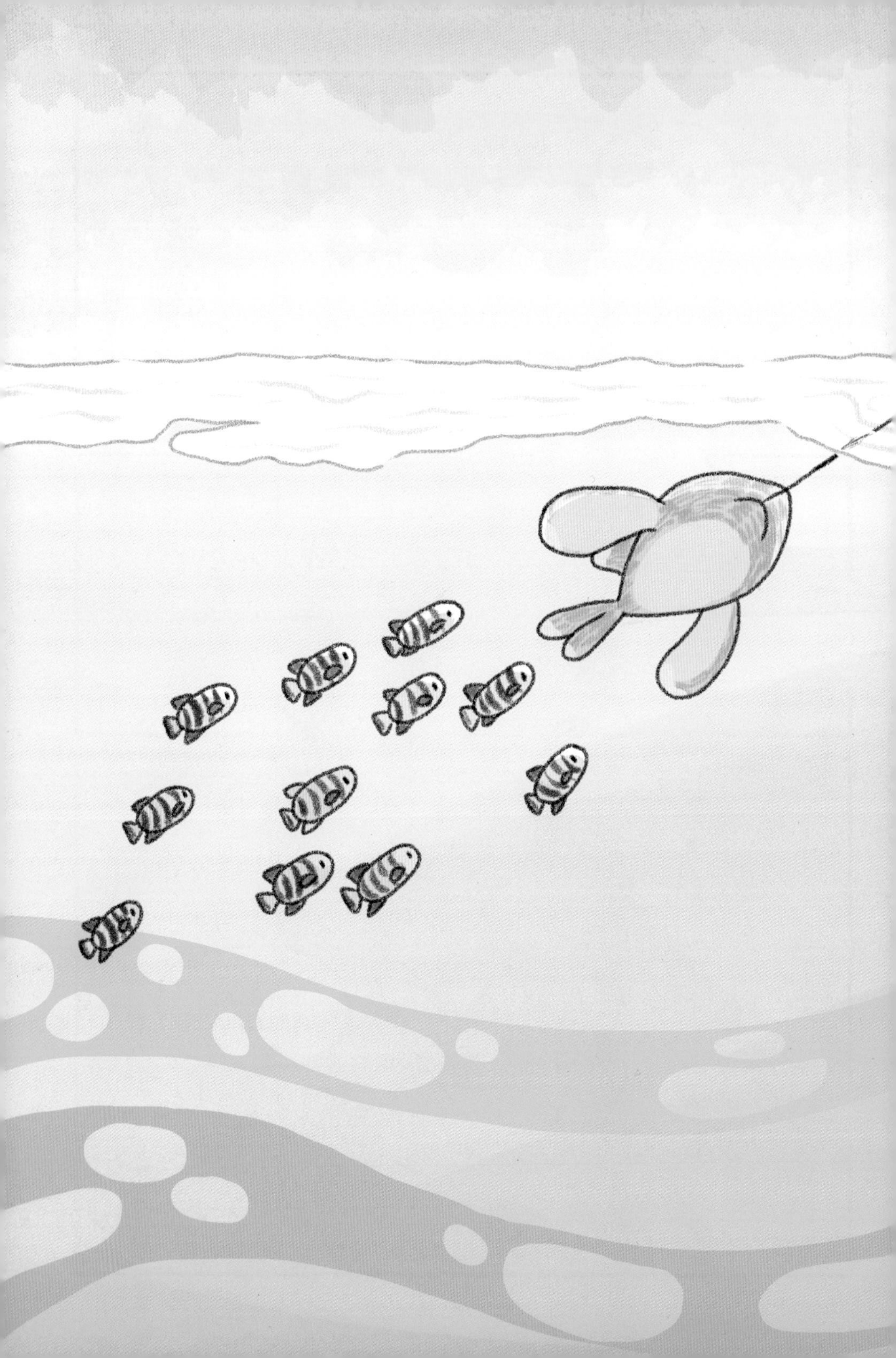

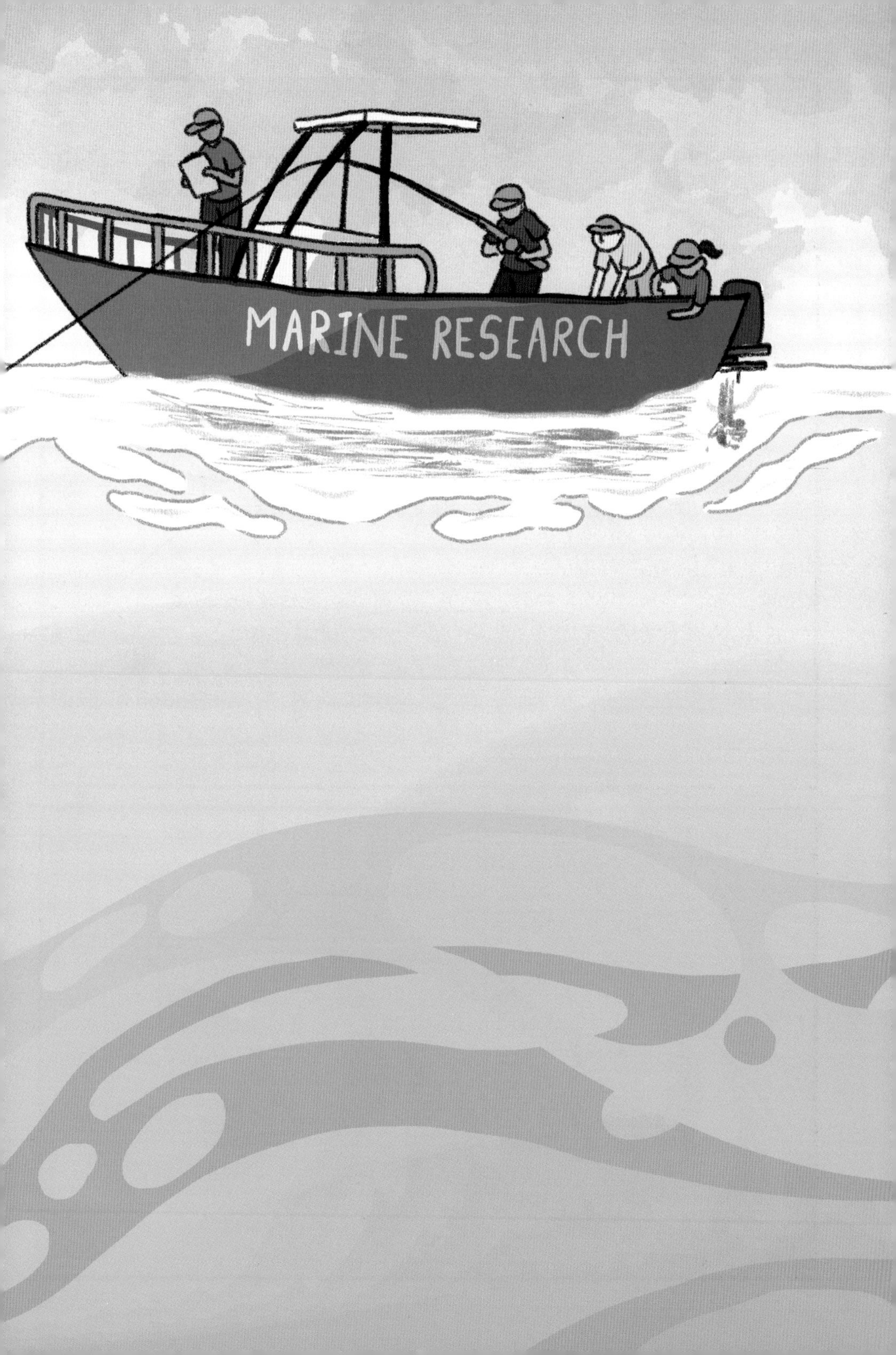
MARINE RESEARCH

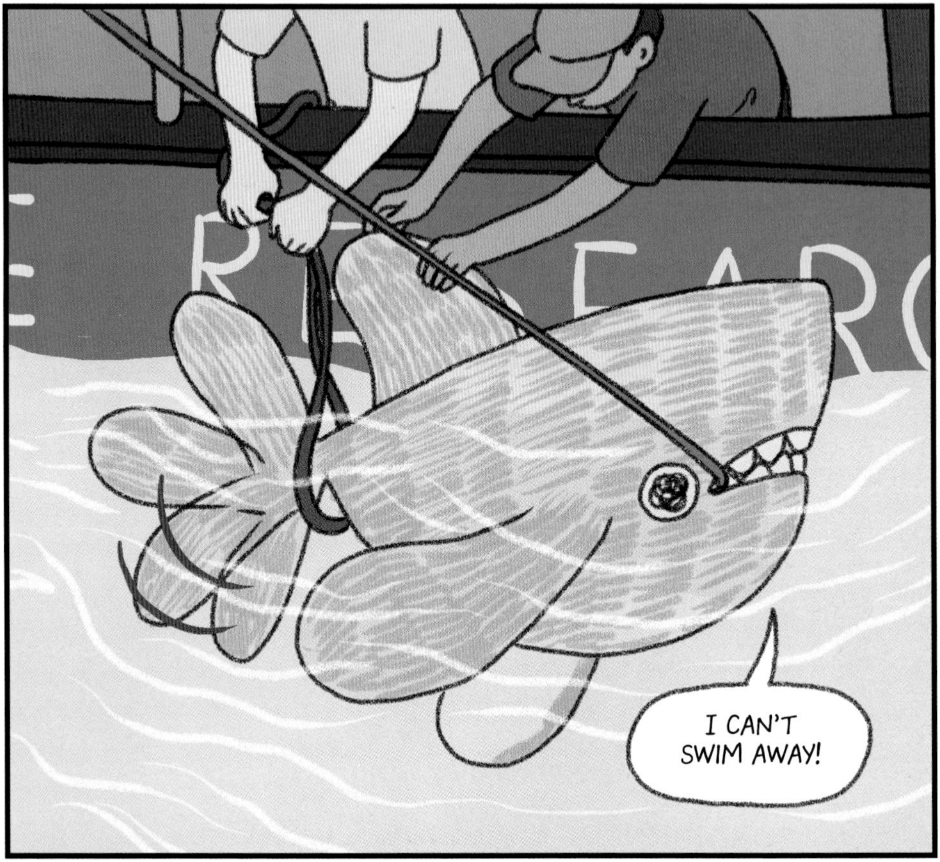
I CAN'T SWIM AWAY!

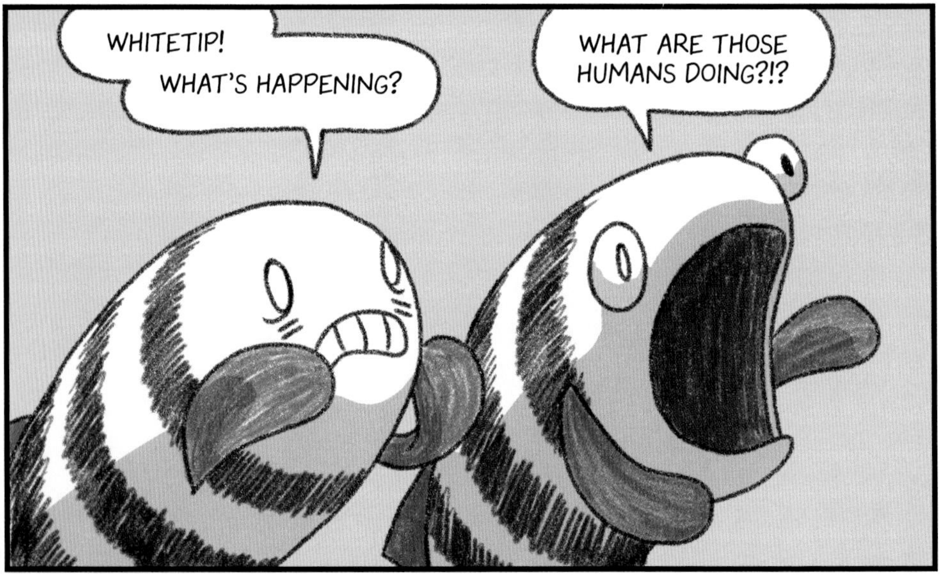
WHITETIP!
WHAT'S HAPPENING?
WHAT ARE THOSE HUMANS DOING?!?

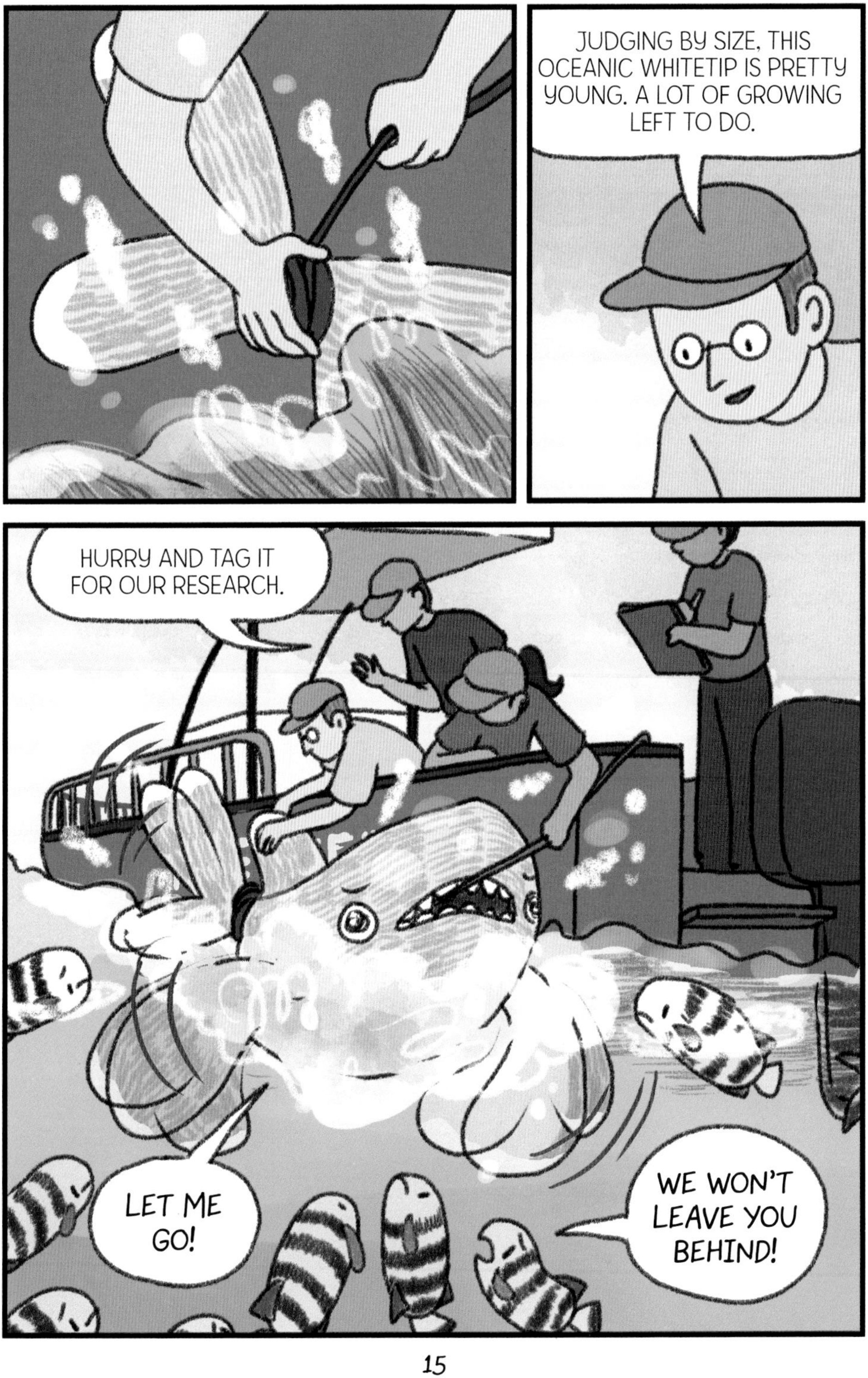
JUDGING BY SIZE, THIS OCEANIC WHITETIP IS PRETTY YOUNG. A LOT OF GROWING LEFT TO DO.
HURRY AND TAG IT FOR OUR RESEARCH.
LET ME GO!
WE WON'T LEAVE YOU BEHIND!

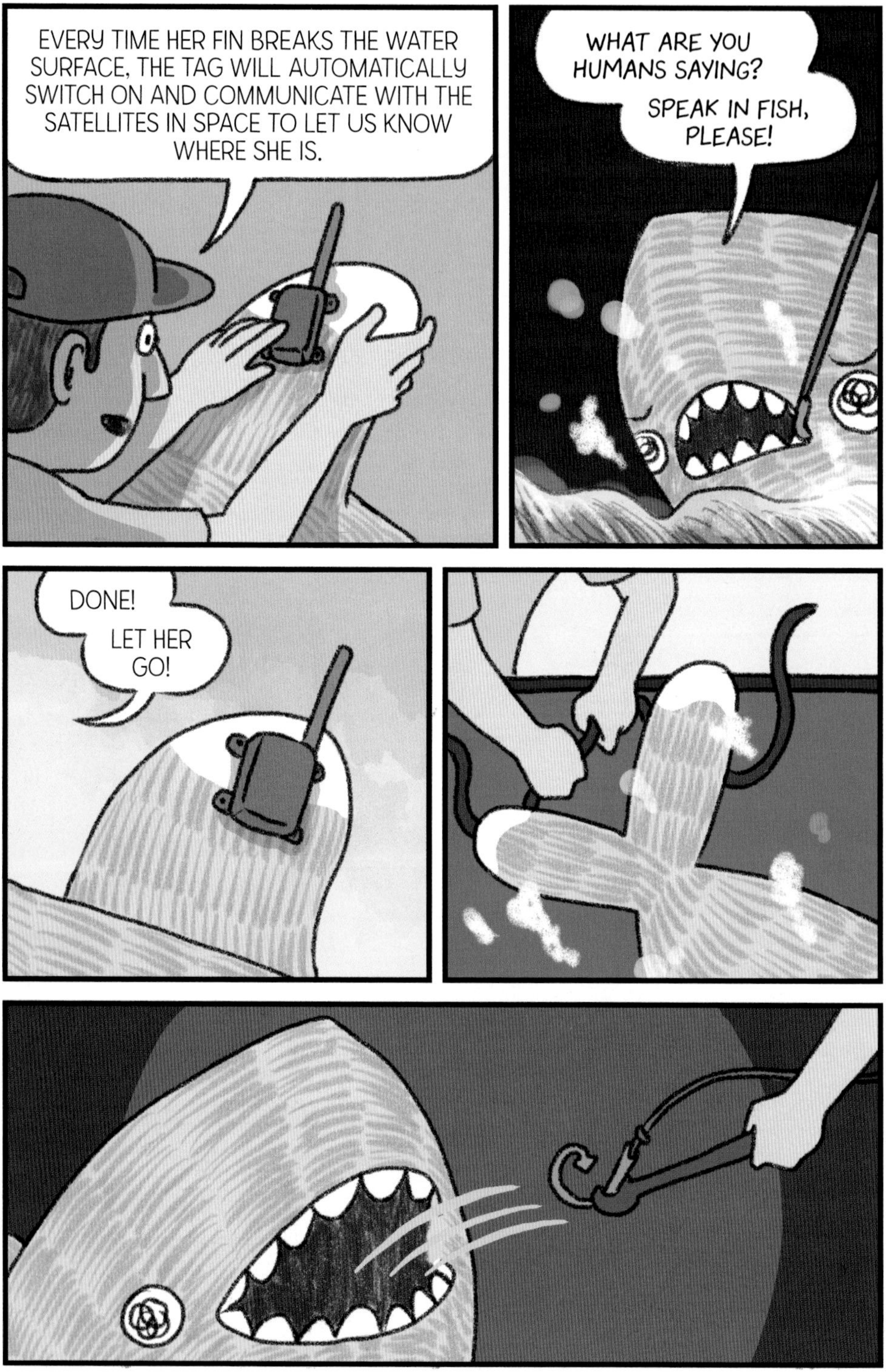
EVERY TIME HER FIN BREAKS THE WATER SURFACE, THE TAG WILL AUTOMATICALLY SWITCH ON AND COMMUNICATE WITH THE SATELLITES IN SPACE TO LET US KNOW WHERE SHE IS.
WHAT ARE YOU HUMANS SAYING?
SPEAK IN FISH, PLEASE!
DONE!
LET HER GO!

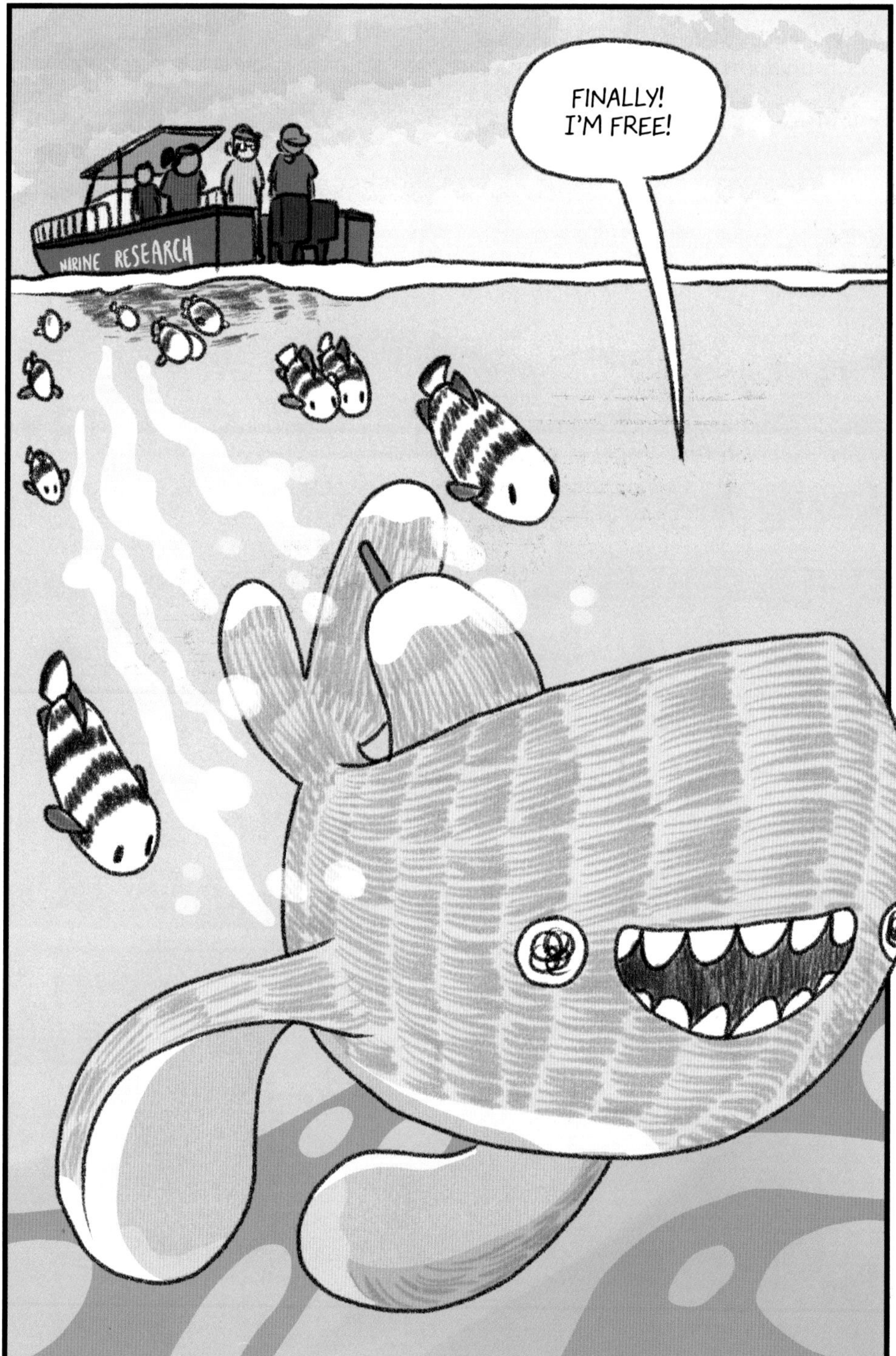
FINALLY!
I'M FREE!
MARINE RESEARCH

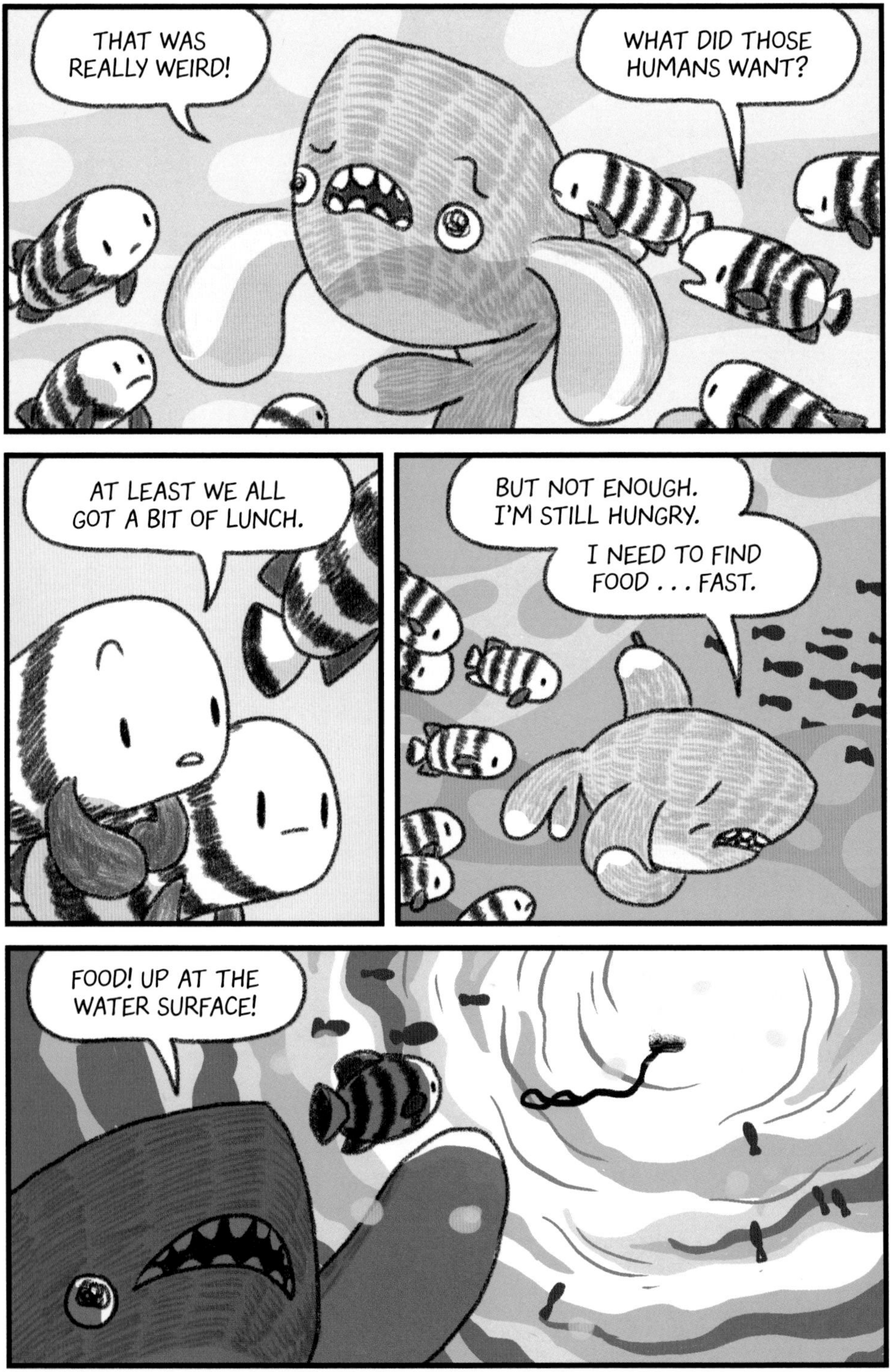
THAT WAS REALLY WEIRD!
WHAT DID THOSE HUMANS WANT?
AT LEAST WE ALL GOT A BIT OF LUNCH.
BUT NOT ENOUGH. I'M STILL HUNGRY.
I NEED TO FIND FOOD . . . FAST.
FOOD! UP AT THE WATER SURFACE!

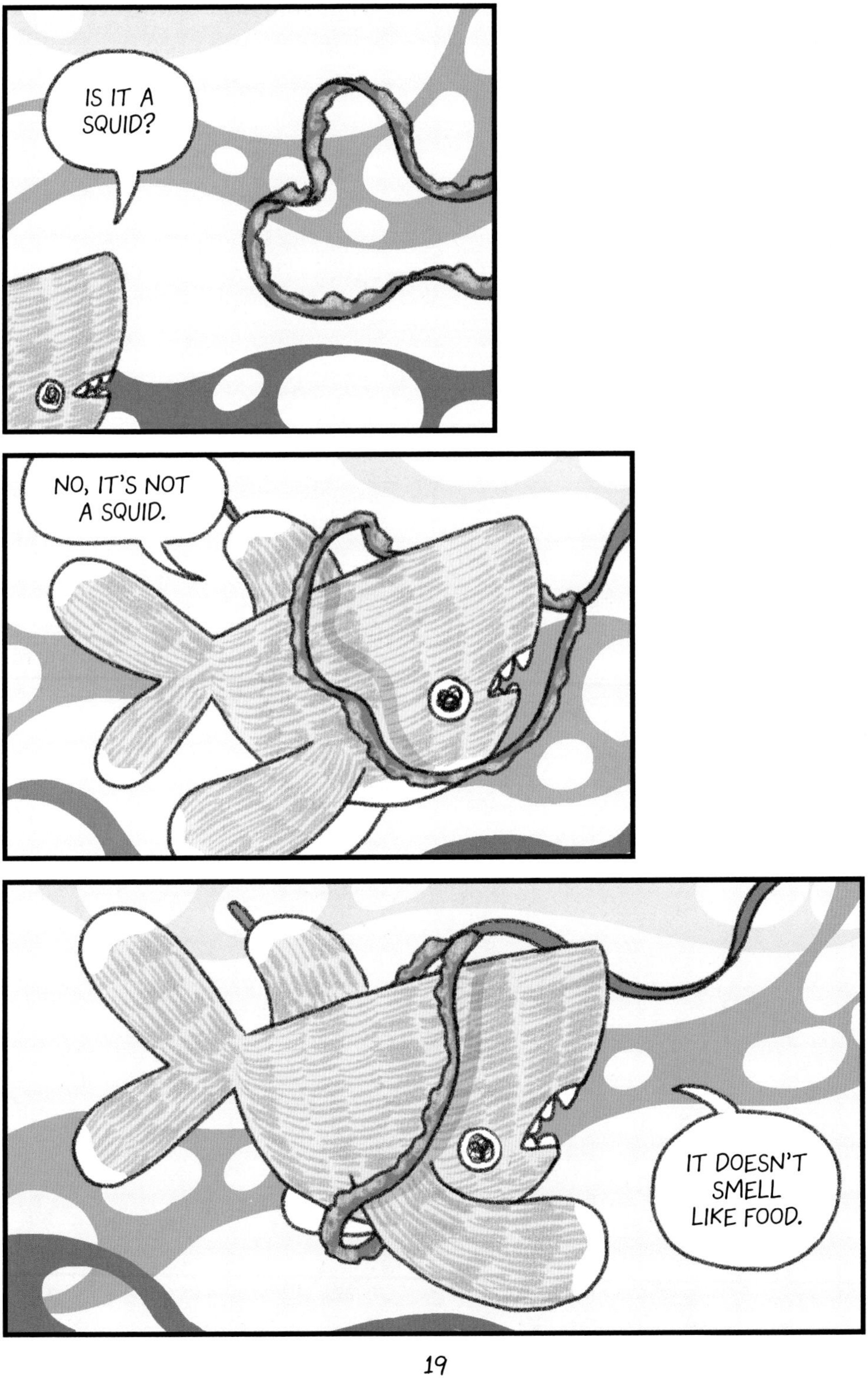

IS IT A SQUID?
NO, IT'S NOT A SQUID.
IT DOESN'T SMELL LIKE FOOD.

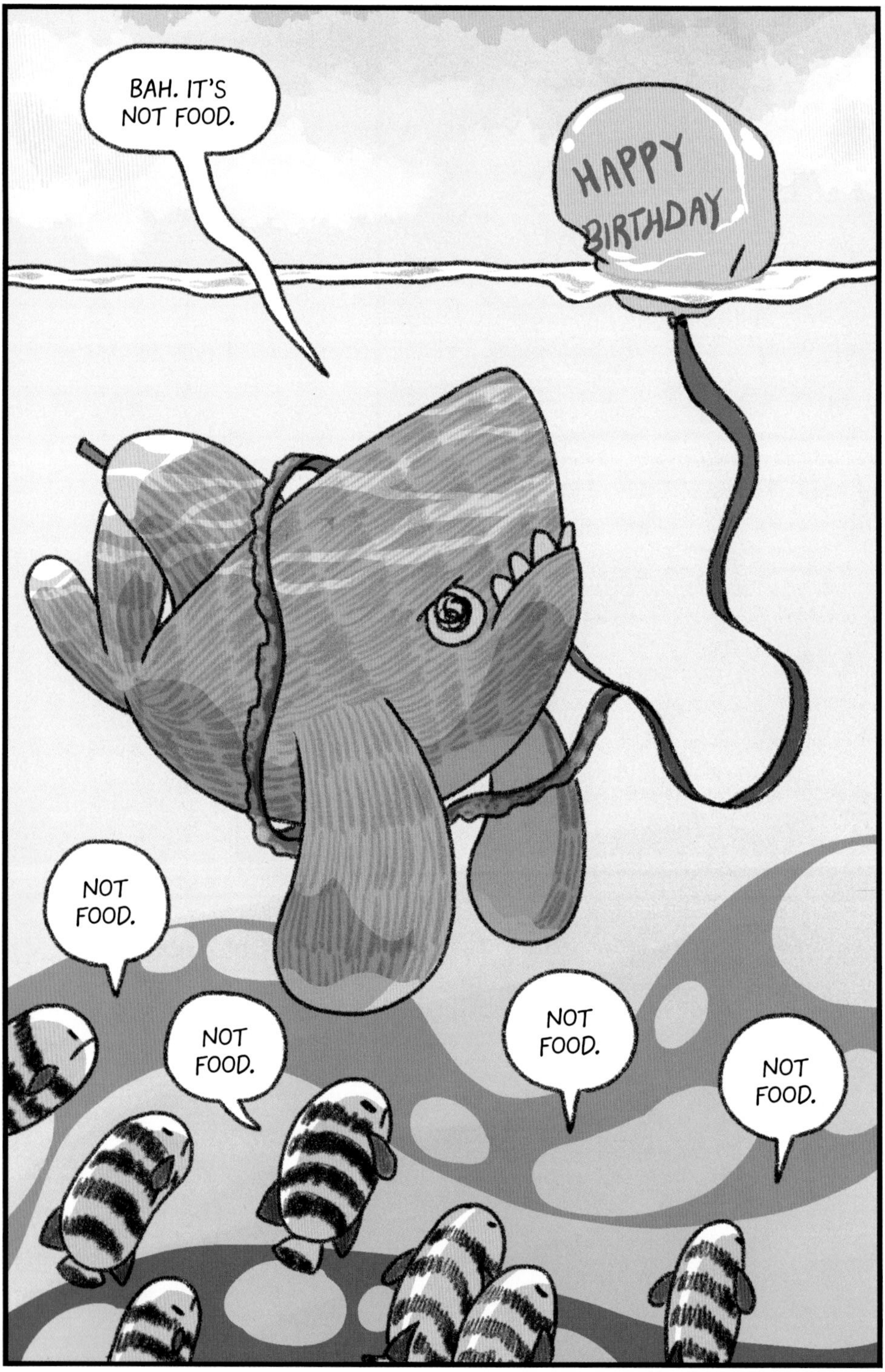
BAH. IT'S NOT FOOD.
HAPPY BIRTHDAY
NOT FOOD.
NOT FOOD.
NOT FOOD.
NOT FOOD.

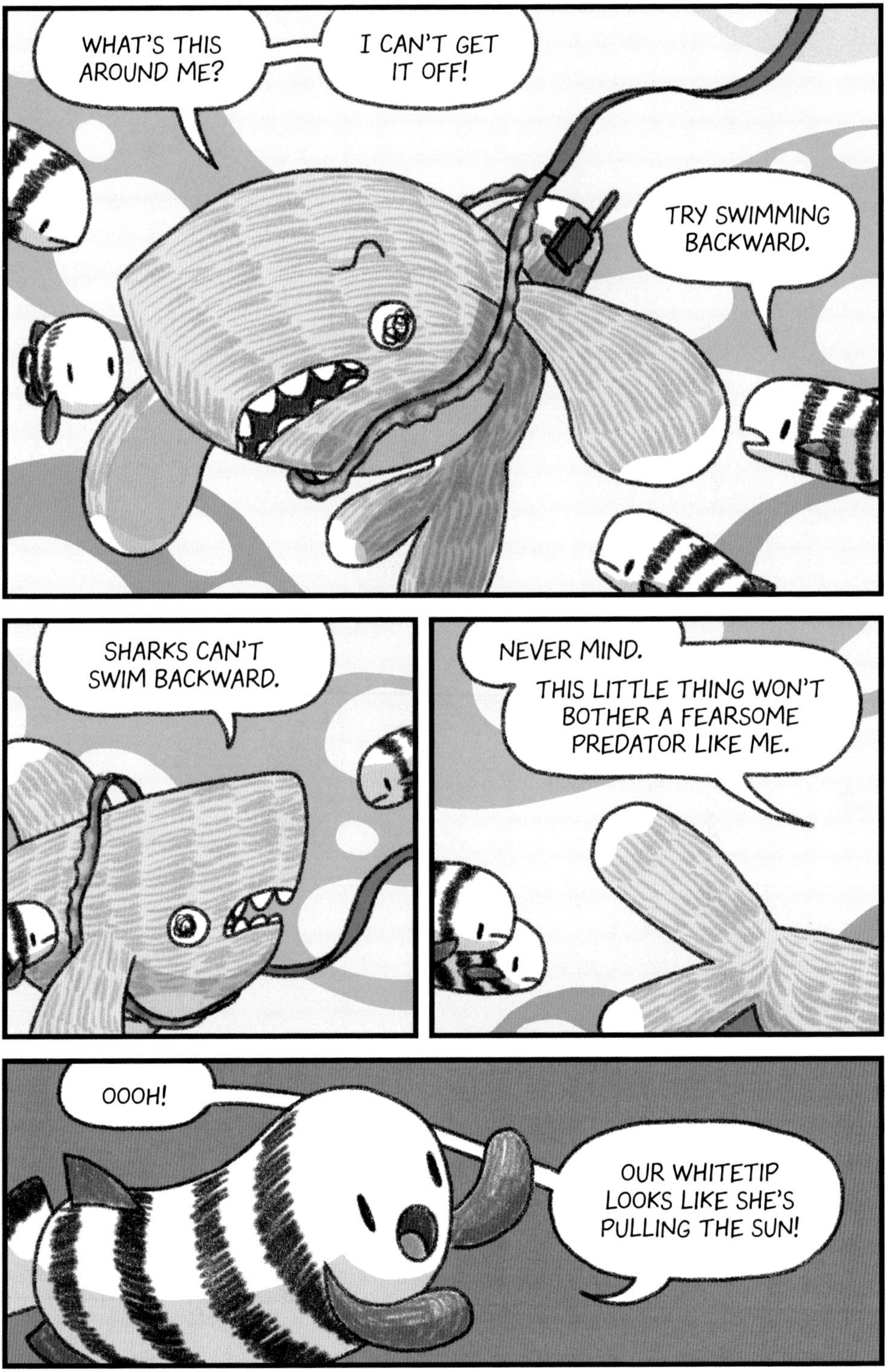
WHAT'S THIS AROUND ME?
I CAN'T GET IT OFF!
TRY SWIMMING BACKWARD.
SHARKS CAN'T SWIM BACKWARD.
NEVER MIND.
THIS LITTLE THING WON'T BOTHER A FEARSOME PREDATOR LIKE ME.
OOOH!
OUR WHITETIP LOOKS LIKE SHE'S PULLING THE SUN!

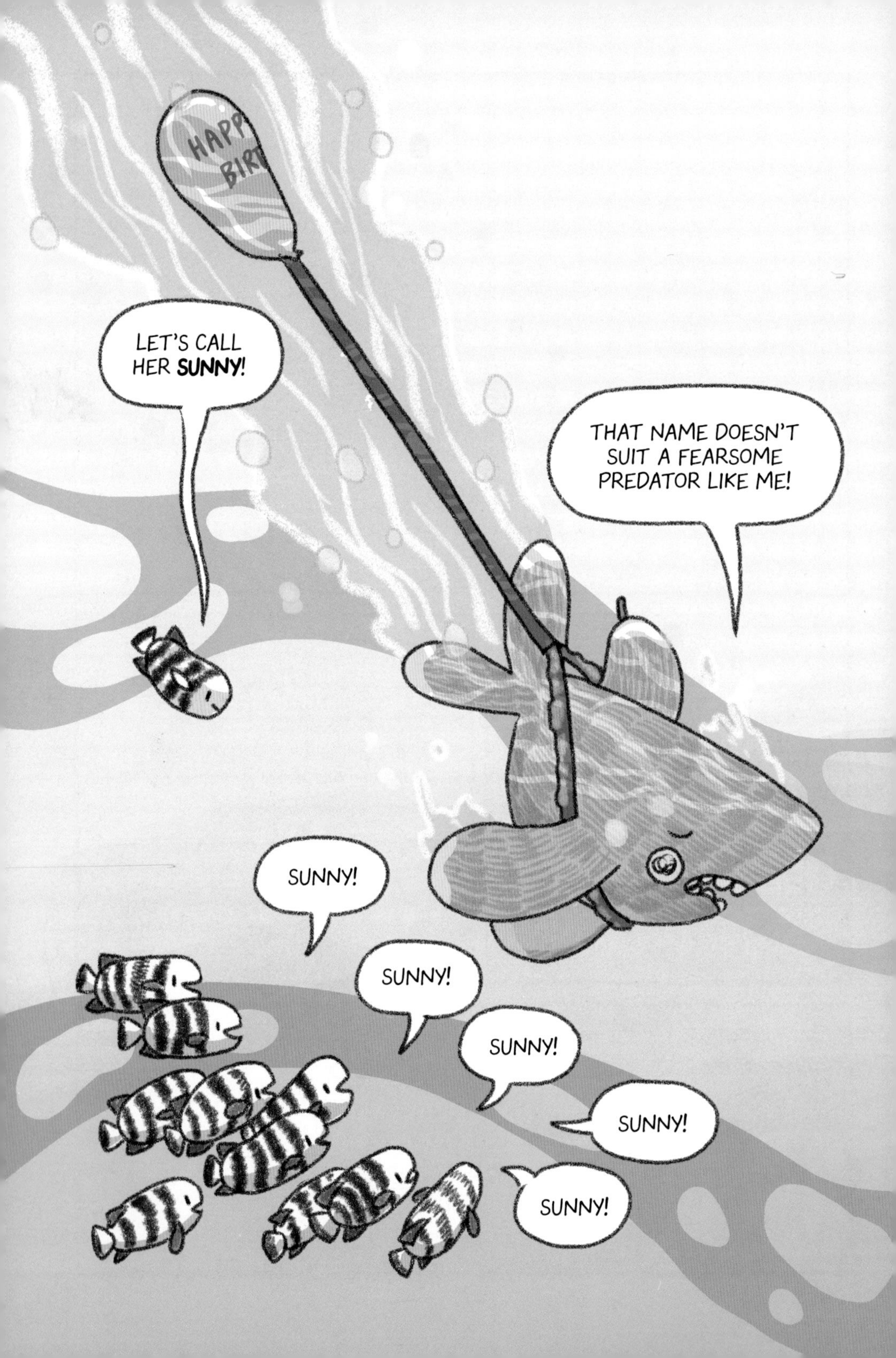
LET'S CALL HER **SUNNY**!
THAT NAME DOESN'T SUIT A FEARSOME PREDATOR LIKE ME!
SUNNY!
SUNNY!
SUNNY!
SUNNY!
SUNNY!

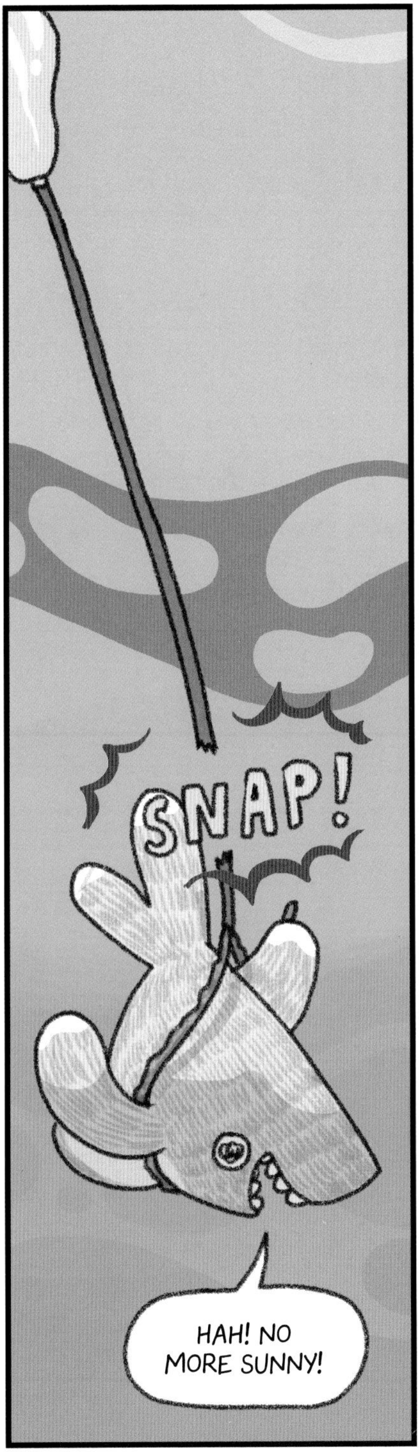
SNAP!
HAH! NO MORE SUNNY!

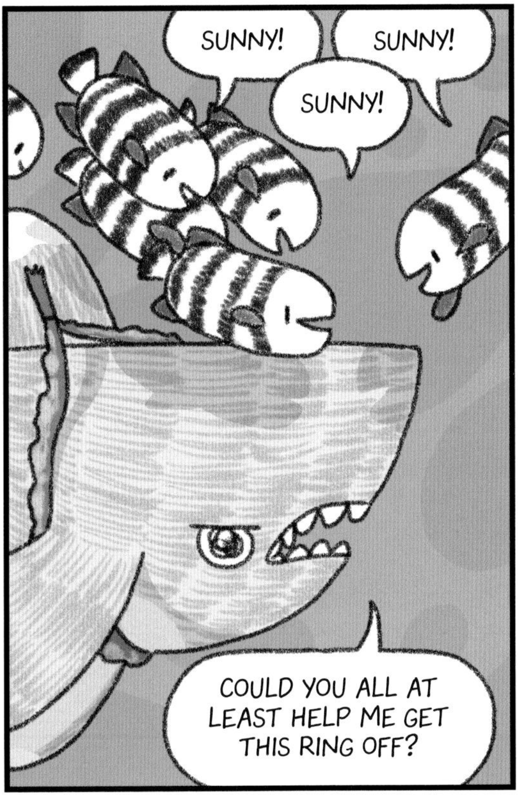
SUNNY!
SUNNY!
SUNNY!
COULD YOU ALL AT LEAST HELP ME GET THIS RING OFF?

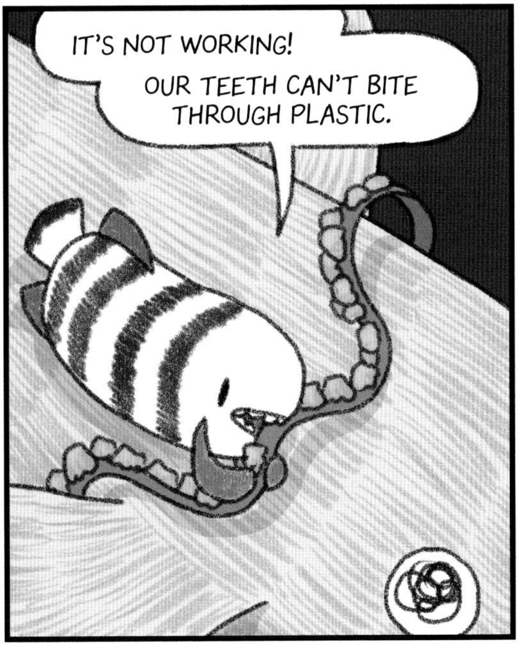
IT'S NOT WORKING!
OUR TEETH CAN'T BITE THROUGH PLASTIC.

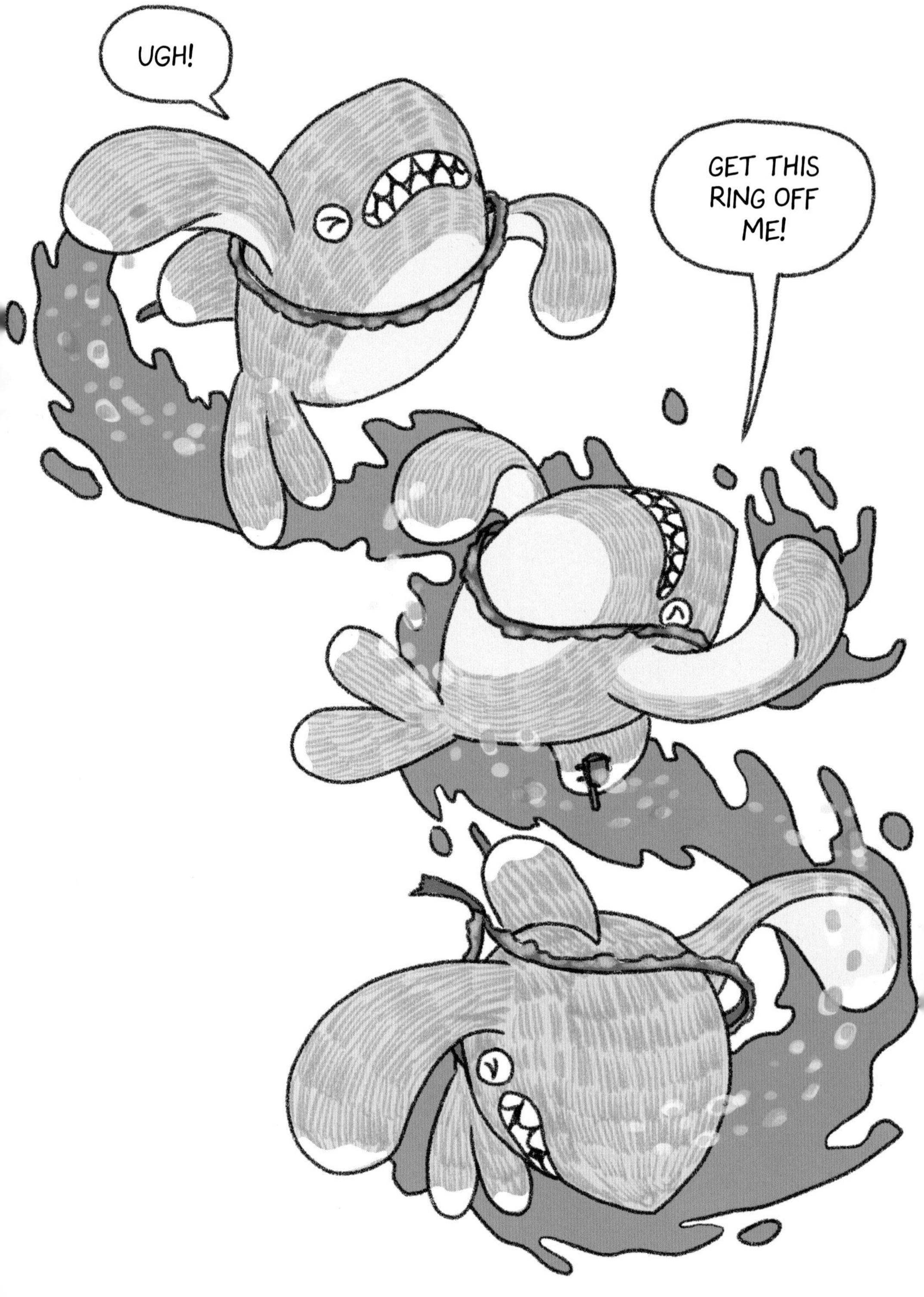
UGH!
GET THIS RING OFF ME!

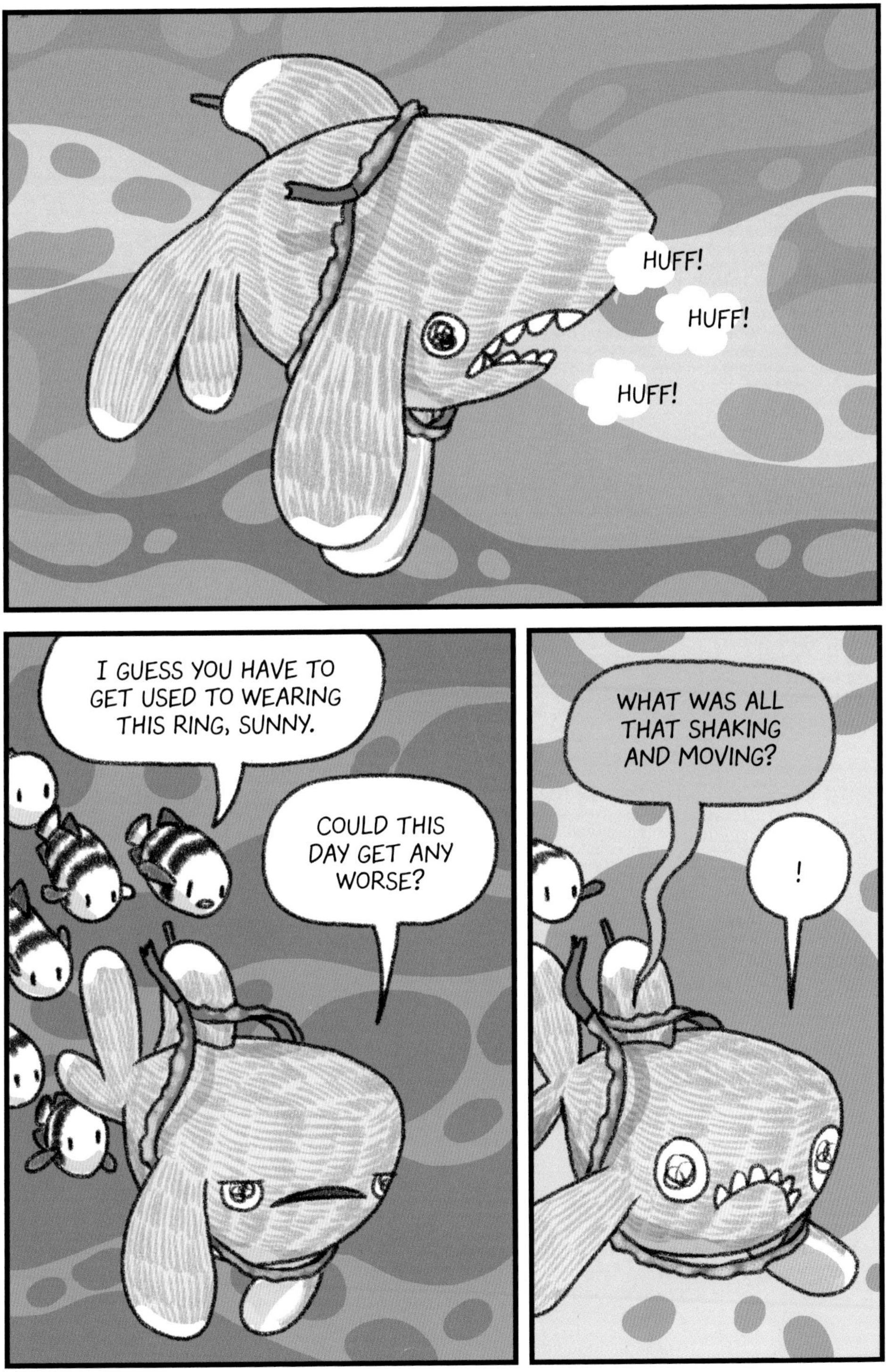
HUFF!
HUFF!
HUFF!
I GUESS YOU HAVE TO GET USED TO WEARING THIS RING, SUNNY.
COULD THIS DAY GET ANY WORSE?
WHAT WAS ALL THAT SHAKING AND MOVING?
!

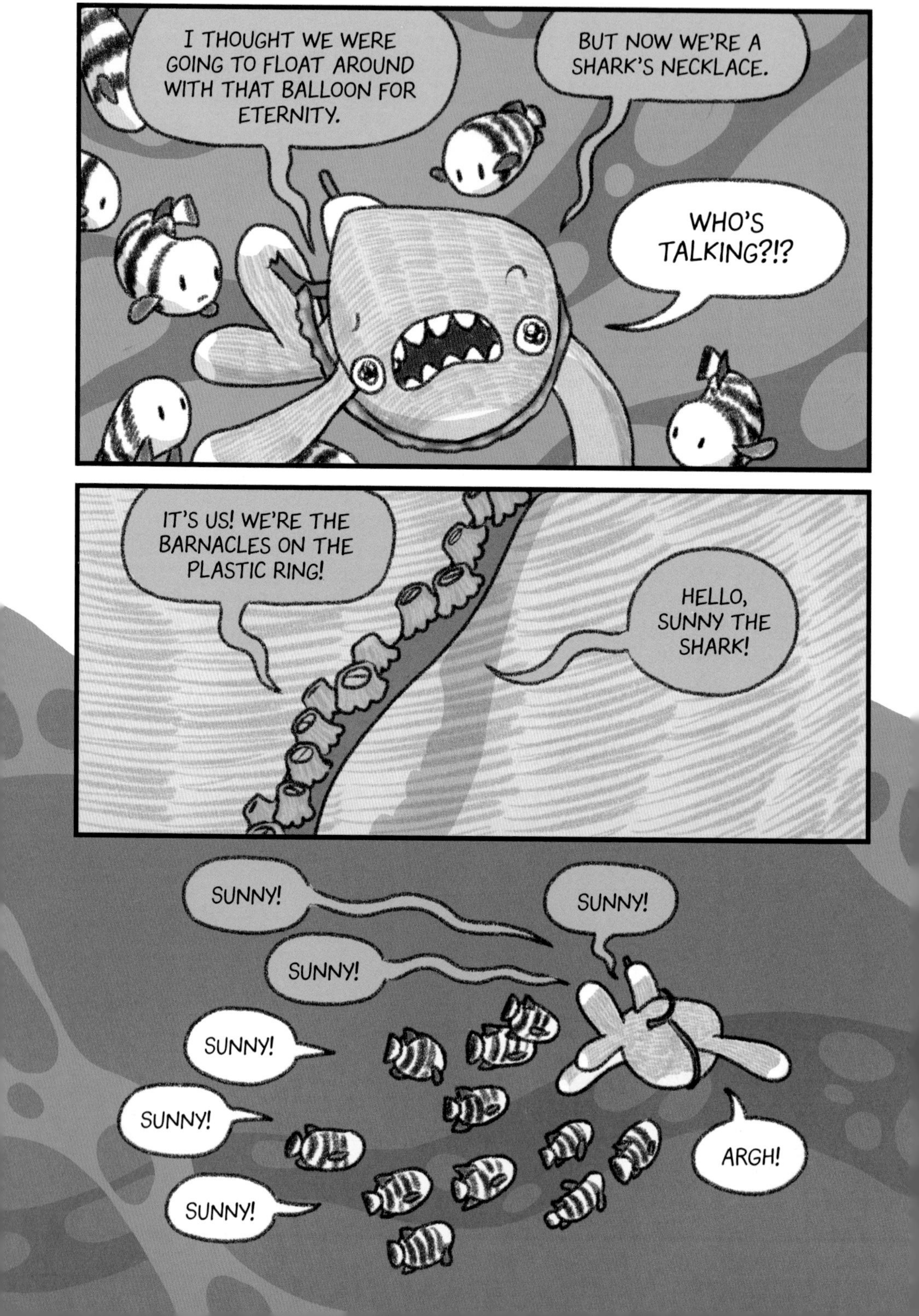
I THOUGHT WE WERE GOING TO FLOAT AROUND WITH THAT BALLOON FOR ETERNITY.
BUT NOW WE'RE A SHARK'S NECKLACE.
WHO'S TALKING?!?
IT'S US! WE'RE THE BARNACLES ON THE PLASTIC RING!
HELLO, SUNNY THE SHARK!
SUNNY!
SUNNY!
SUNNY!
SUNNY!
SUNNY!
SUNNY!
ARGH!

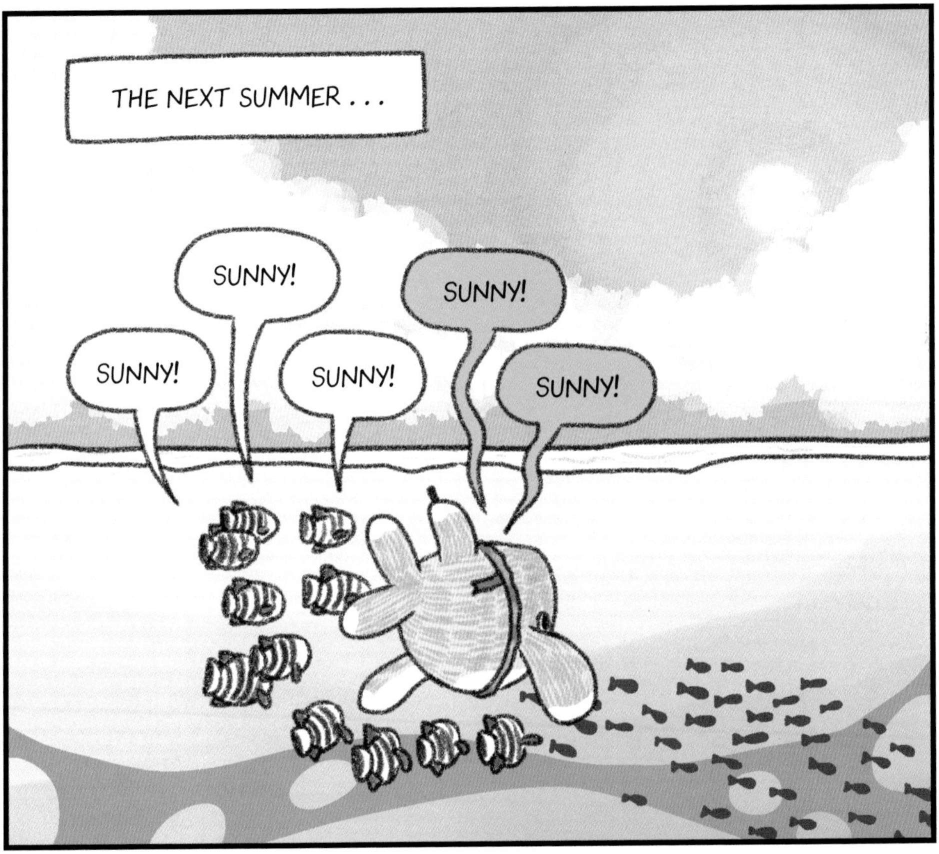
THE NEXT SUMMER . . .
SUNNY!
SUNNY!
SUNNY!
SUNNY!
SUNNY!

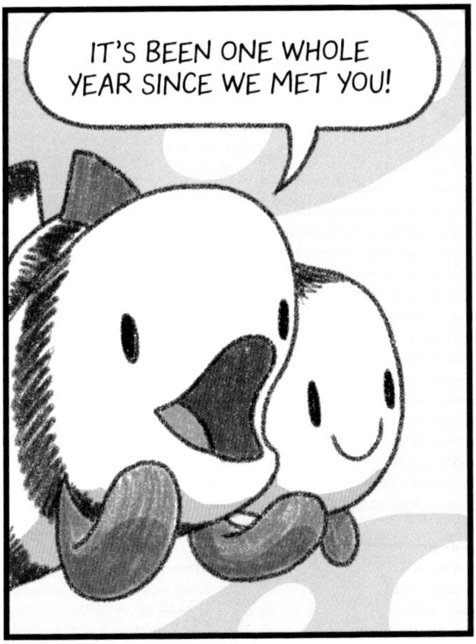
IT'S BEEN ONE WHOLE YEAR SINCE WE MET YOU!

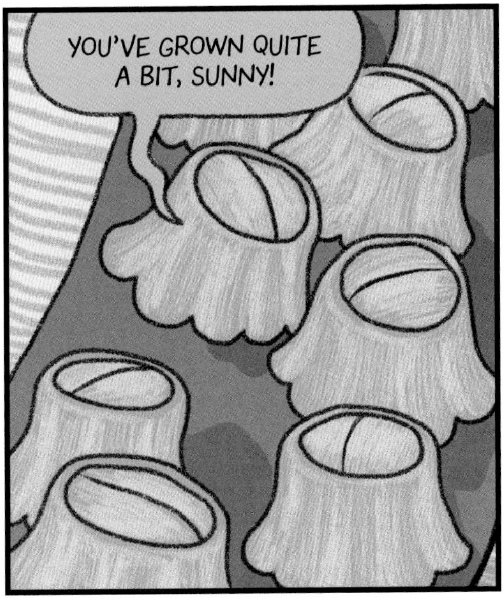
YOU'VE GROWN QUITE A BIT, SUNNY!

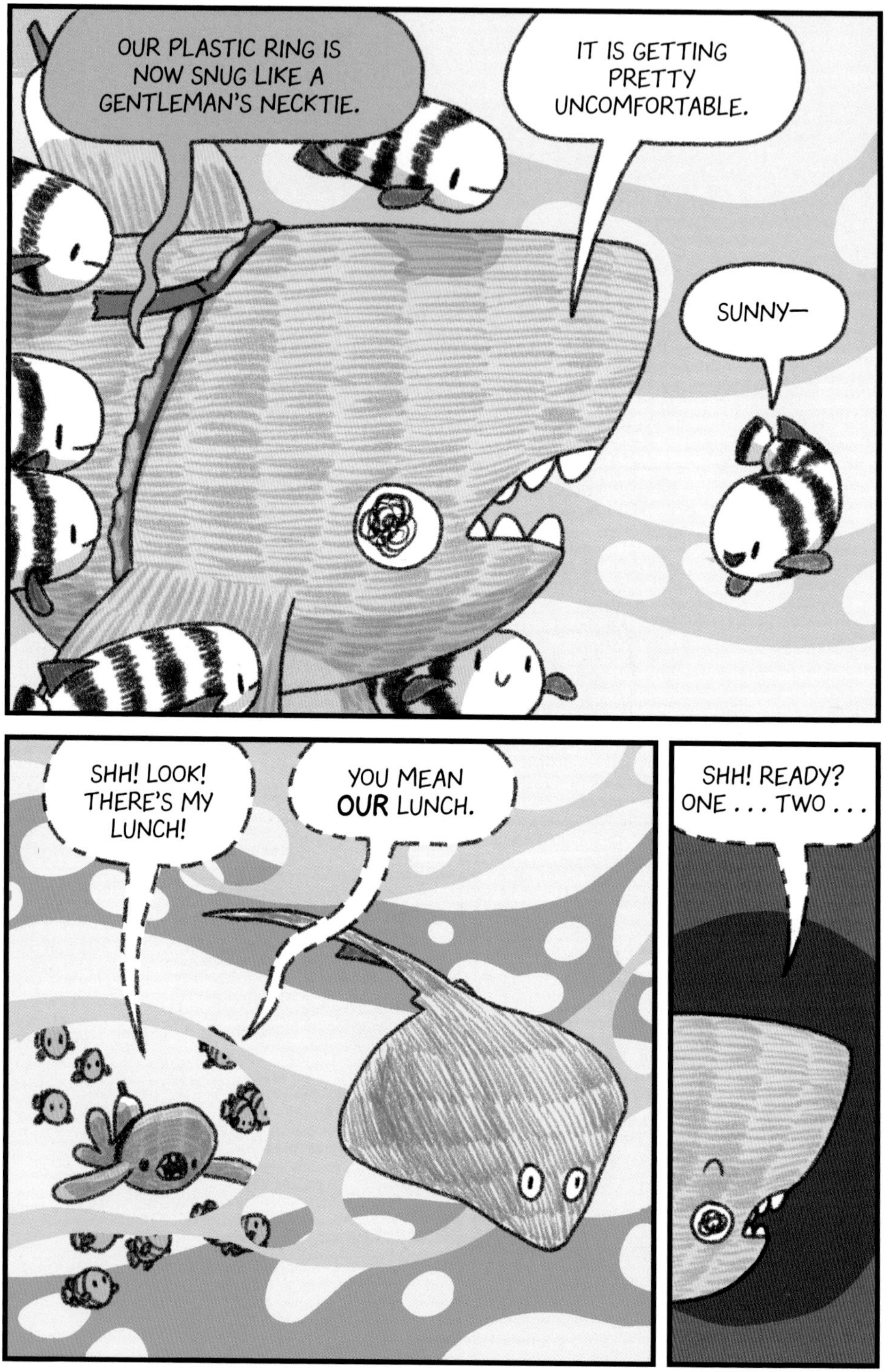

OUR PLASTIC RING IS NOW SNUG LIKE A GENTLEMAN'S NECKTIE.
IT IS GETTING PRETTY UNCOMFORTABLE.
SUNNY—
SHH! LOOK! THERE'S MY LUNCH!
YOU MEAN **OUR** LUNCH.
SHH! READY? ONE . . . TWO . . .

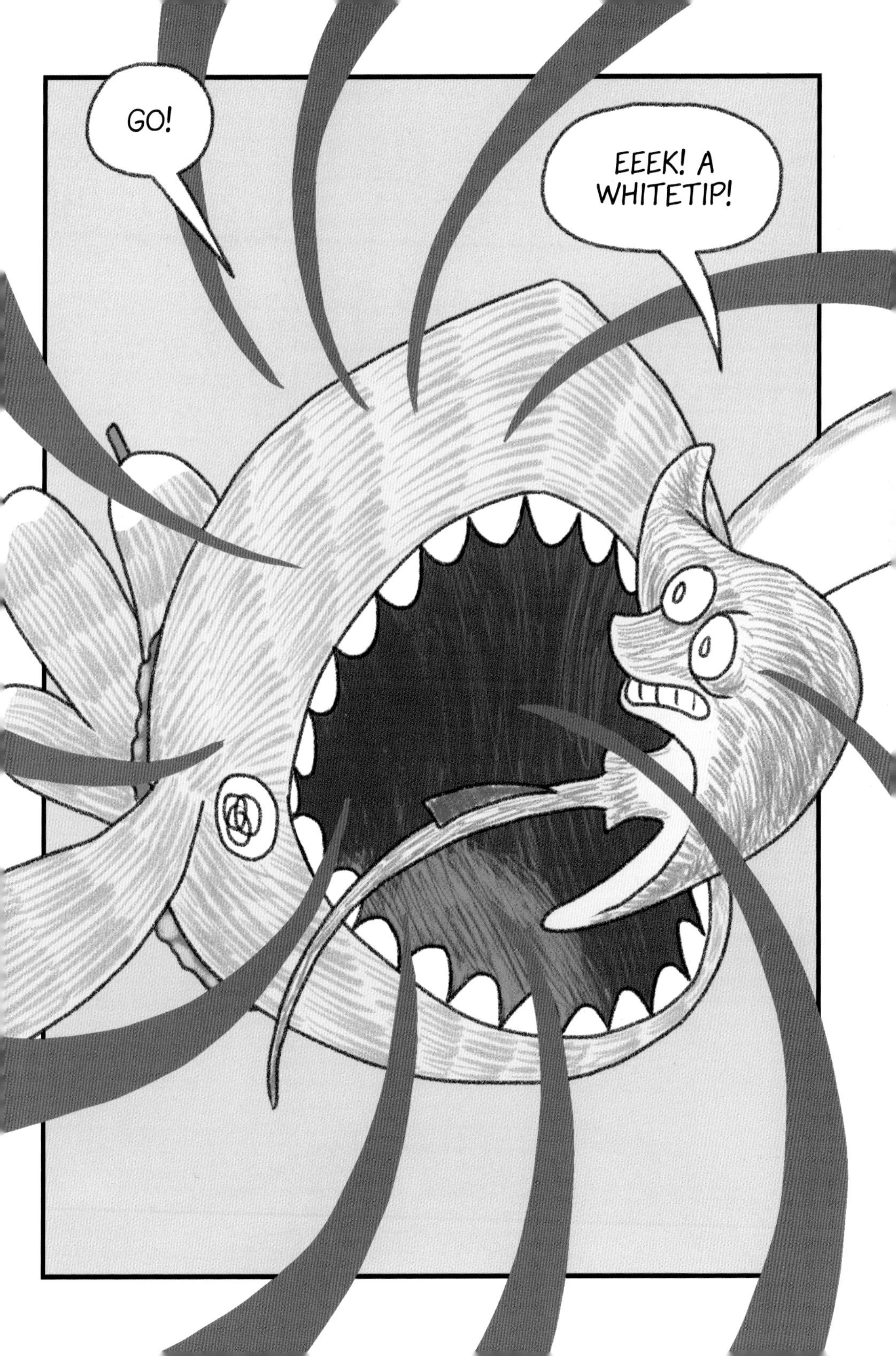
GO!
EEEK! A WHITETIP!

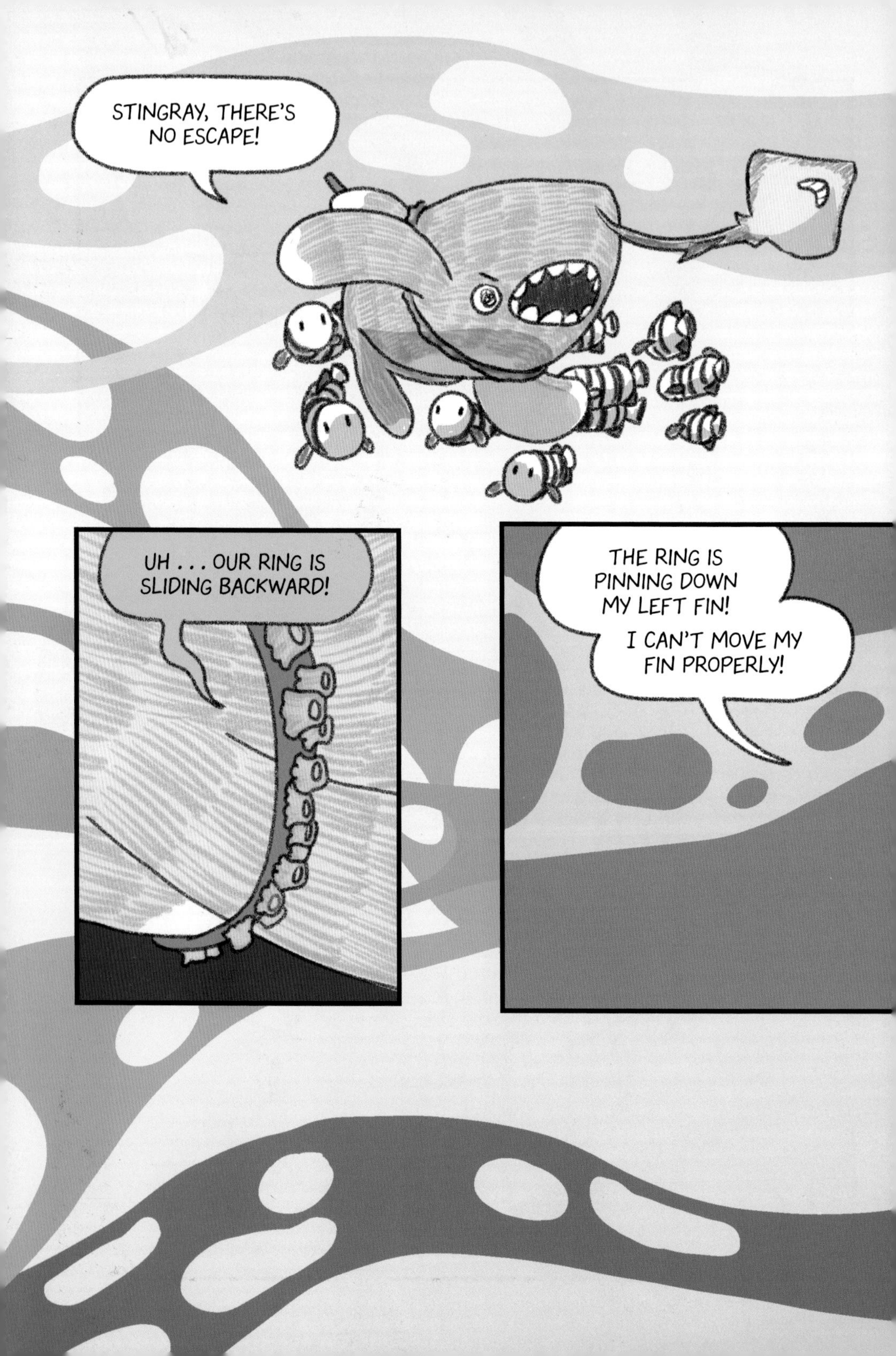
STINGRAY, THERE'S NO ESCAPE!
UH . . . OUR RING IS SLIDING BACKWARD!
THE RING IS PINNING DOWN MY LEFT FIN!
I CAN'T MOVE MY FIN PROPERLY!

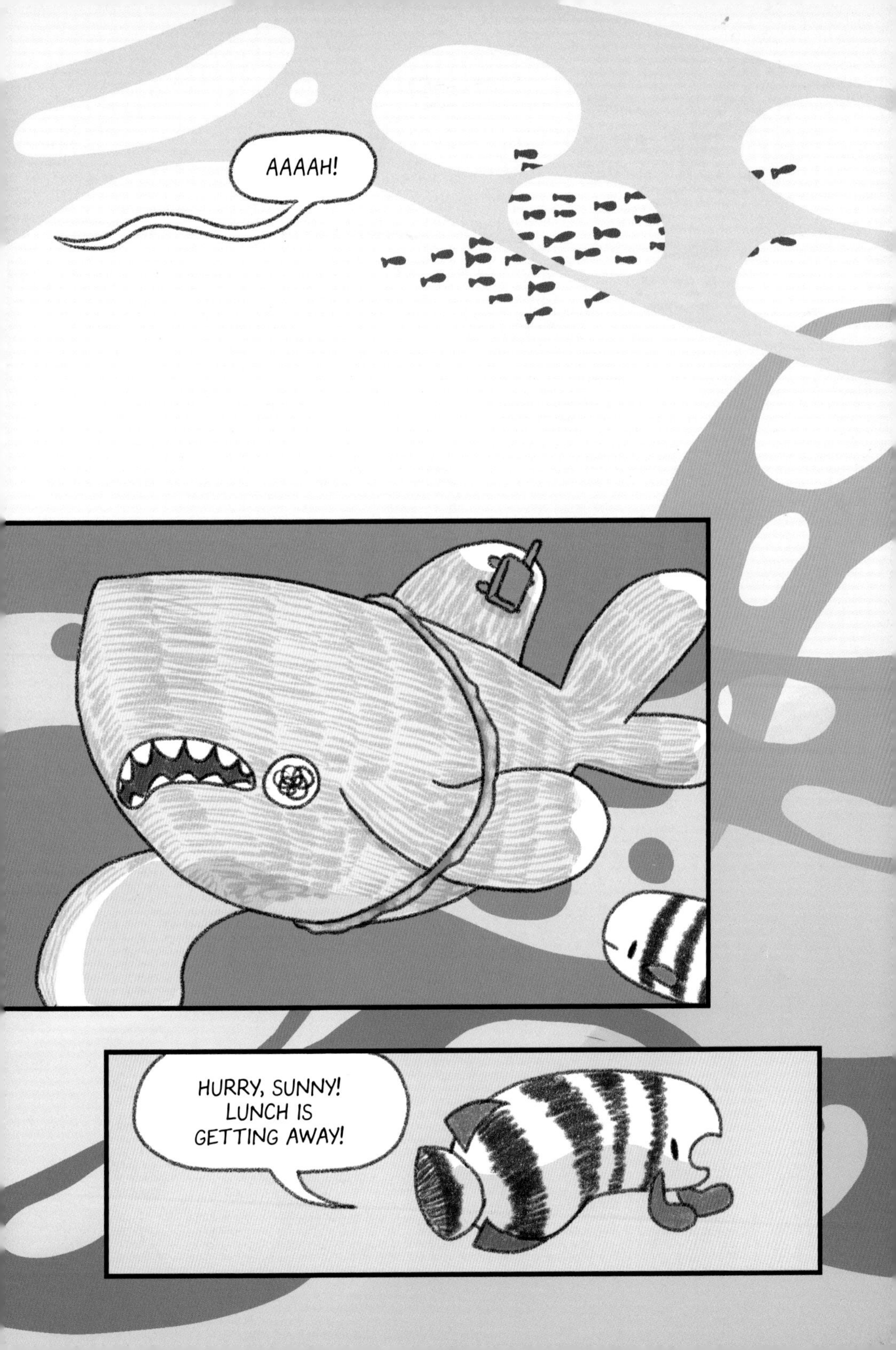
AAAAH!
HURRY, SUNNY! LUNCH IS GETTING AWAY!

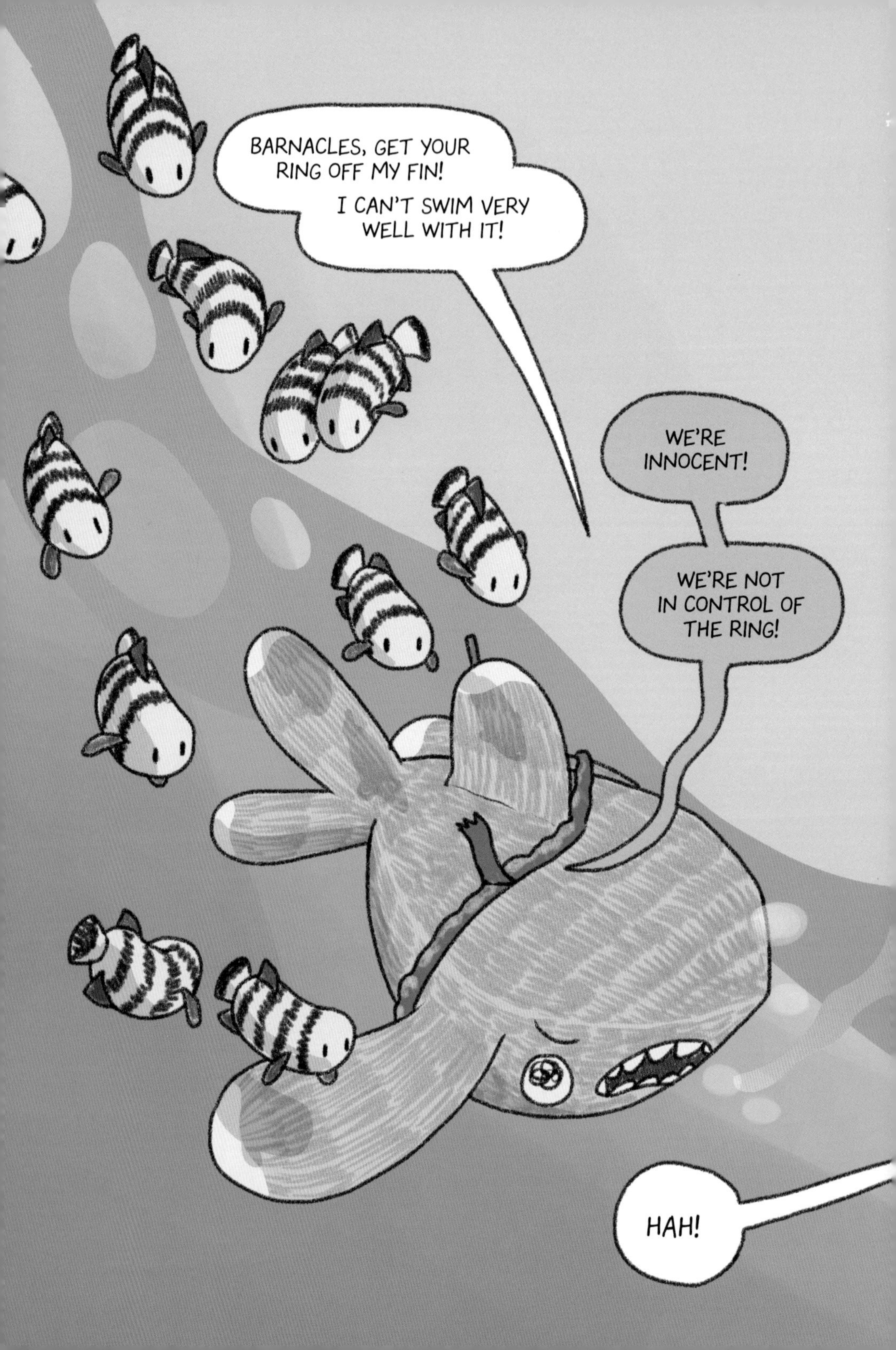
BARNACLES, GET YOUR RING OFF MY FIN!
I CAN'T SWIM VERY WELL WITH IT!
WE'RE INNOCENT!
WE'RE NOT IN CONTROL OF THE RING!
HAH!

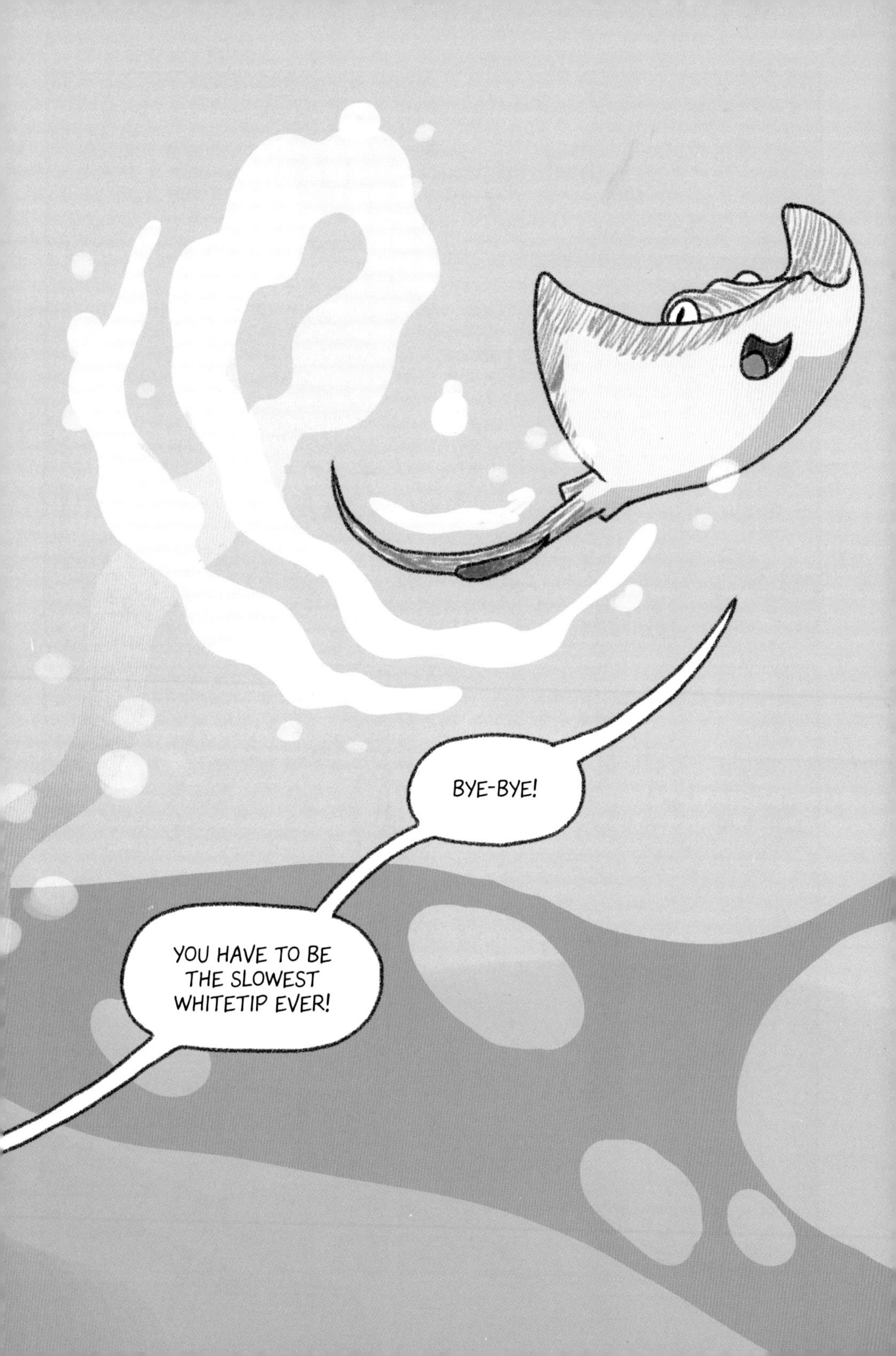
BYE-BYE!
YOU HAVE TO BE THE SLOWEST WHITETIP EVER!

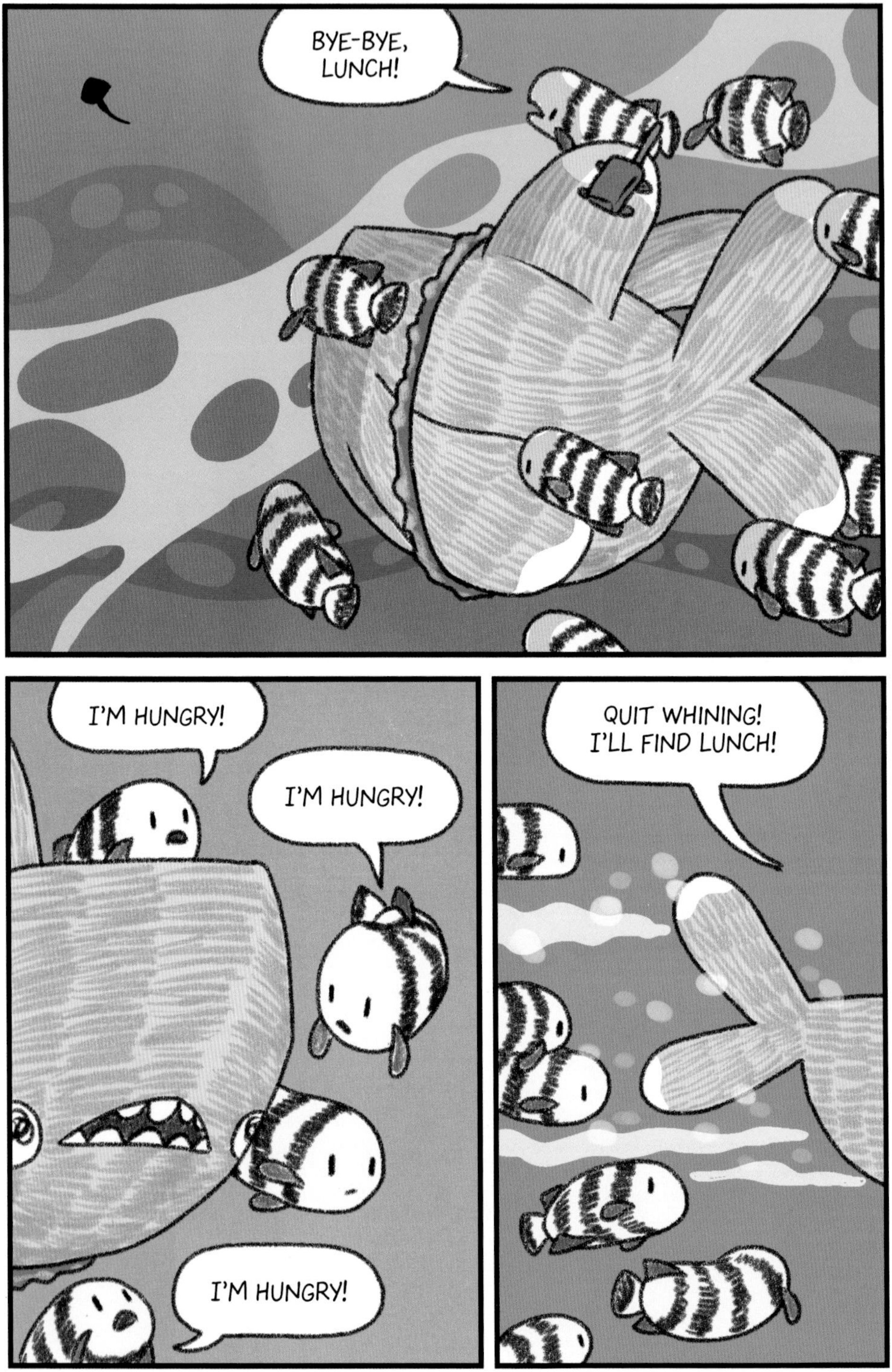
BYE-BYE, LUNCH!
I'M HUNGRY!
I'M HUNGRY!
I'M HUNGRY!
QUIT WHINING! I'LL FIND LUNCH!

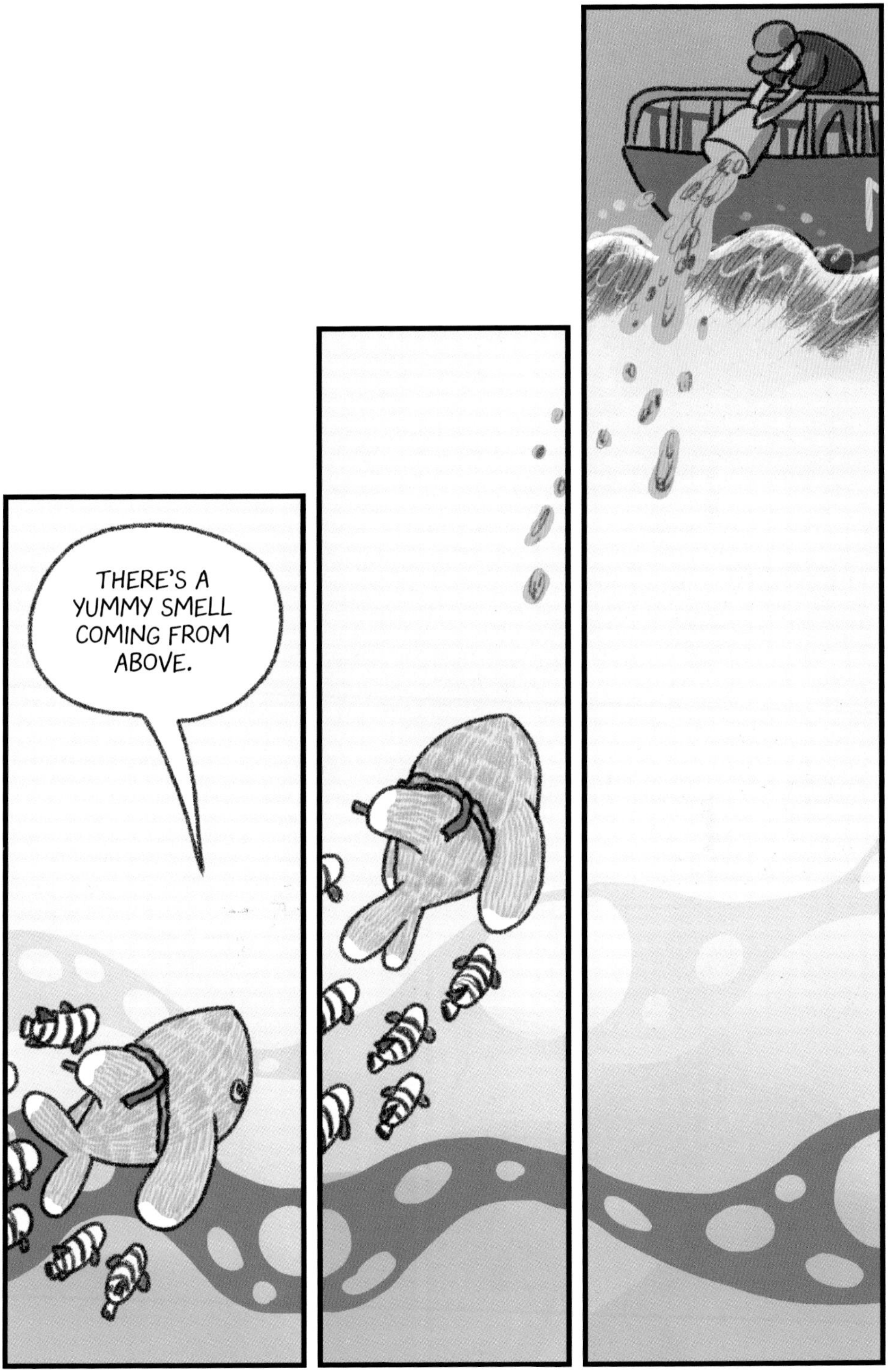
THERE'S A YUMMY SMELL COMING FROM ABOVE.

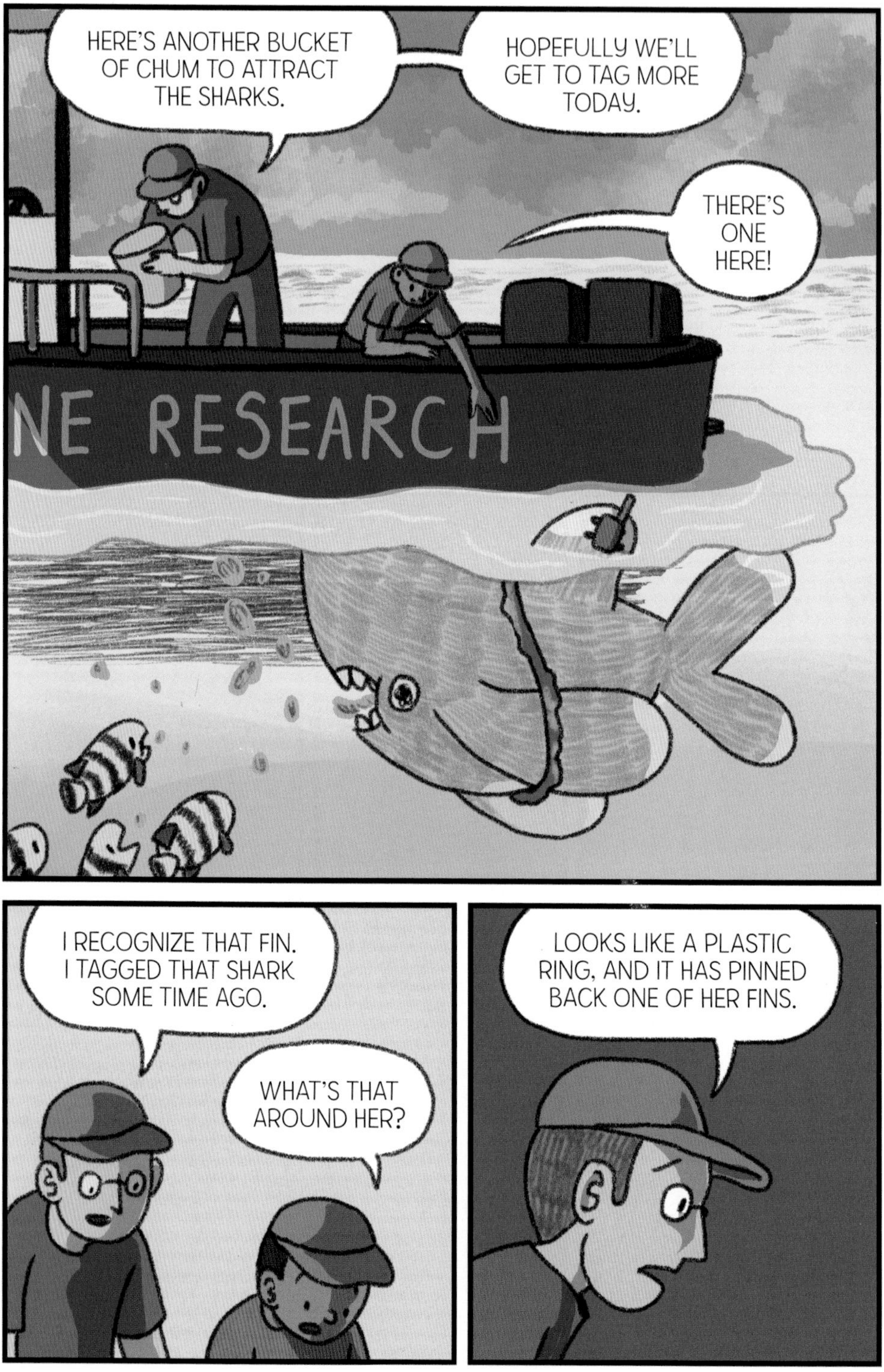
HERE'S ANOTHER BUCKET OF CHUM TO ATTRACT THE SHARKS.
HOPEFULLY WE'LL GET TO TAG MORE TODAY.
THERE'S ONE HERE!
NE RESEARCH
I RECOGNIZE THAT FIN. I TAGGED THAT SHARK SOME TIME AGO.
WHAT'S THAT AROUND HER?
LOOKS LIKE A PLASTIC RING, AND IT HAS PINNED BACK ONE OF HER FINS.

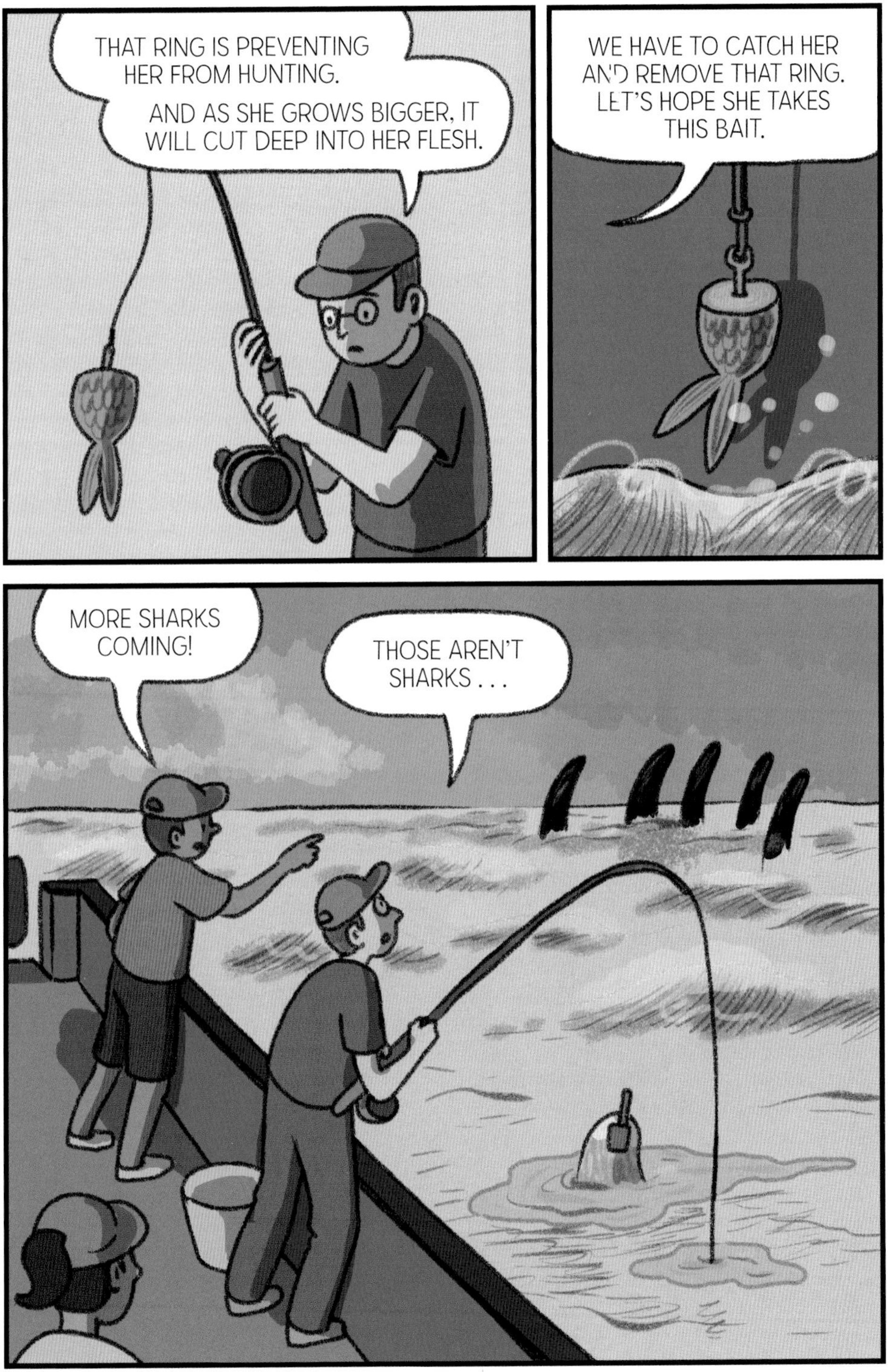
THAT RING IS PREVENTING HER FROM HUNTING.
AND AS SHE GROWS BIGGER, IT WILL CUT DEEP INTO HER FLESH.
WE HAVE TO CATCH HER AND REMOVE THAT RING. LET'S HOPE SHE TAKES THIS BAIT.
MORE SHARKS COMING!
THOSE AREN'T SHARKS . . .

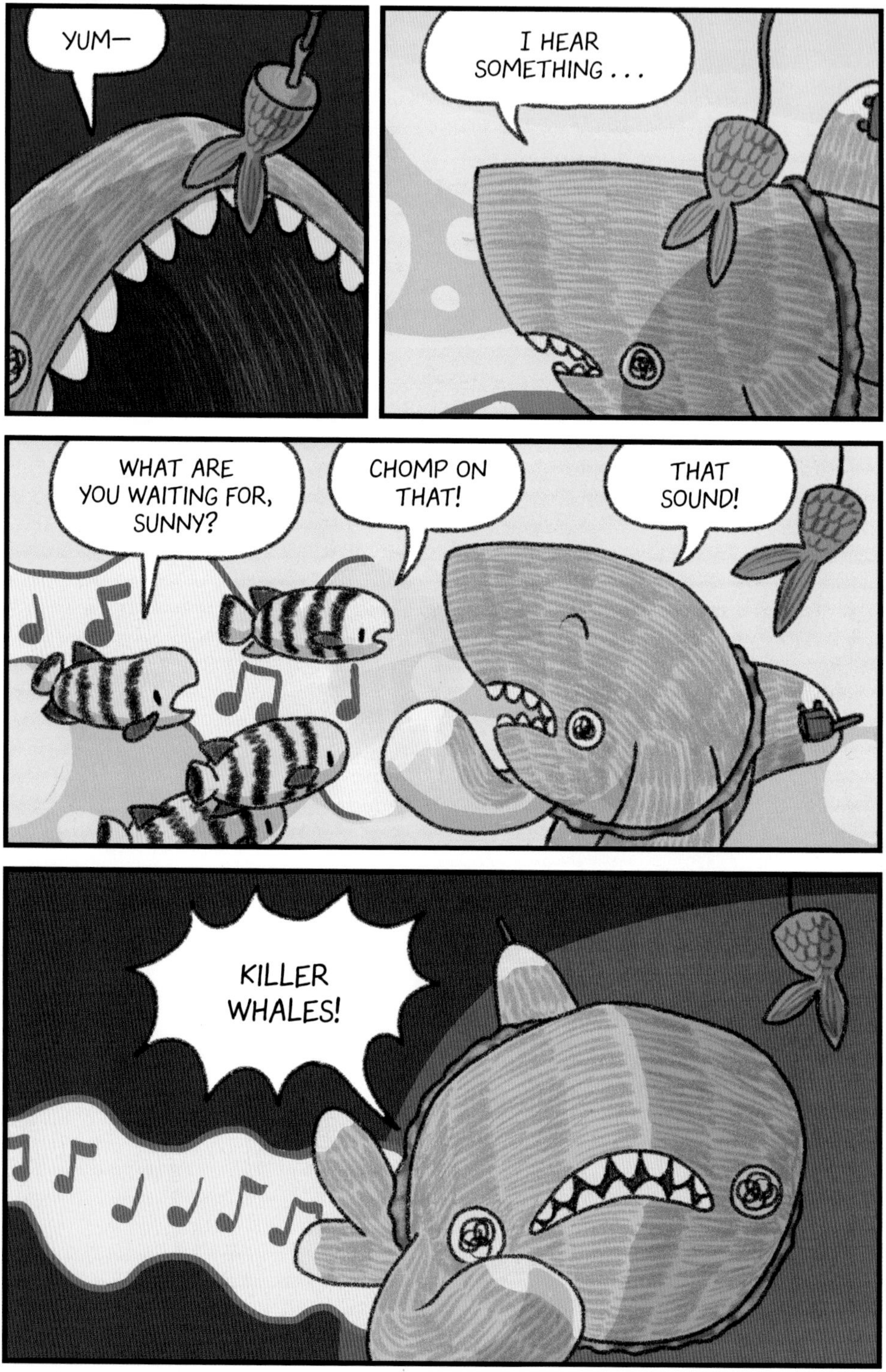
YUM—
I HEAR SOMETHING . . .
WHAT ARE YOU WAITING FOR, SUNNY?
CHOMP ON THAT!
THAT SOUND!
KILLER WHALES!

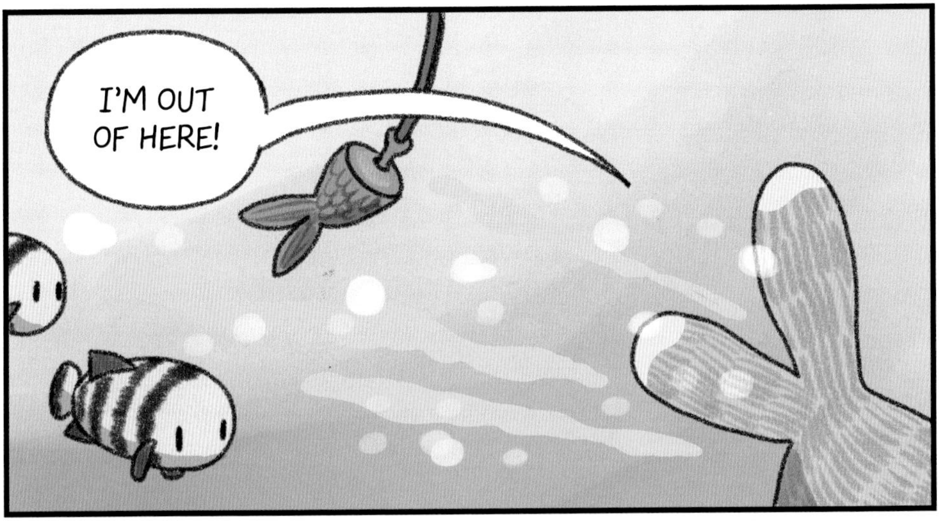
I'M OUT OF HERE!

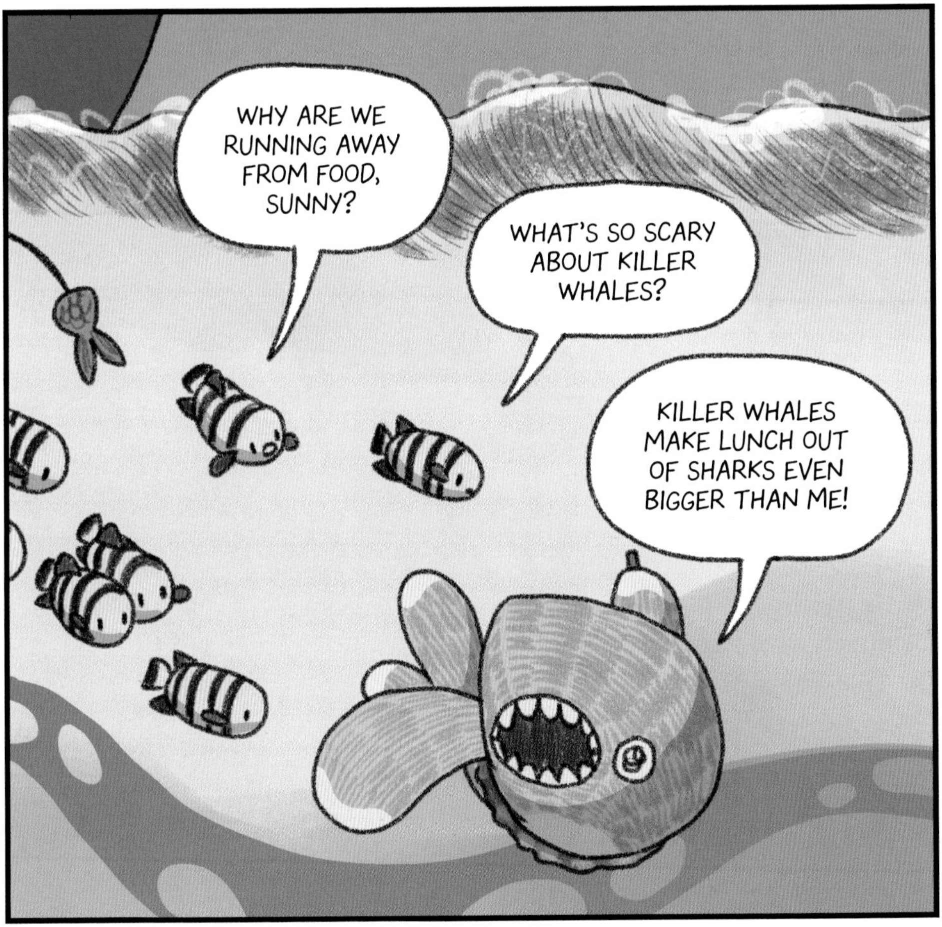
WHY ARE WE RUNNING AWAY FROM FOOD, SUNNY?
WHAT'S SO SCARY ABOUT KILLER WHALES?
KILLER WHALES MAKE LUNCH OUT OF SHARKS EVEN BIGGER THAN ME!

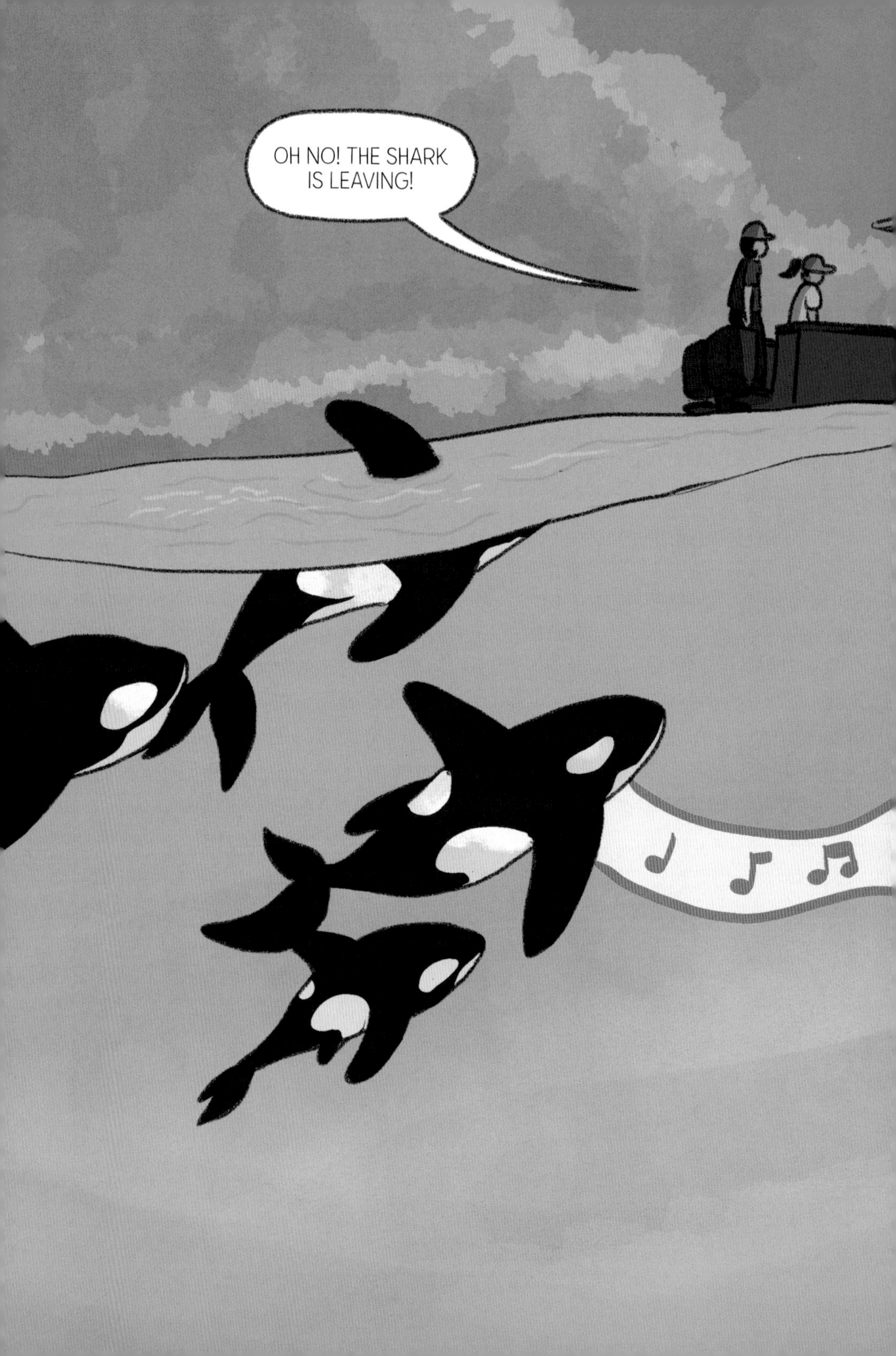
OH NO! THE SHARK IS LEAVING!

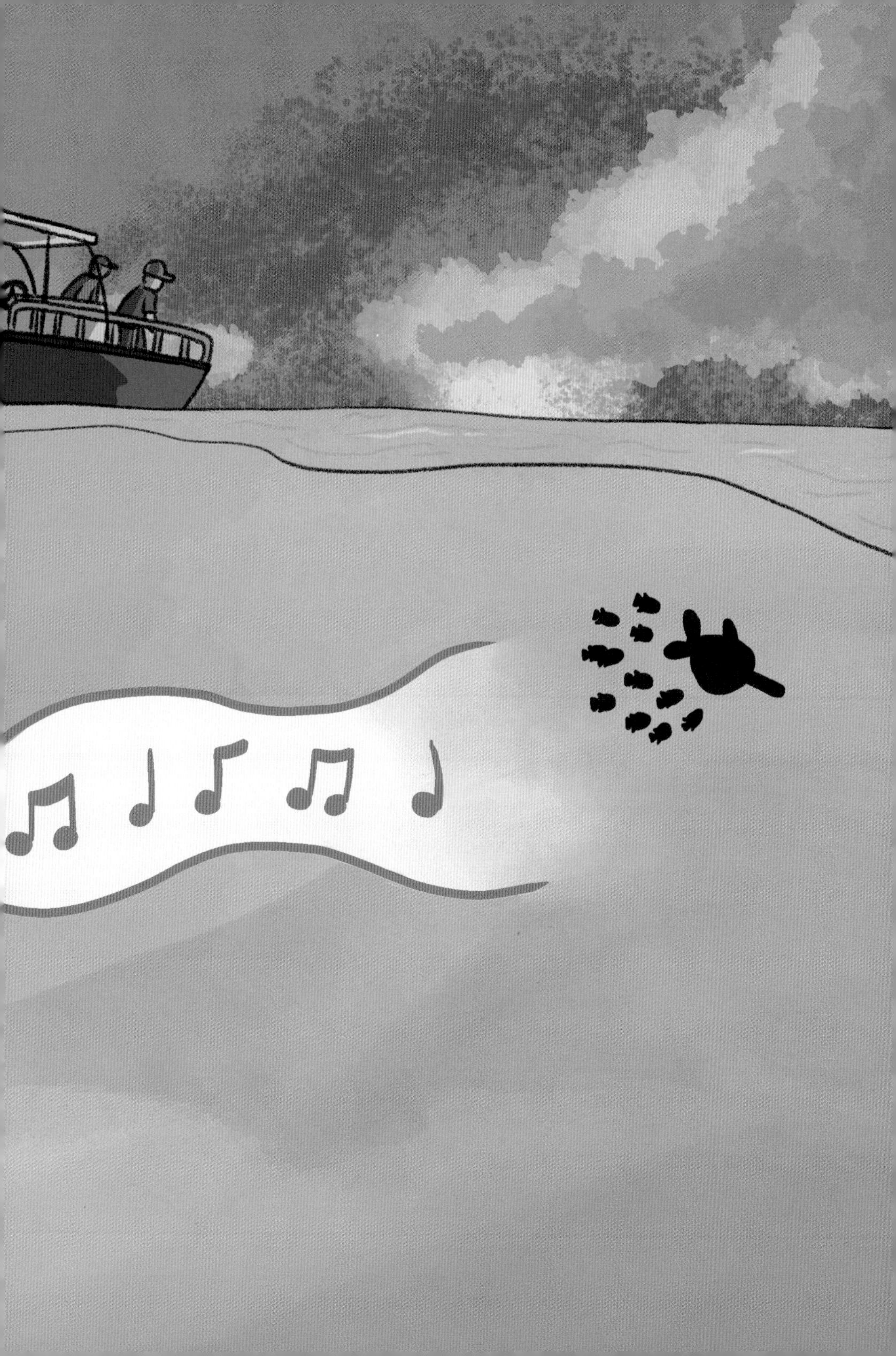

THE PLASTIC RING WILL MAKE IT HARD FOR THAT SHARK TO HUNT.

BY MY ESTIMATION, IF SHE DOESN'T GET IF OFF, SHE WON'T SURVIVE BEYOND THE FIRST SNOWFALL.

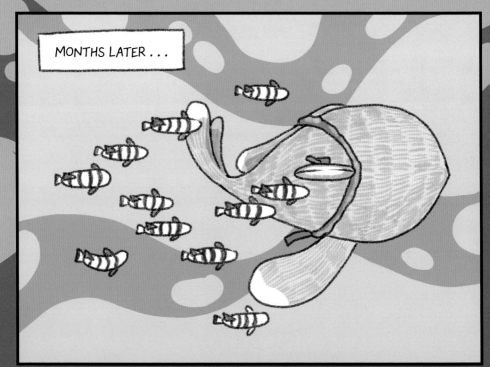

MONTHS LATER . . .

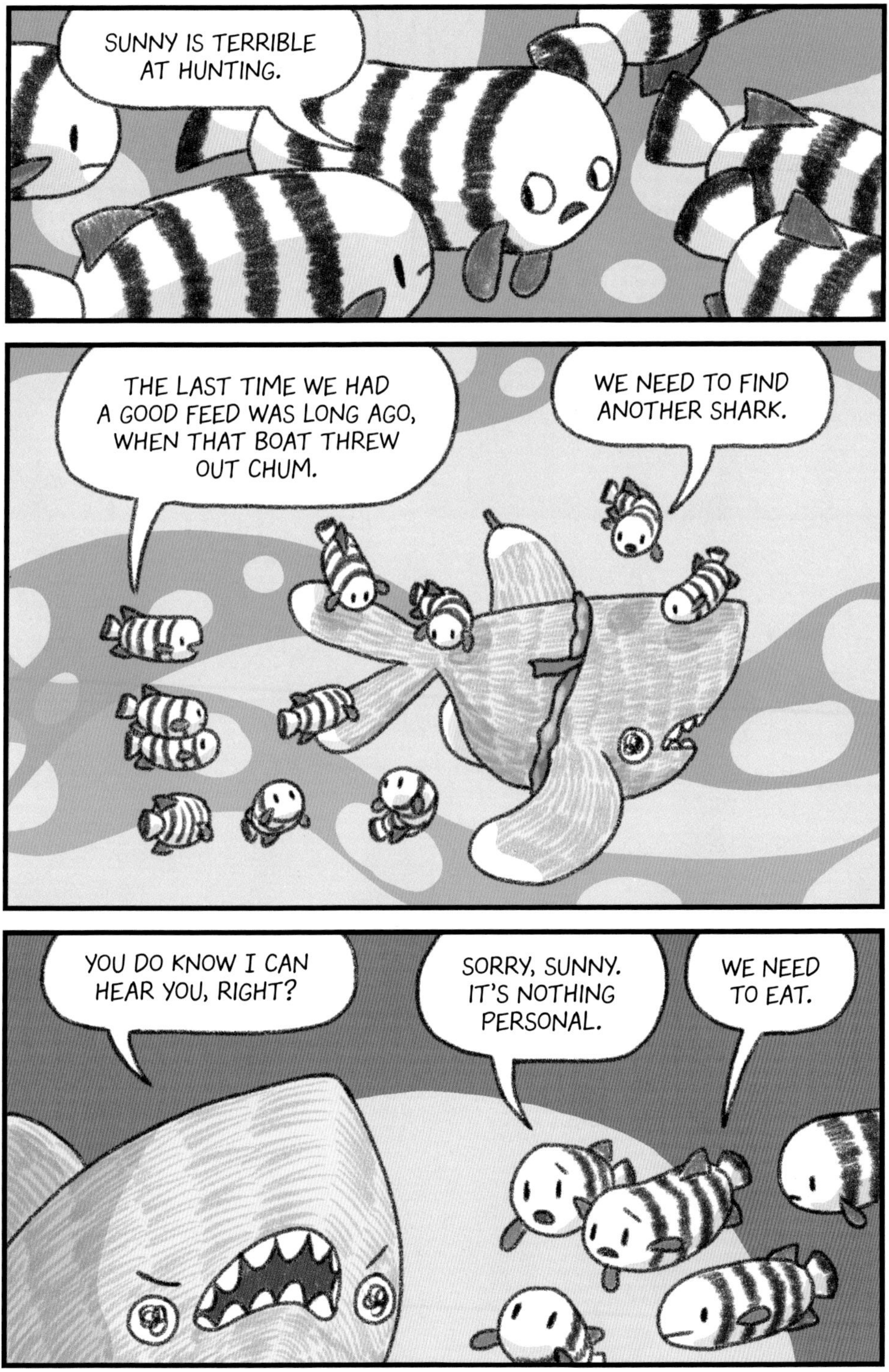
SUNNY IS TERRIBLE AT HUNTING.
THE LAST TIME WE HAD A GOOD FEED WAS LONG AGO, WHEN THAT BOAT THREW OUT CHUM.
WE NEED TO FIND ANOTHER SHARK.
YOU DO KNOW I CAN HEAR YOU, RIGHT?
SORRY, SUNNY. IT'S NOTHING PERSONAL.
WE NEED TO EAT.

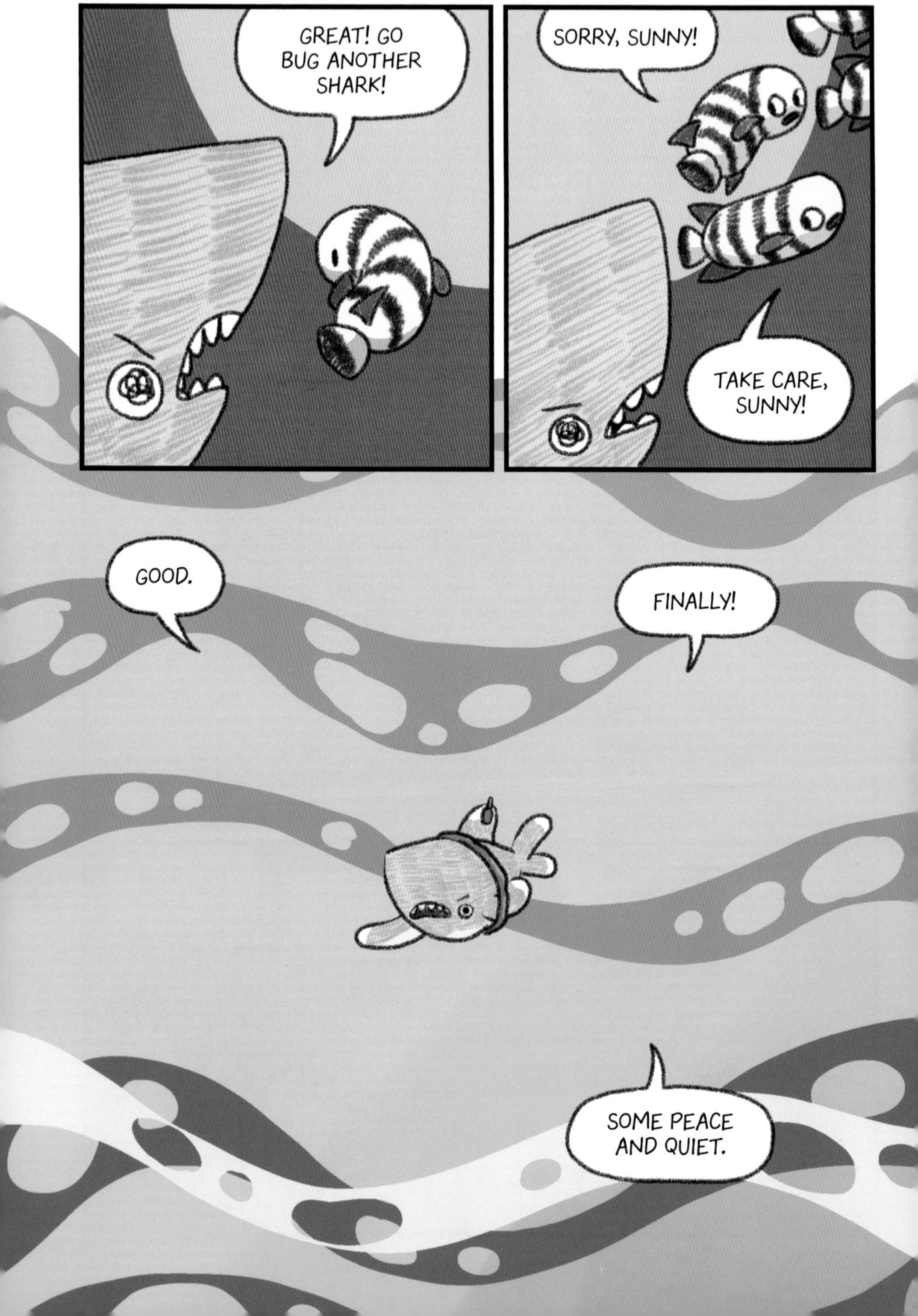
GREAT! GO BUG ANOTHER SHARK!
SORRY, SUNNY!
TAKE CARE, SUNNY!
GOOD.
FINALLY!
SOME PEACE AND QUIET.

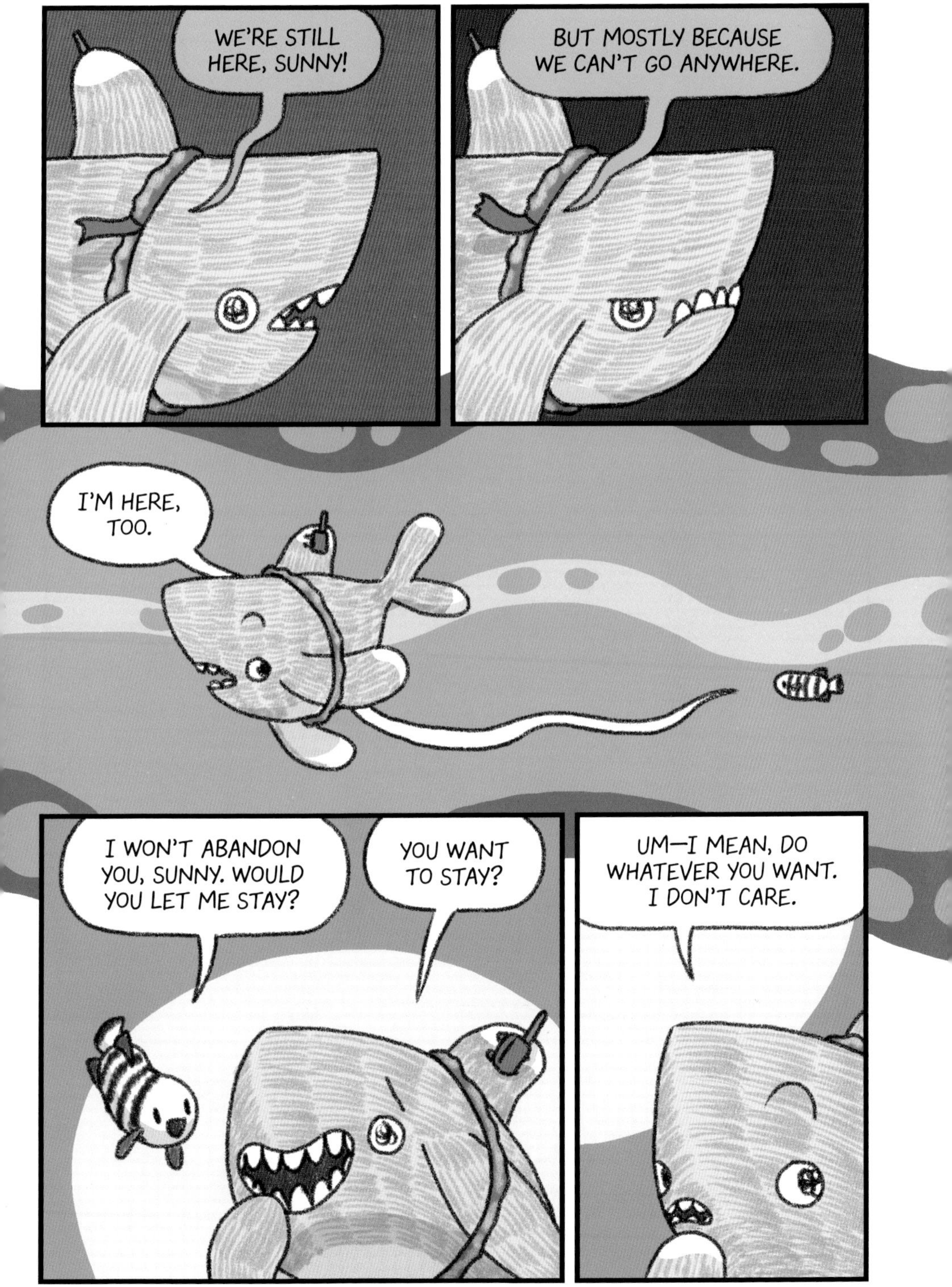
WE'RE STILL HERE, SUNNY!
BUT MOSTLY BECAUSE WE CAN'T GO ANYWHERE.
I'M HERE, TOO.
I WON'T ABANDON YOU, SUNNY. WOULD YOU LET ME STAY?
YOU WANT TO STAY?
UM—I MEAN, DO WHATEVER YOU WANT. I DON'T CARE.

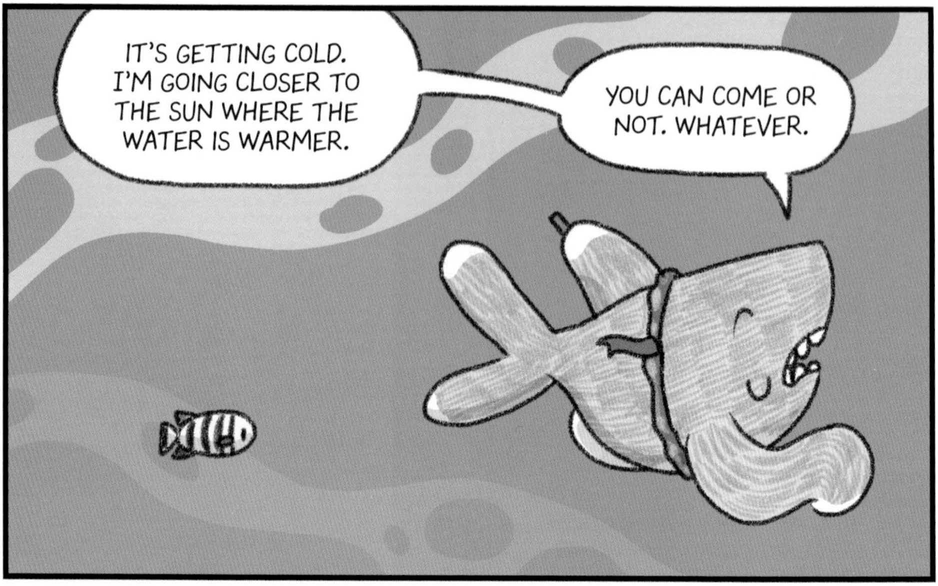
IT'S GETTING COLD. I'M GOING CLOSER TO THE SUN WHERE THE WATER IS WARMER.
YOU CAN COME OR NOT. WHATEVER.

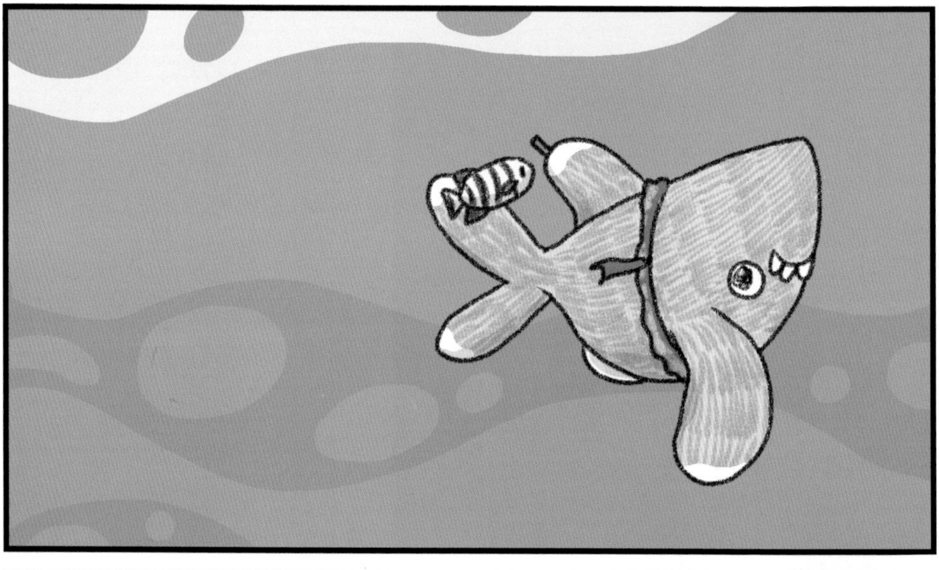

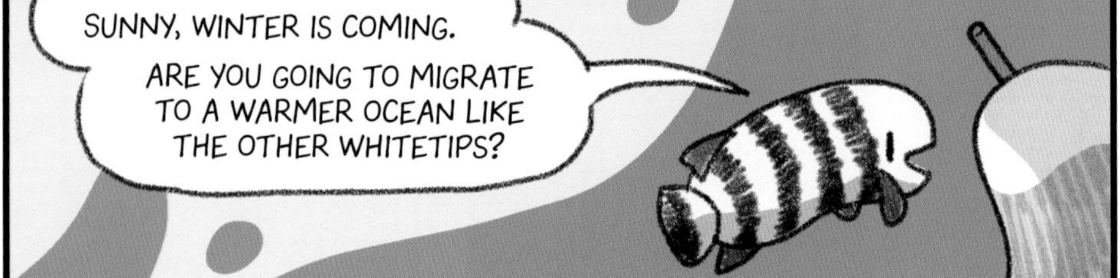
SUNNY, WINTER IS COMING.
ARE YOU GOING TO MIGRATE TO A WARMER OCEAN LIKE THE OTHER WHITETIPS?

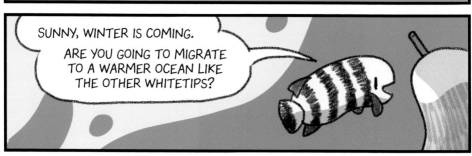

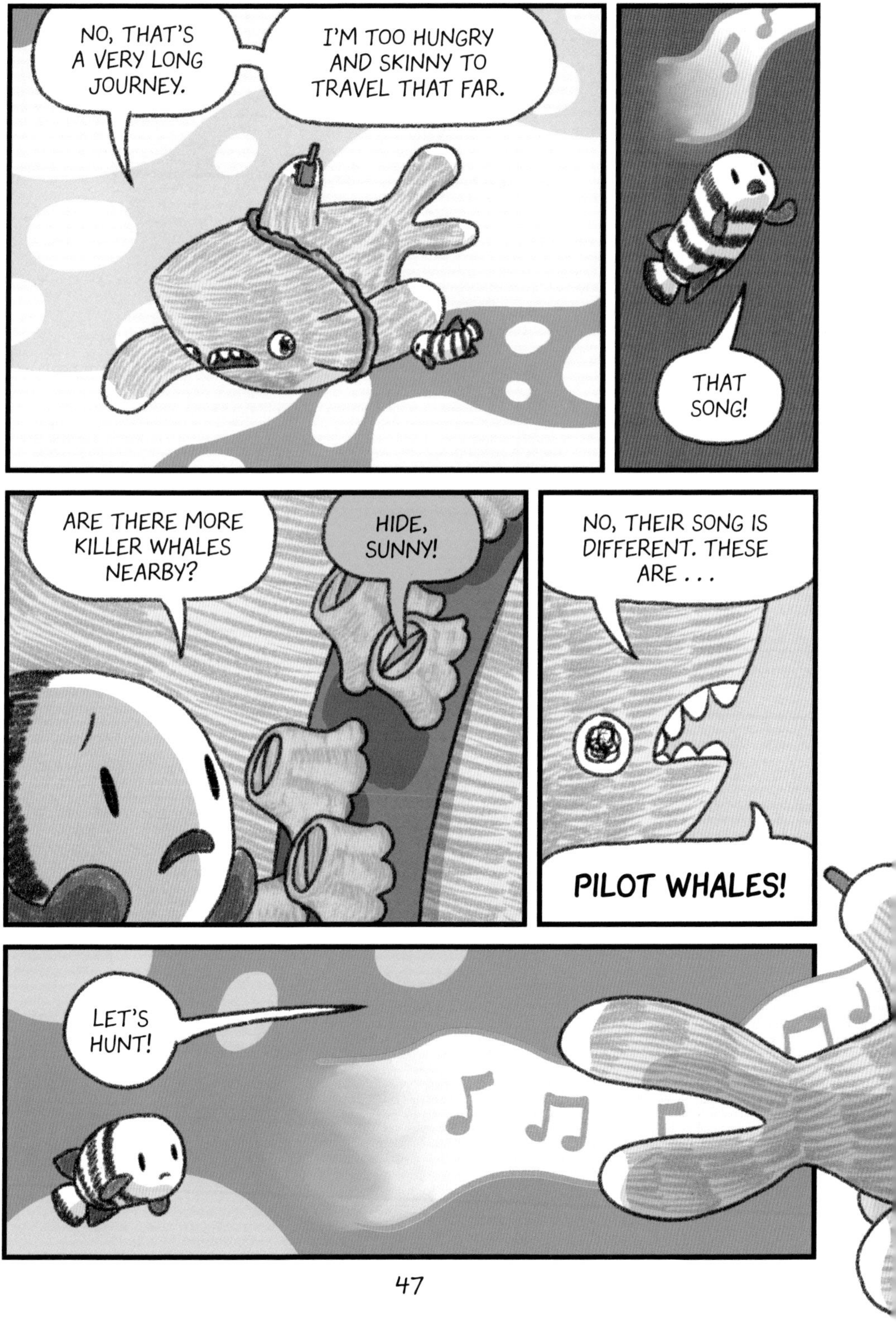
NO, THAT'S A VERY LONG JOURNEY.
I'M TOO HUNGRY AND SKINNY TO TRAVEL THAT FAR.
THAT SONG!
ARE THERE MORE KILLER WHALES NEARBY?
HIDE, SUNNY!
NO, THEIR SONG IS DIFFERENT. THESE ARE . . .
PILOT WHALES!
LET'S HUNT!

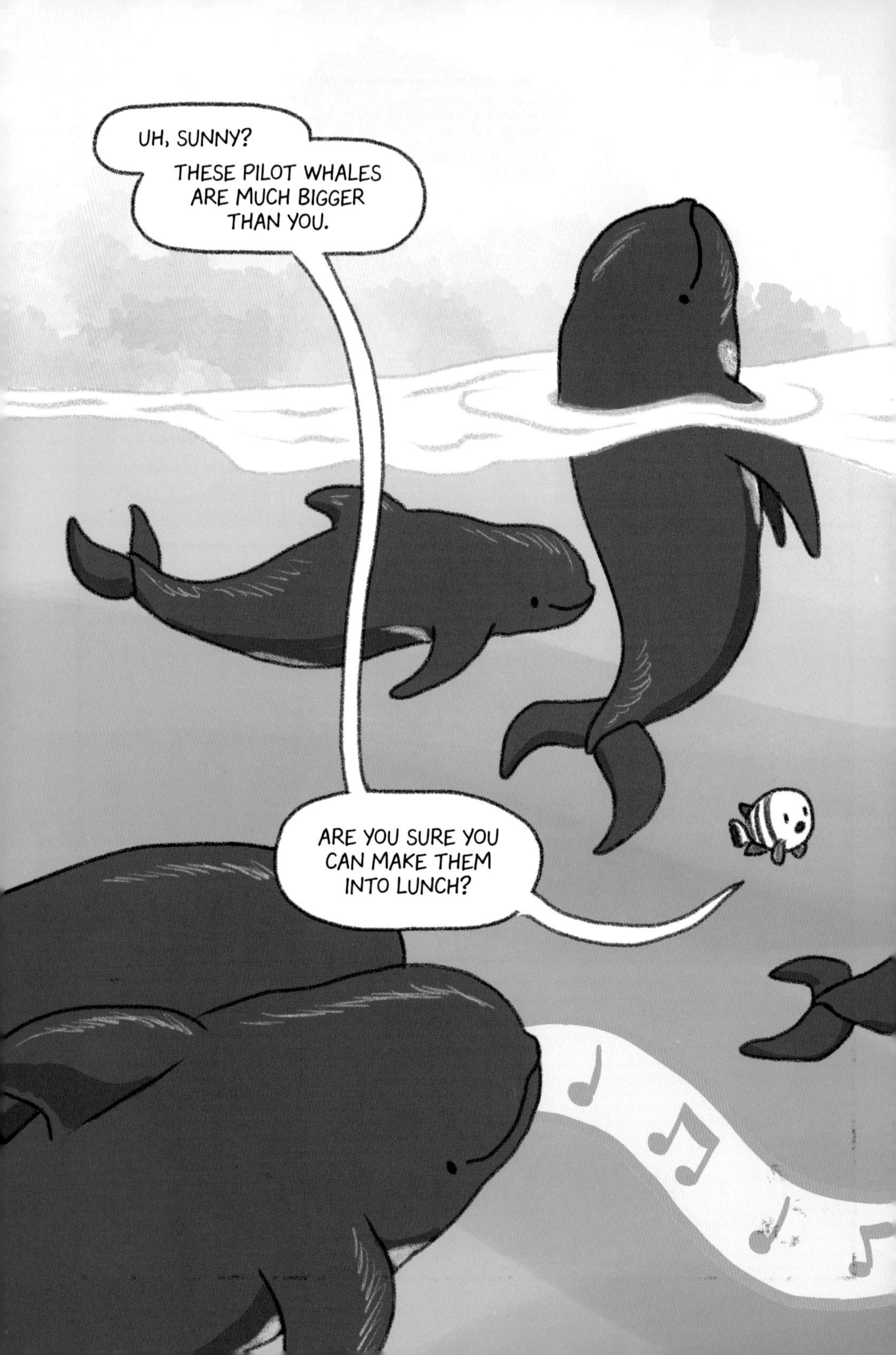
UH, SUNNY?
THESE PILOT WHALES ARE MUCH BIGGER THAN YOU.
ARE YOU SURE YOU CAN MAKE THEM INTO LUNCH?

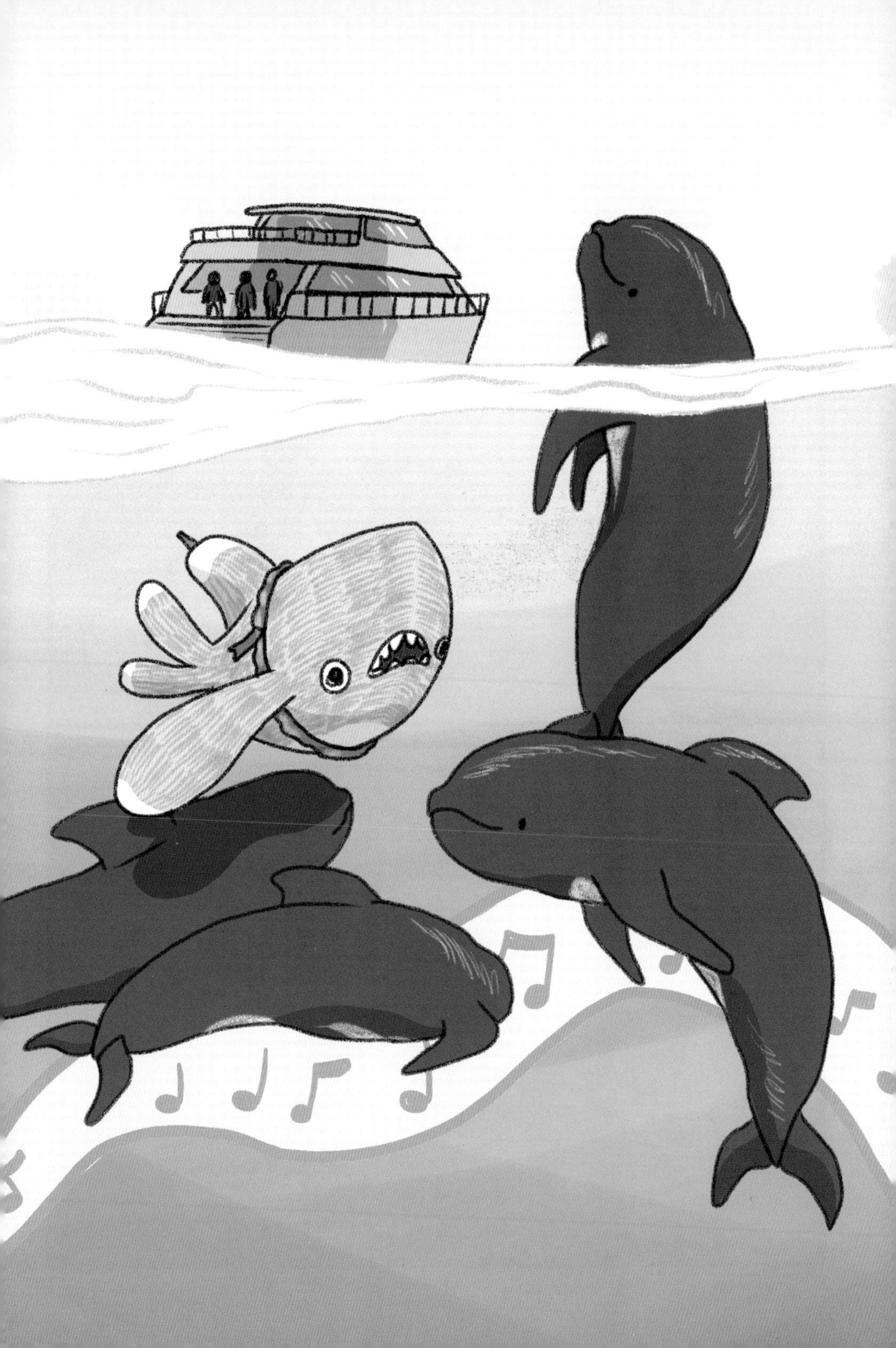

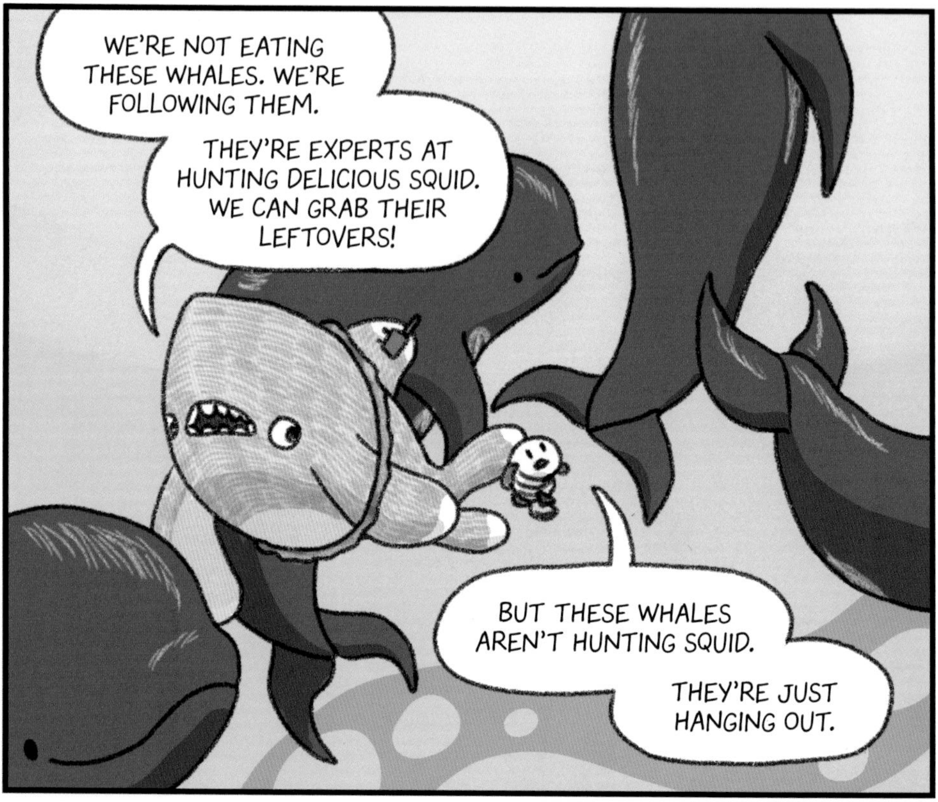
WE'RE NOT EATING THESE WHALES. WE'RE FOLLOWING THEM.
THEY'RE EXPERTS AT HUNTING DELICIOUS SQUID. WE CAN GRAB THEIR LEFTOVERS!
BUT THESE WHALES AREN'T HUNTING SQUID.
THEY'RE JUST HANGING OUT.

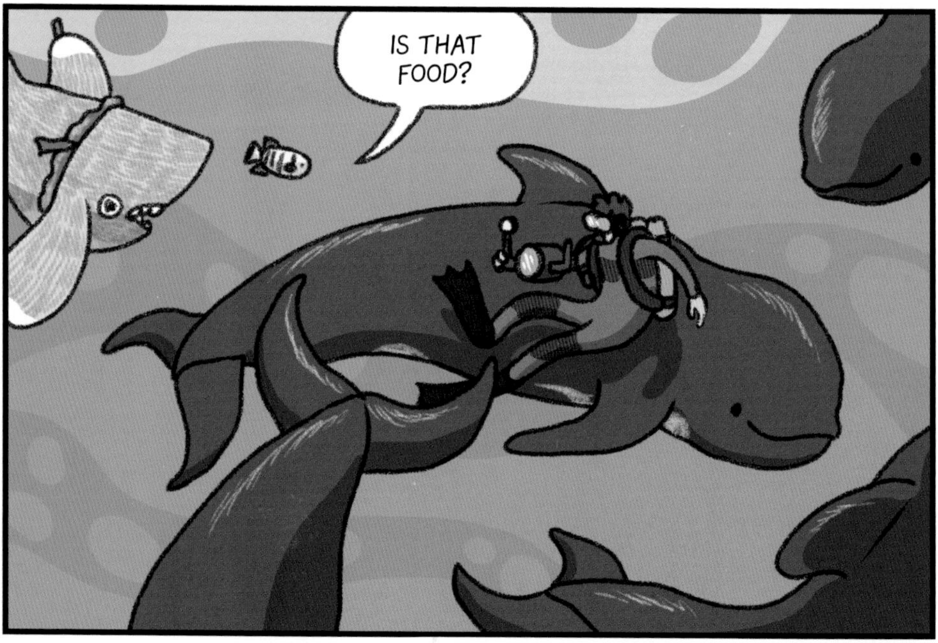
IS THAT FOOD?

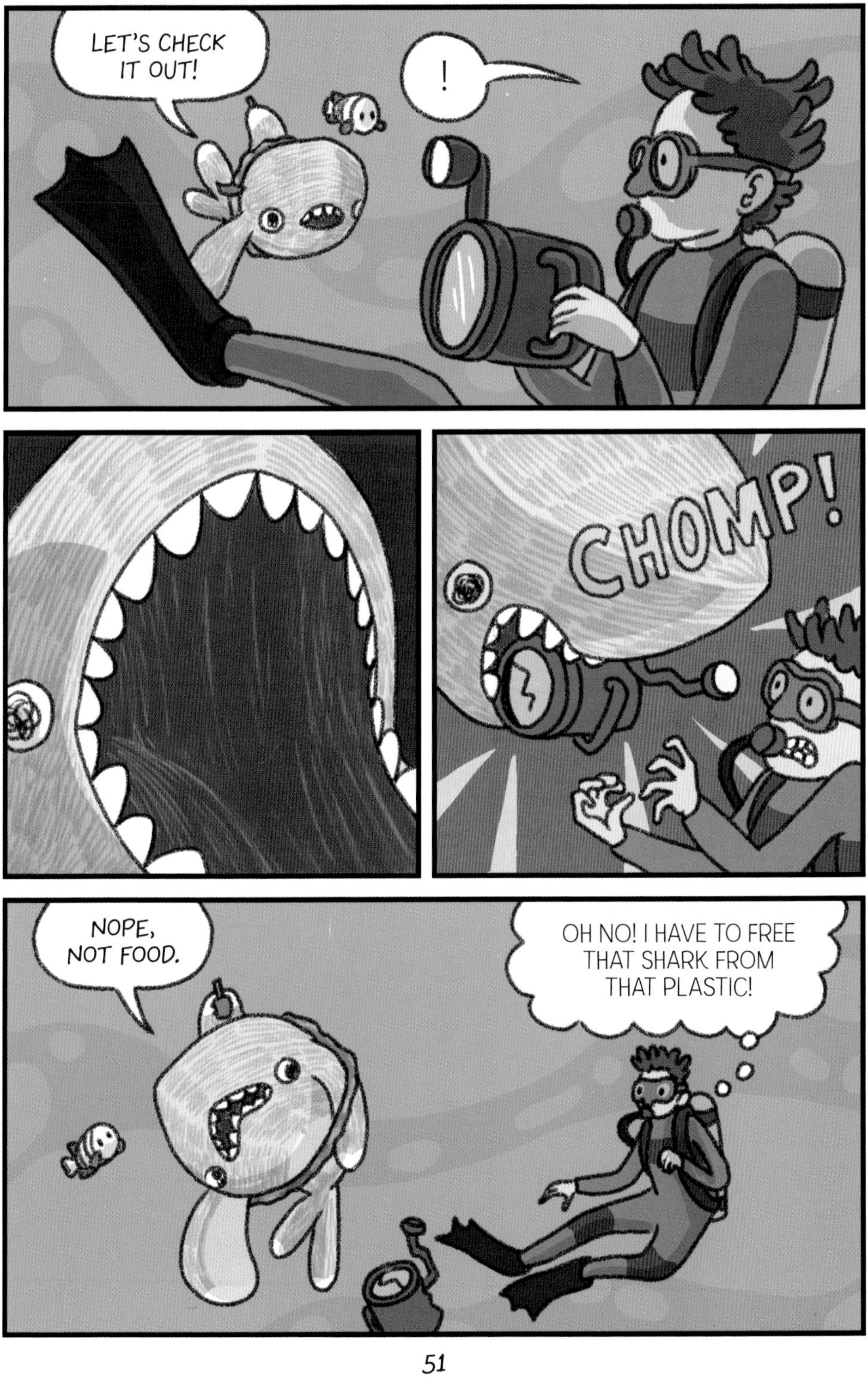
LET'S CHECK IT OUT!
!
CHOMP!
NOPE, NOT FOOD.
OH NO! I HAVE TO FREE THAT SHARK FROM THAT PLASTIC!

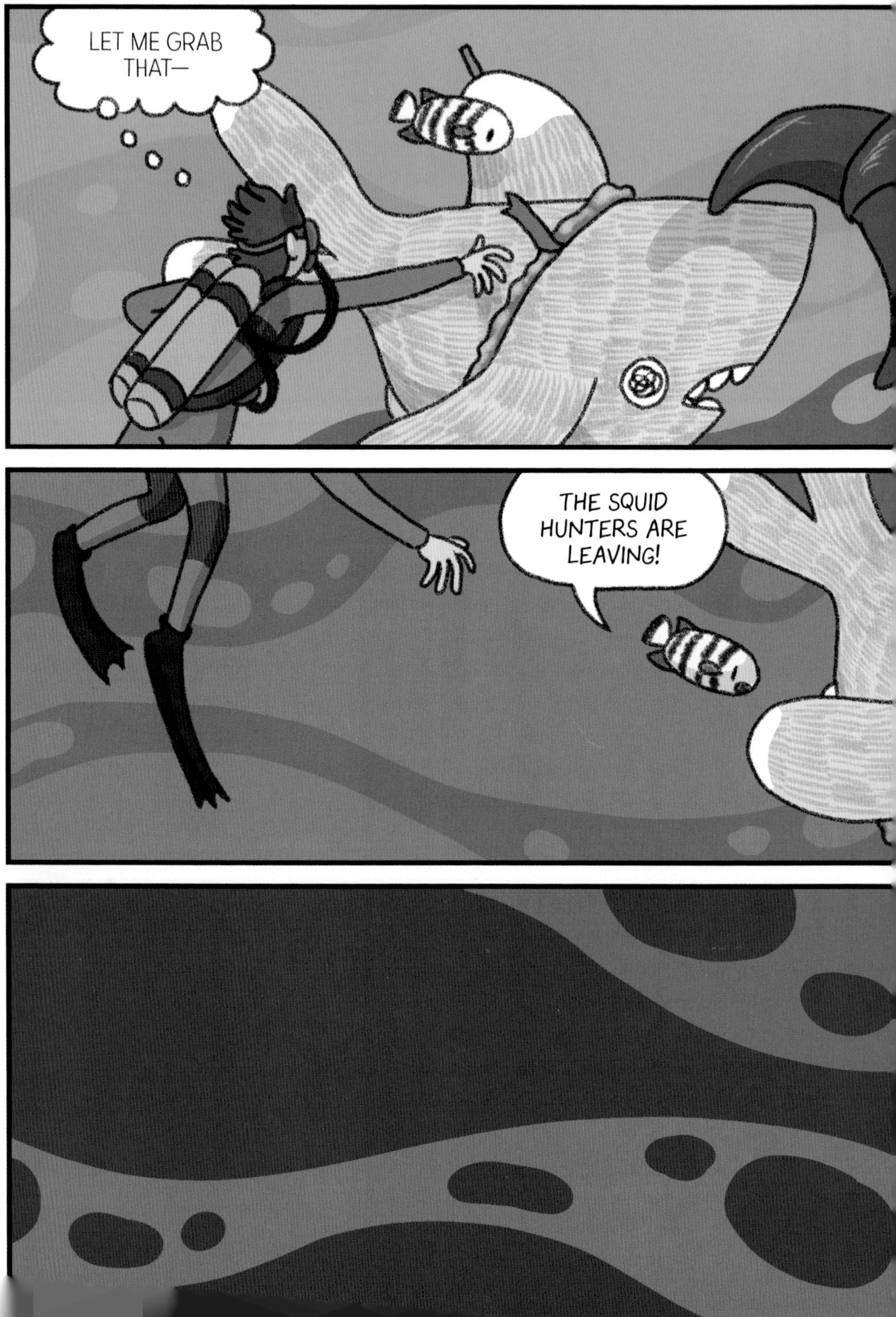
LET ME GRAB THAT—
THE SQUID HUNTERS ARE LEAVING!

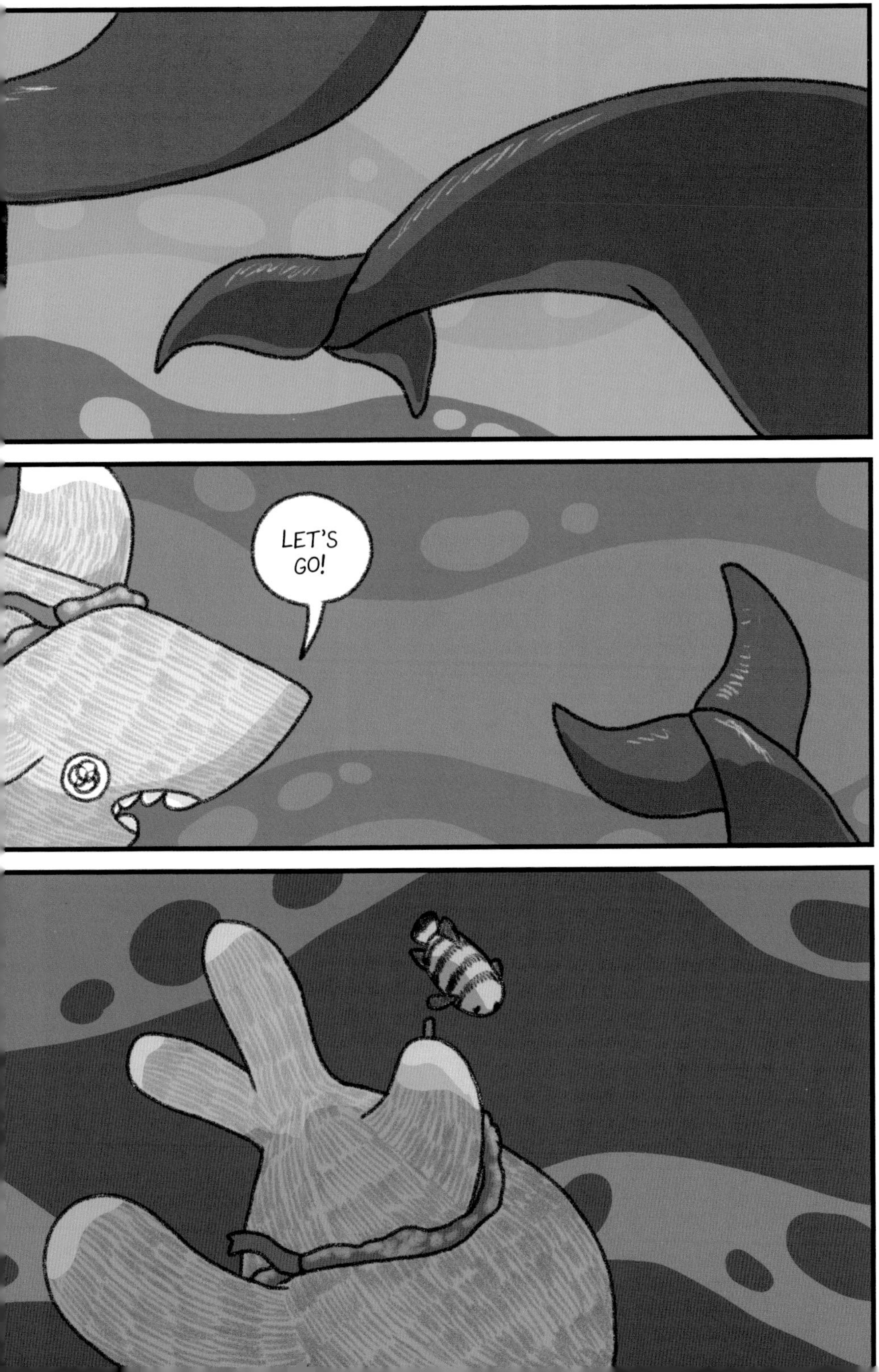
LET'S GO!

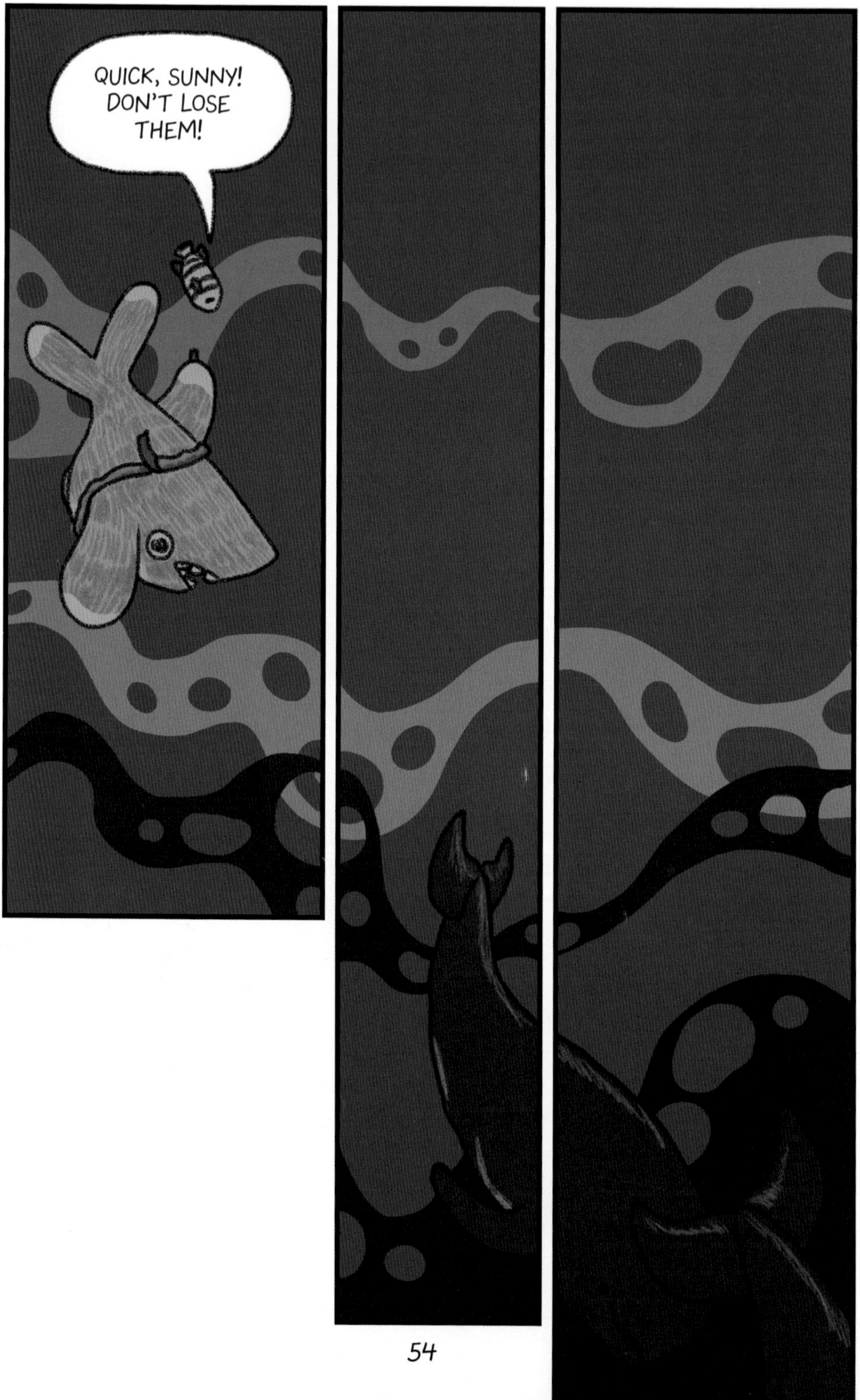
QUICK, SUNNY! DON'T LOSE THEM!

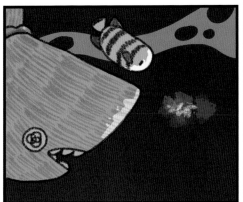

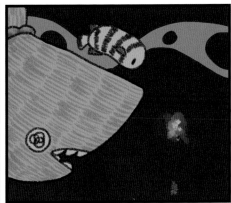

WHAT'S THAT FLASHING STREAK OF LIGHT?

IT'S A SMALL SQUID!

SQUIDS MAKE LIGHT LIKE THE SUN???

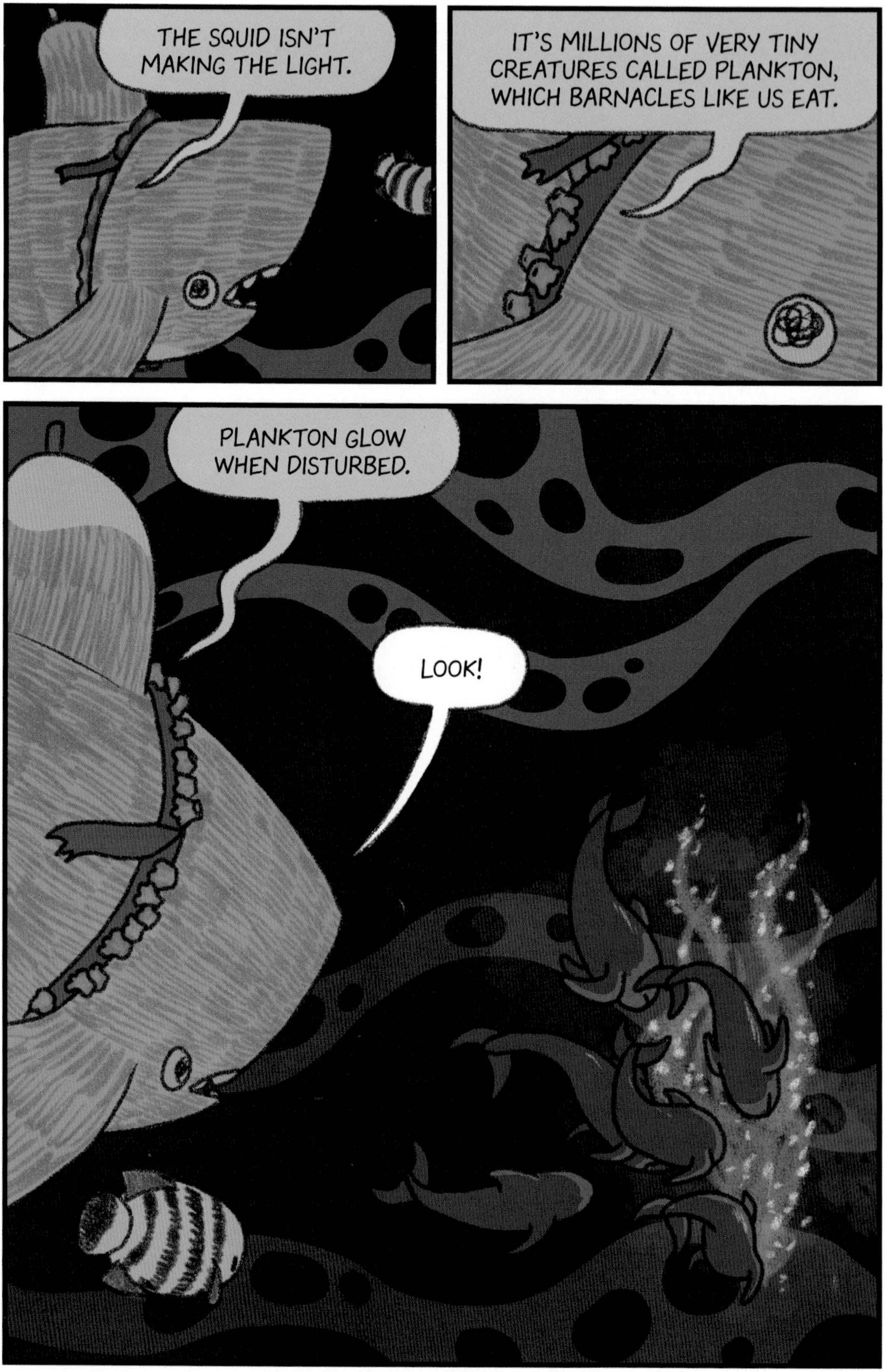
THE SQUID ISN'T MAKING THE LIGHT.
IT'S MILLIONS OF VERY TINY CREATURES CALLED PLANKTON, WHICH BARNACLES LIKE US EAT.
PLANKTON GLOW WHEN DISTURBED.
LOOK!

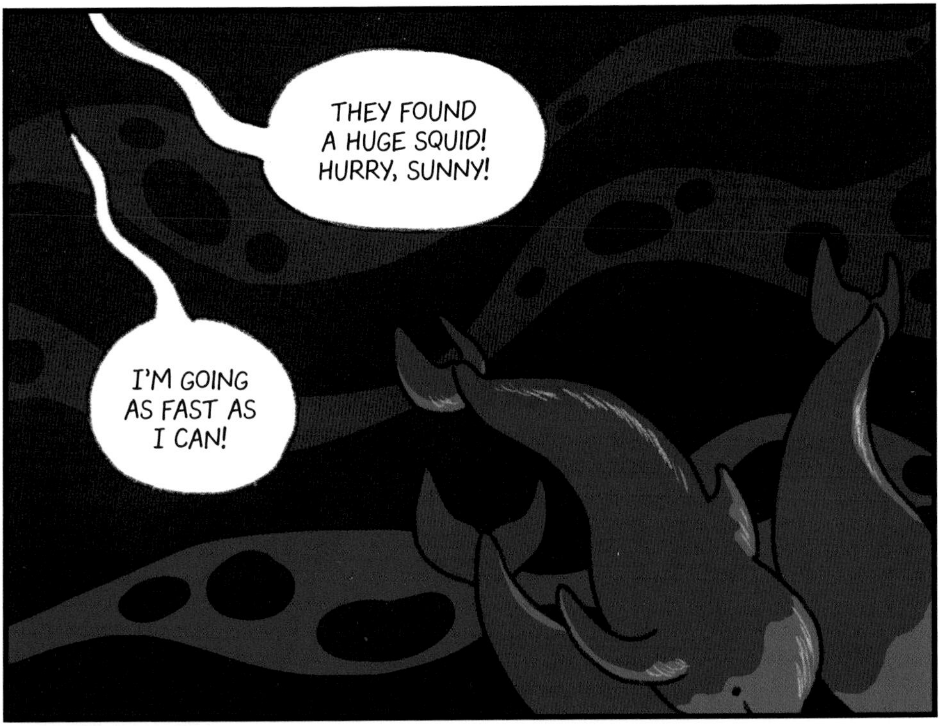
THEY FOUND A HUGE SQUID! HURRY, SUNNY!
I'M GOING AS FAST AS I CAN!

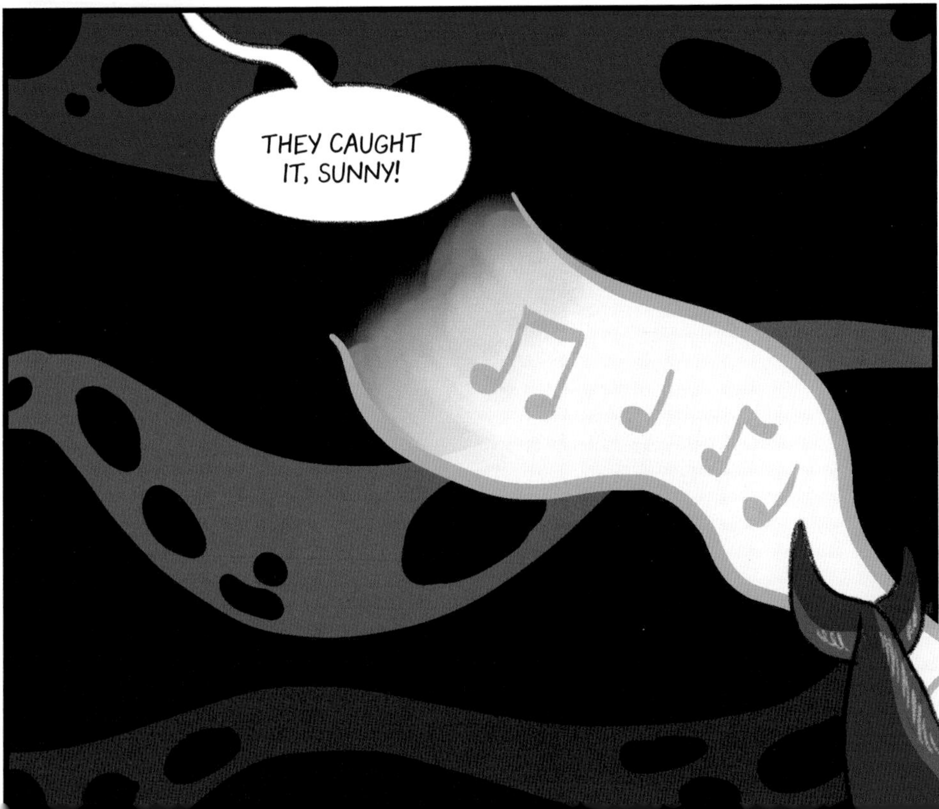
THEY CAUGHT IT, SUNNY!

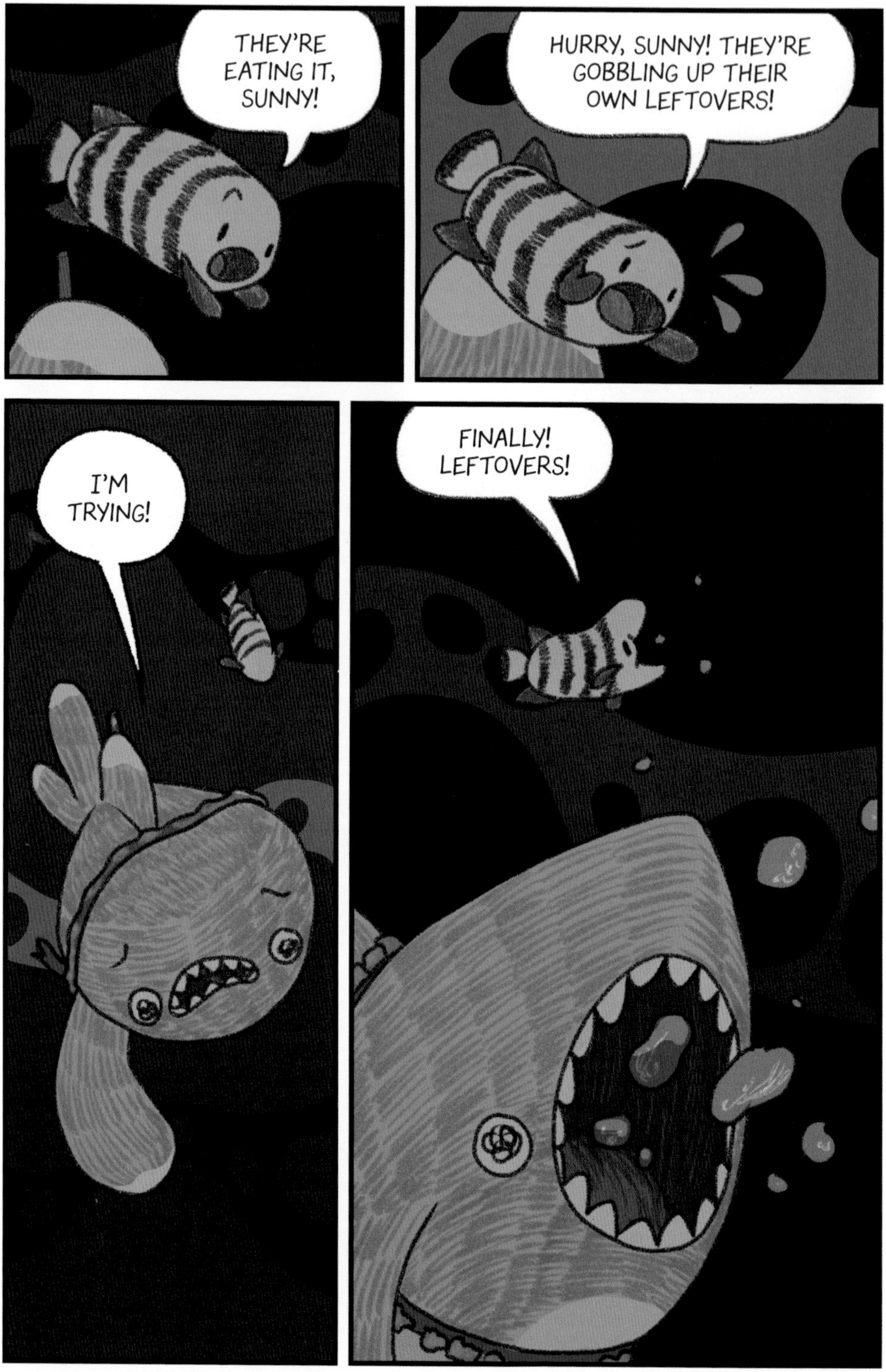
THEY'RE EATING IT, SUNNY!
HURRY, SUNNY! THEY'RE GOBBLING UP THEIR OWN LEFTOVERS!
I'M TRYING!
FINALLY! LEFTOVERS!

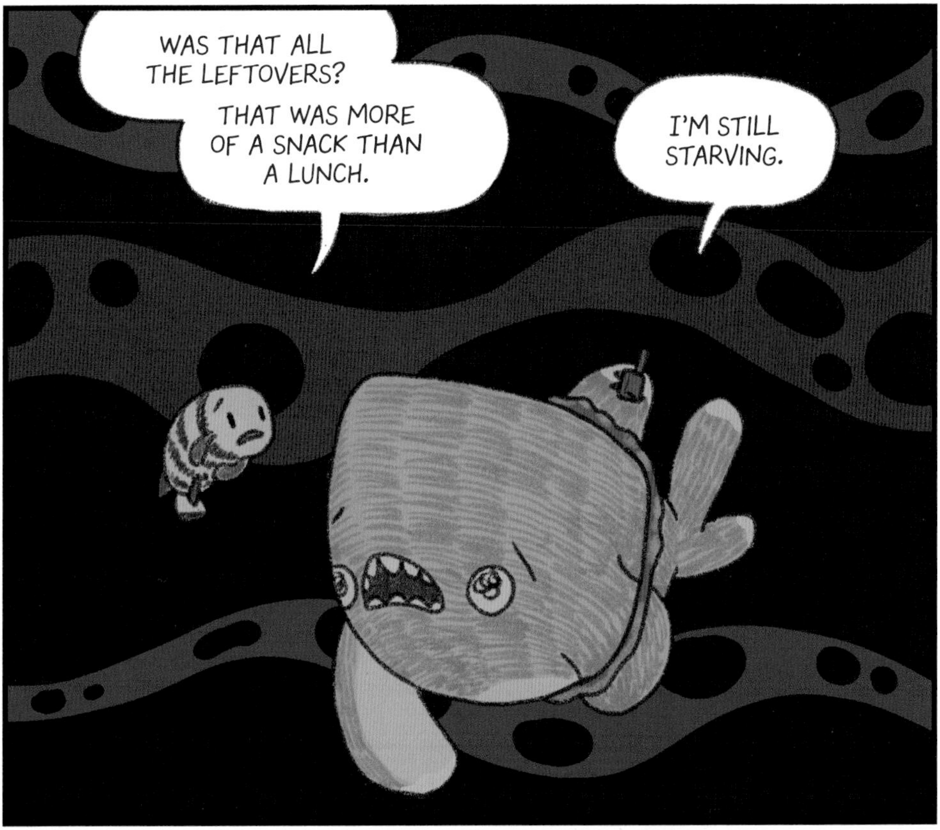
WAS THAT ALL THE LEFTOVERS?
THAT WAS MORE OF A SNACK THAN A LUNCH.
I'M STILL STARVING.

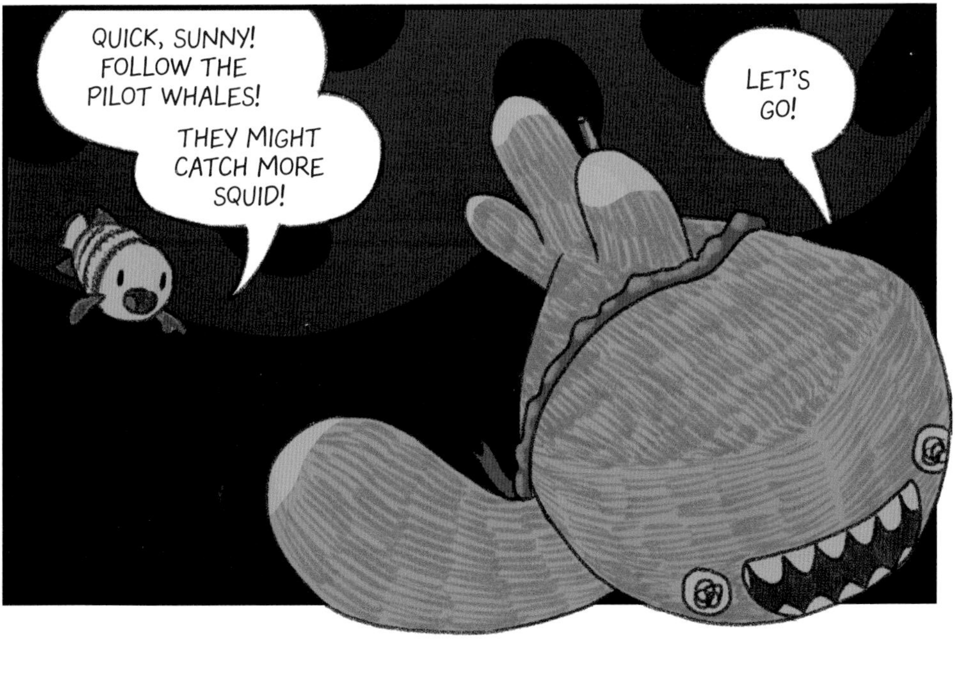
QUICK, SUNNY! FOLLOW THE PILOT WHALES!
THEY MIGHT CATCH MORE SQUID!
LET'S GO!

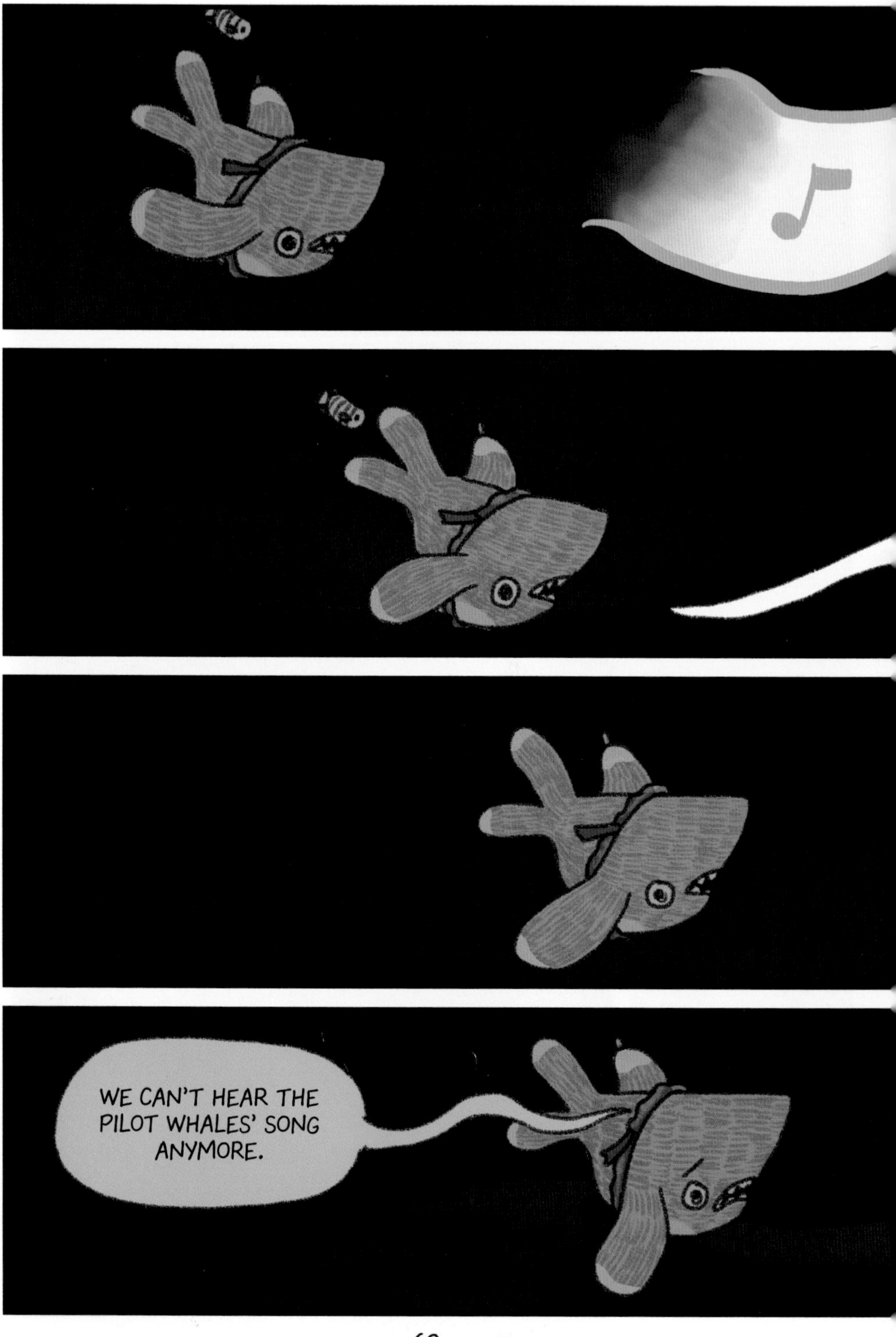
WE CAN'T HEAR THE PILOT WHALES' SONG ANYMORE.

I'M TOO TIRED. I CAN'T GO ON ANYMORE.

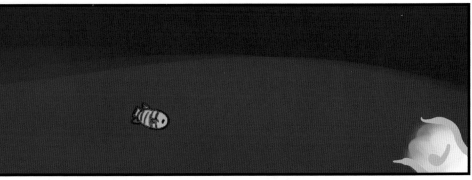

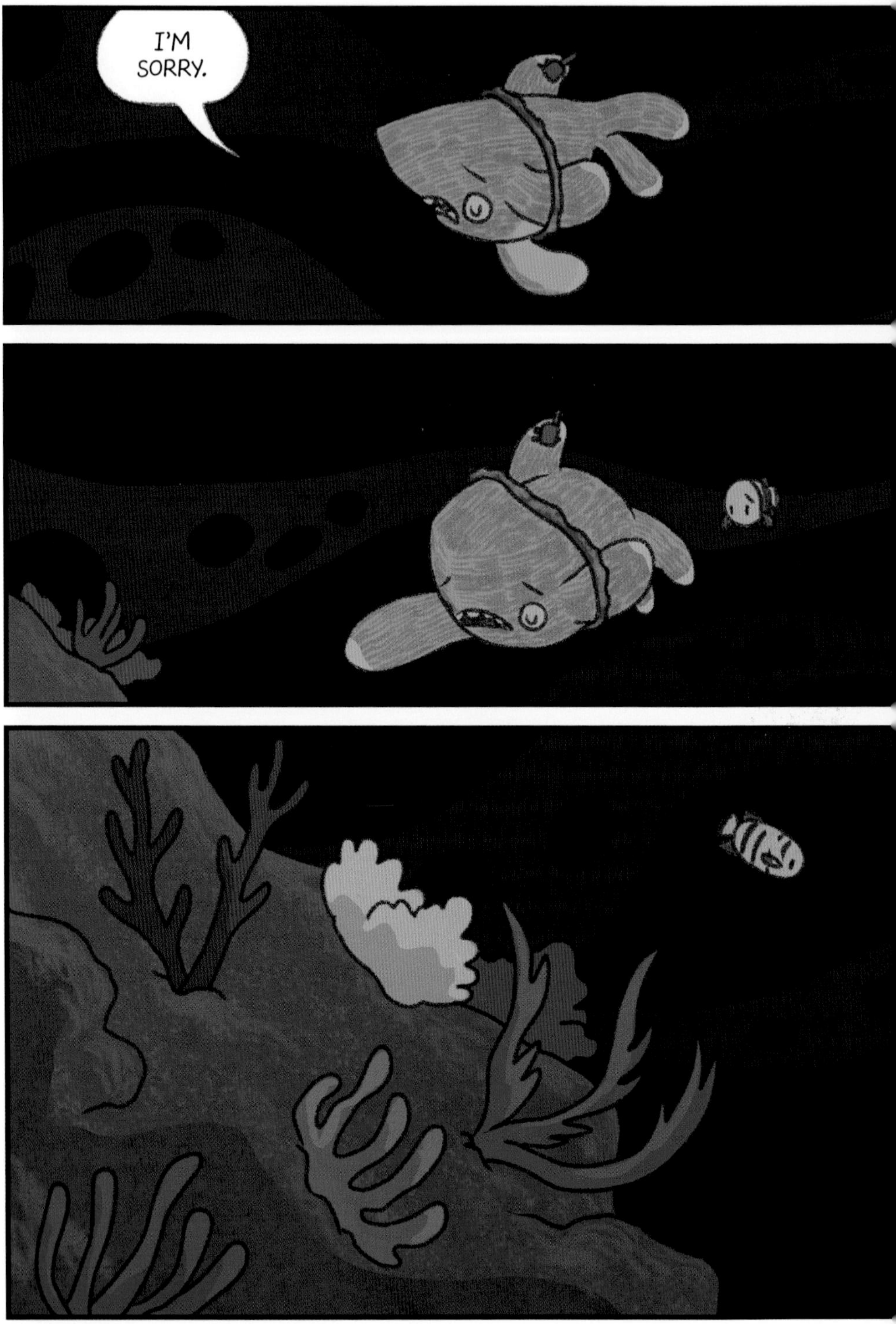
I'M SORRY.

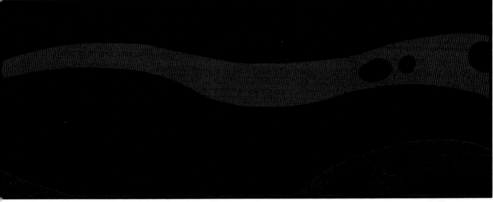

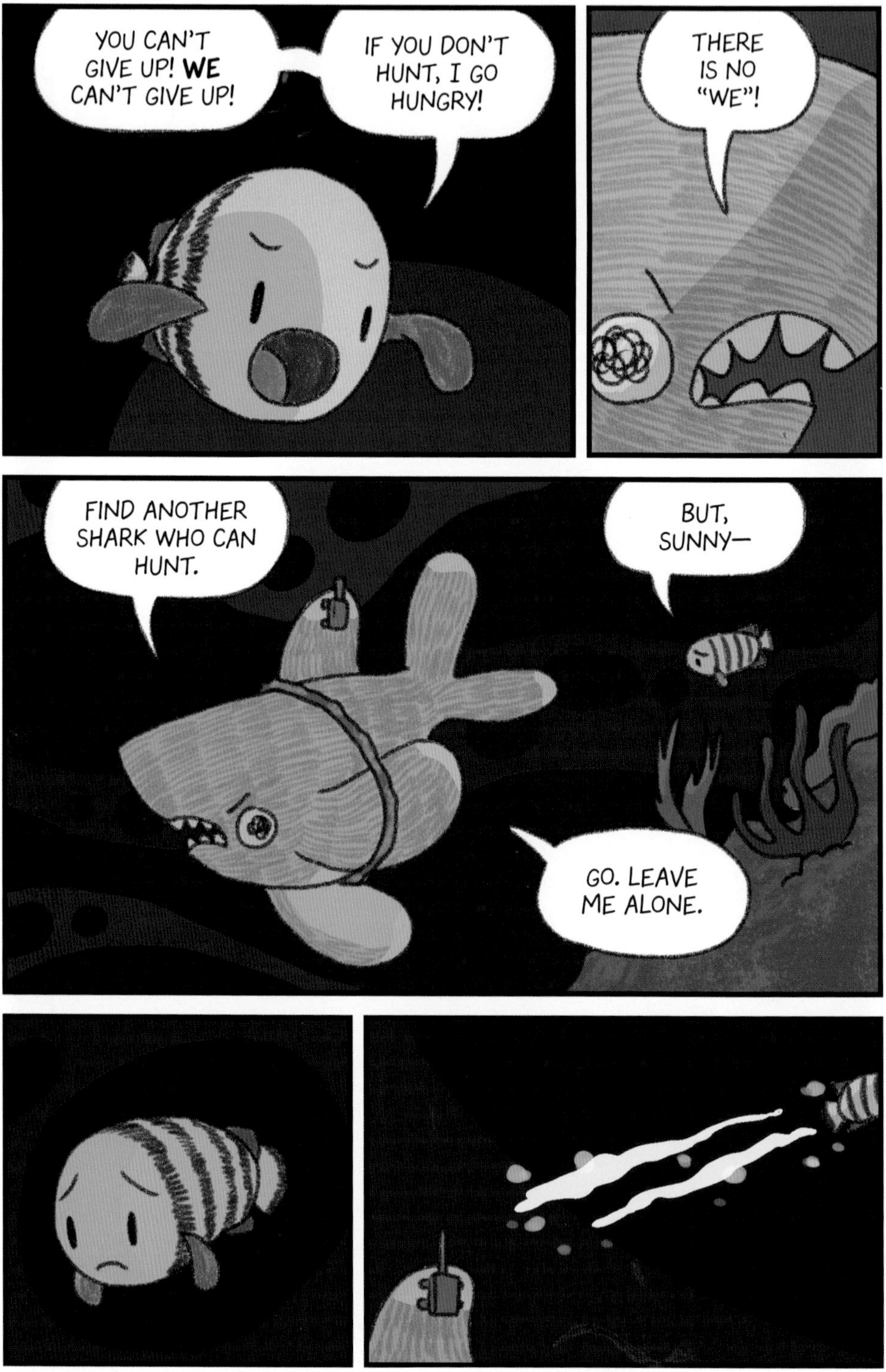
YOU CAN'T GIVE UP! **WE** CAN'T GIVE UP!
IF YOU DON'T HUNT, I GO HUNGRY!
THERE IS NO "WE"!
FIND ANOTHER SHARK WHO CAN HUNT.
BUT, SUNNY—
GO. LEAVE ME ALONE.

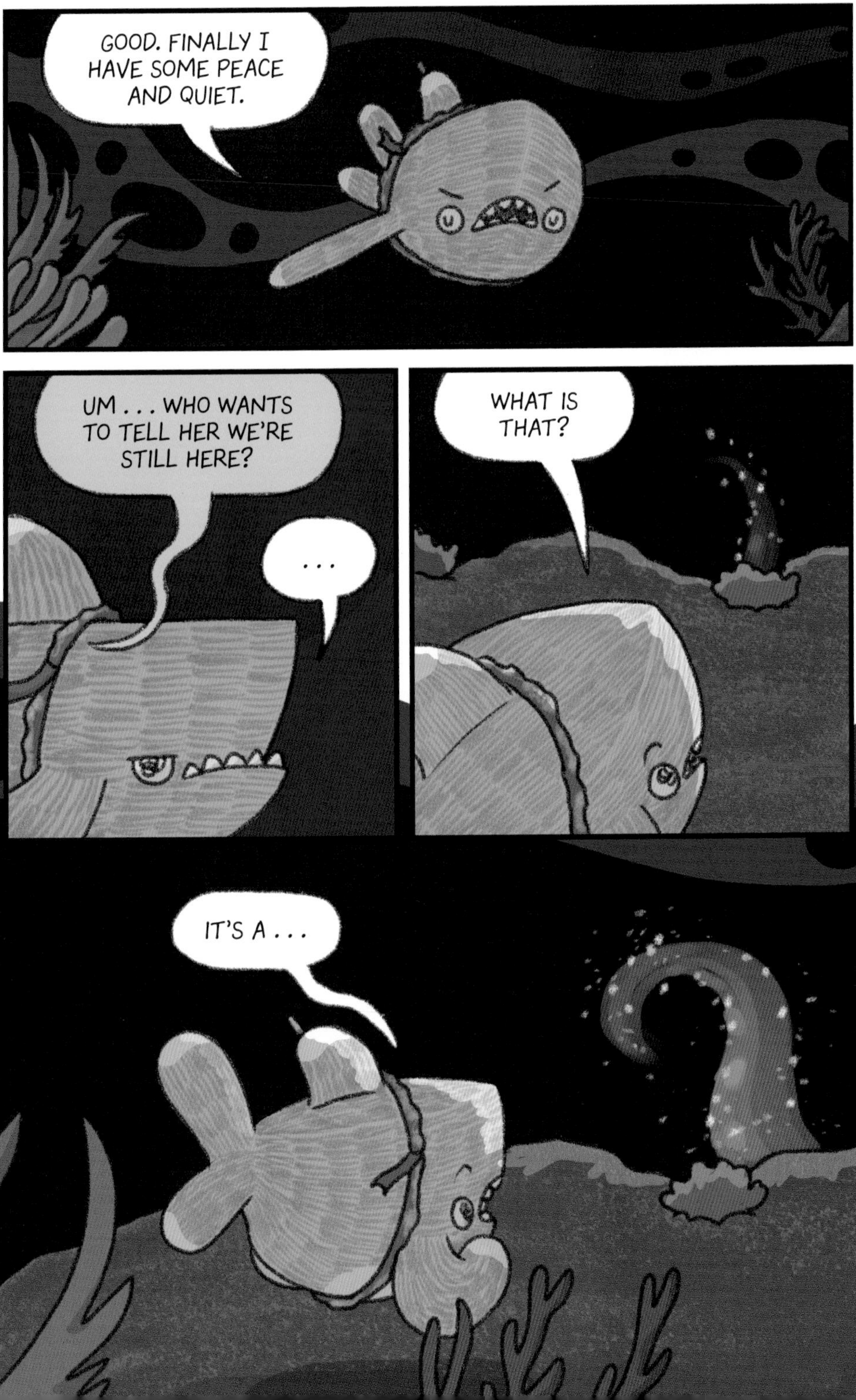
GOOD. FINALLY I HAVE SOME PEACE AND QUIET.
UM . . . WHO WANTS TO TELL HER WE'RE STILL HERE?
. . .
WHAT IS THAT?
IT'S A . . .

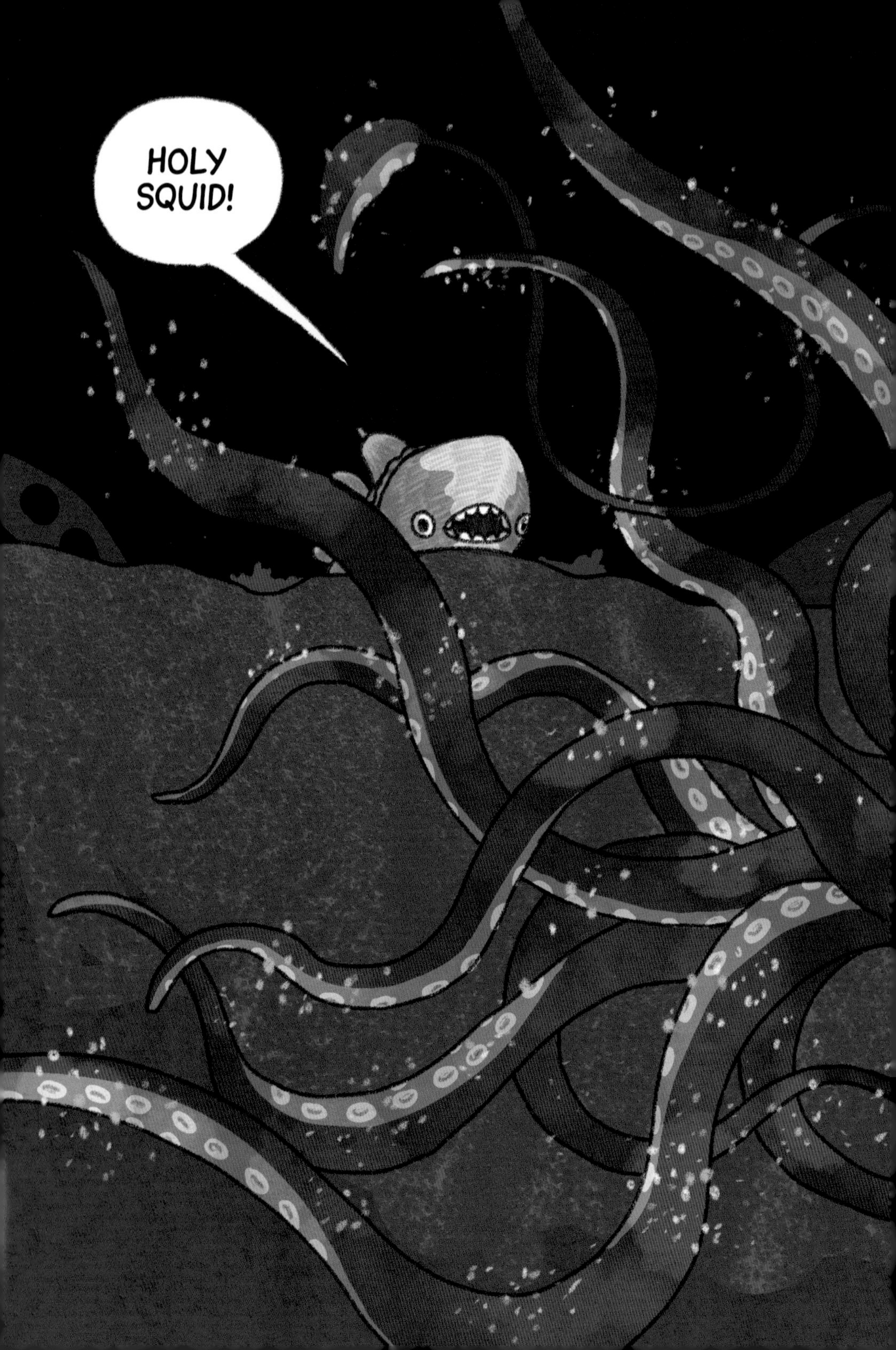
HOLY SQUID!

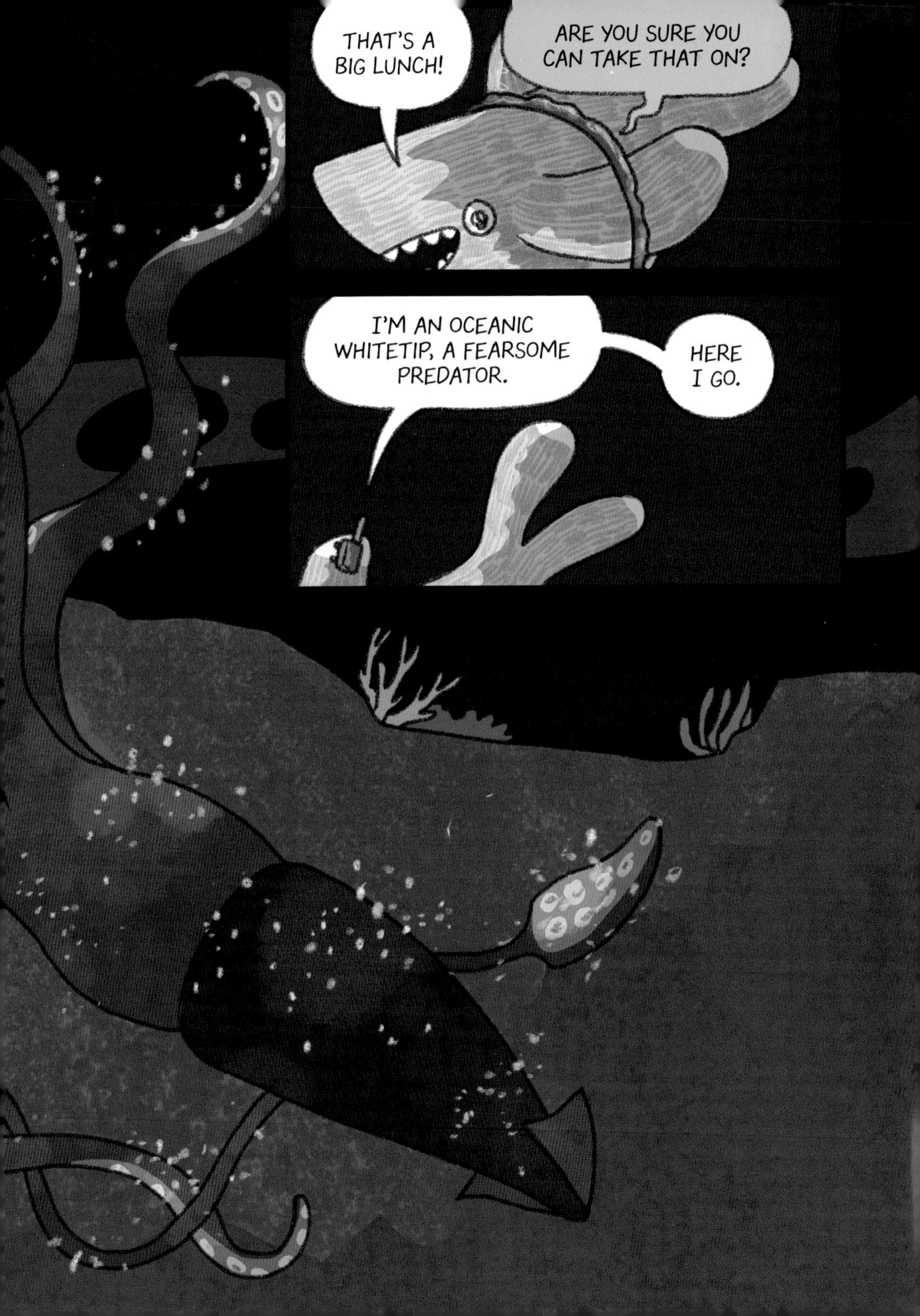
THAT'S A BIG LUNCH!
ARE YOU SURE YOU CAN TAKE THAT ON?
I'M AN OCEANIC WHITETIP, A FEARSOME PREDATOR.
HERE I GO.

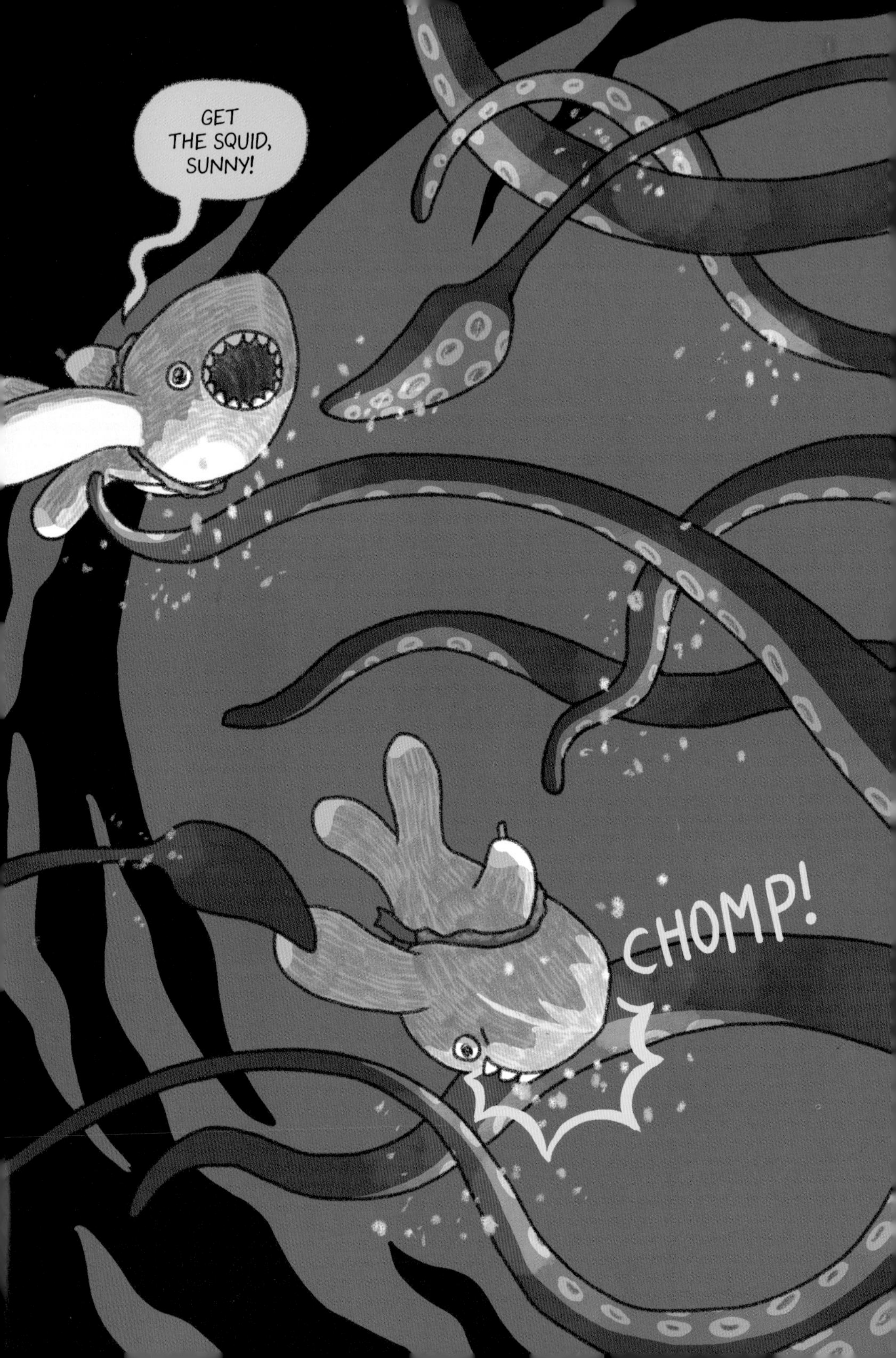
GET THE SQUID, SUNNY!
CHOMP!

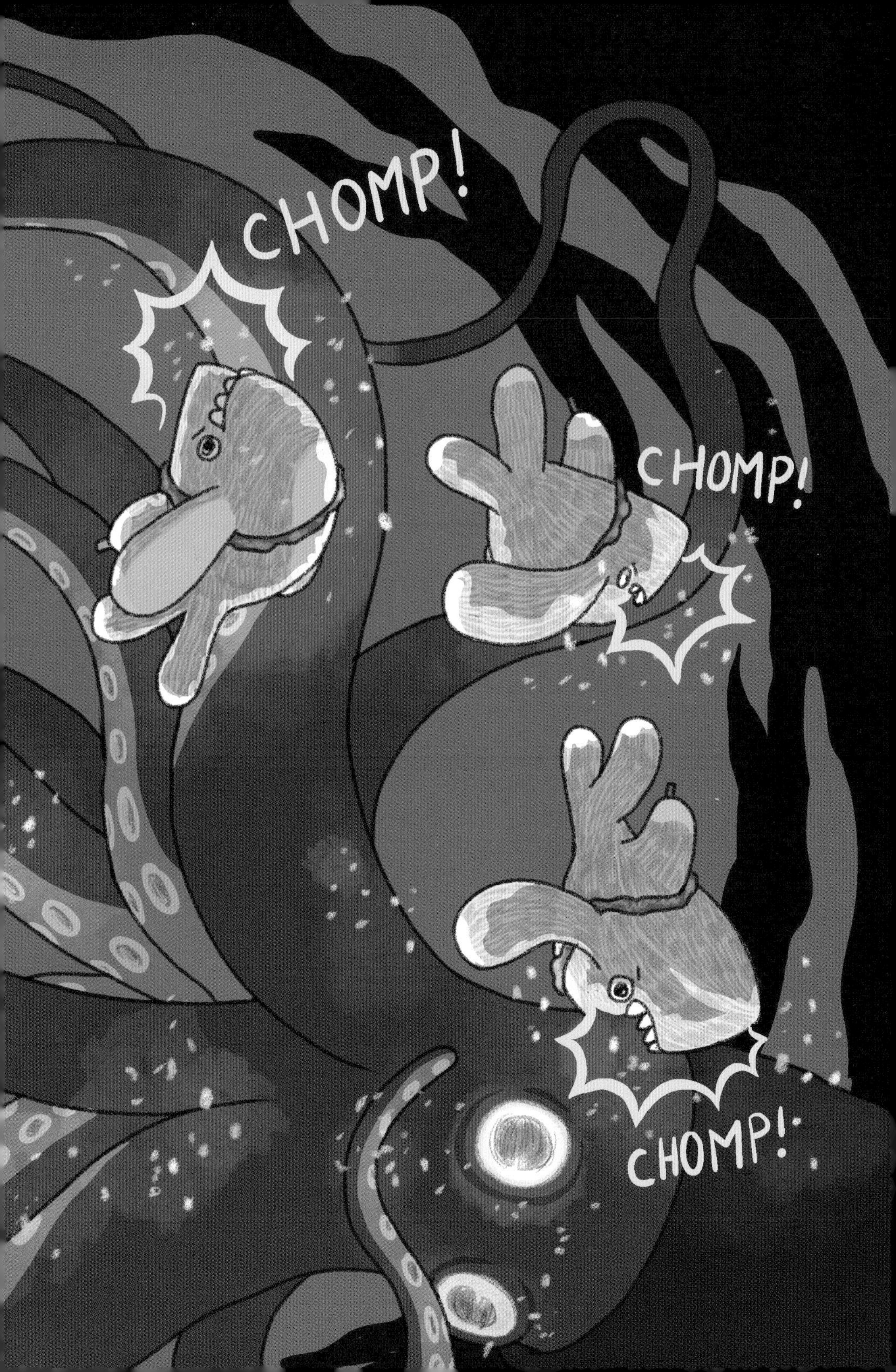
CHOMP!
CHOMP!
CHOMP!

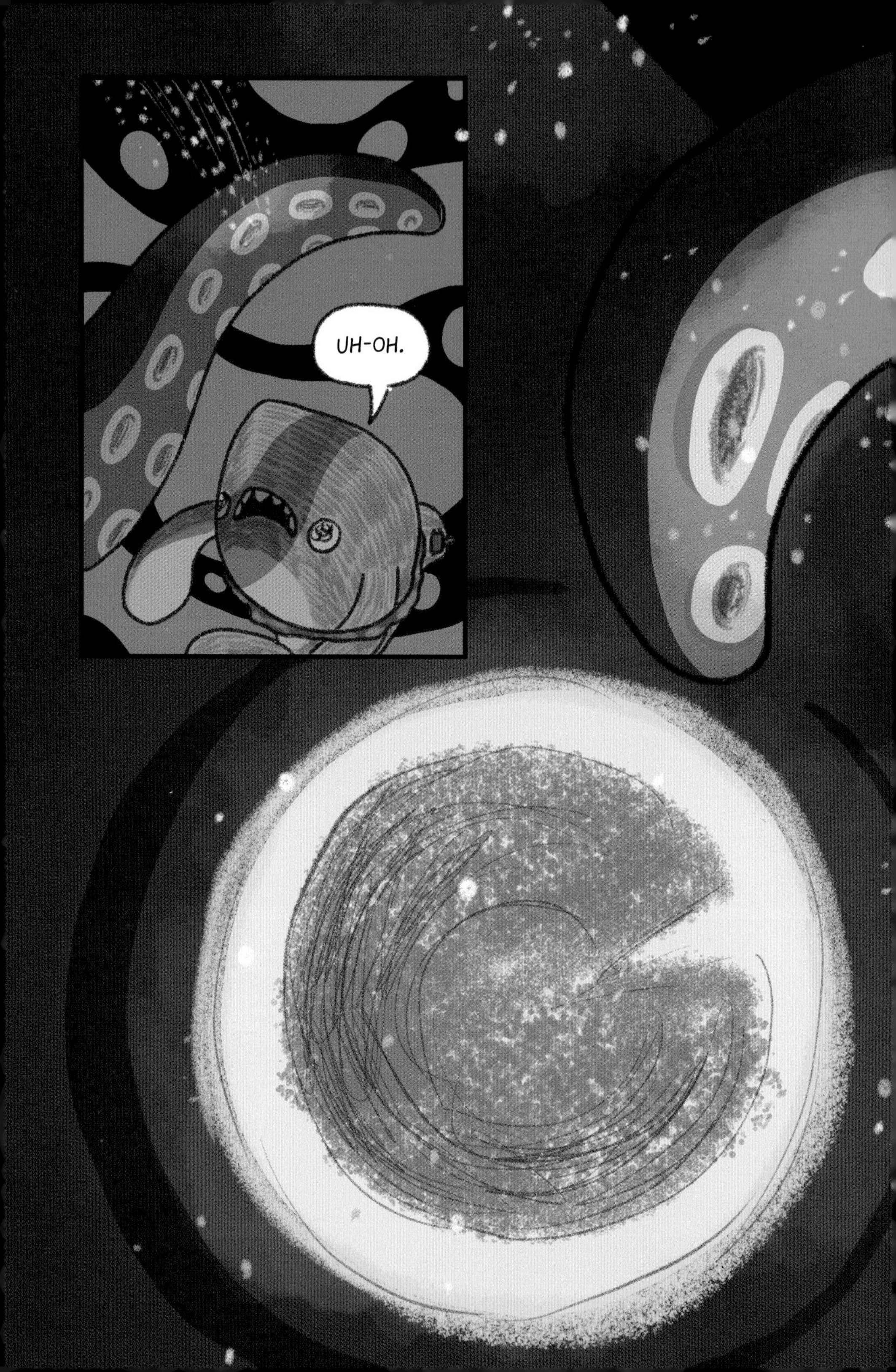
UH-OH.

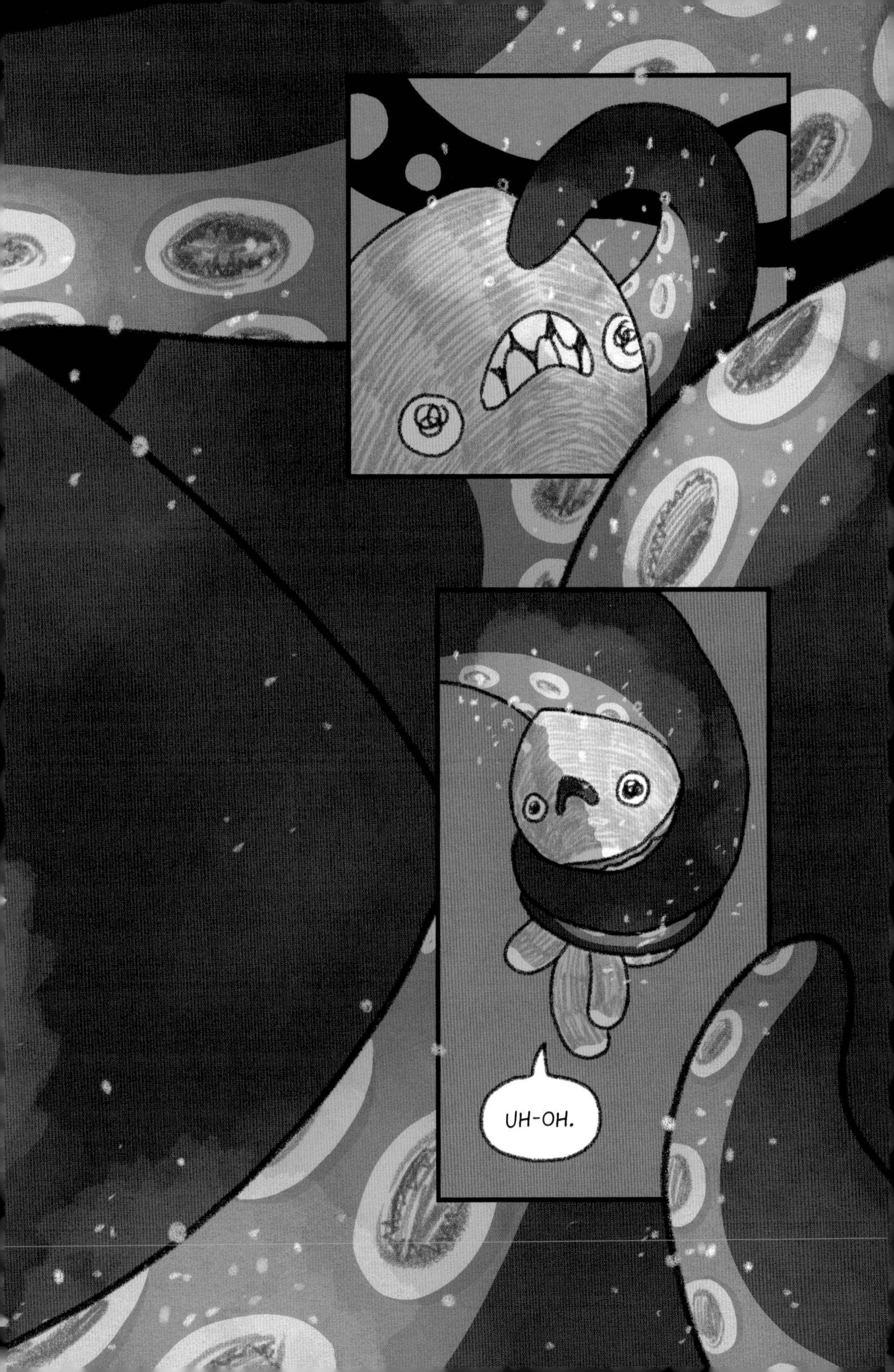
UH-OH.

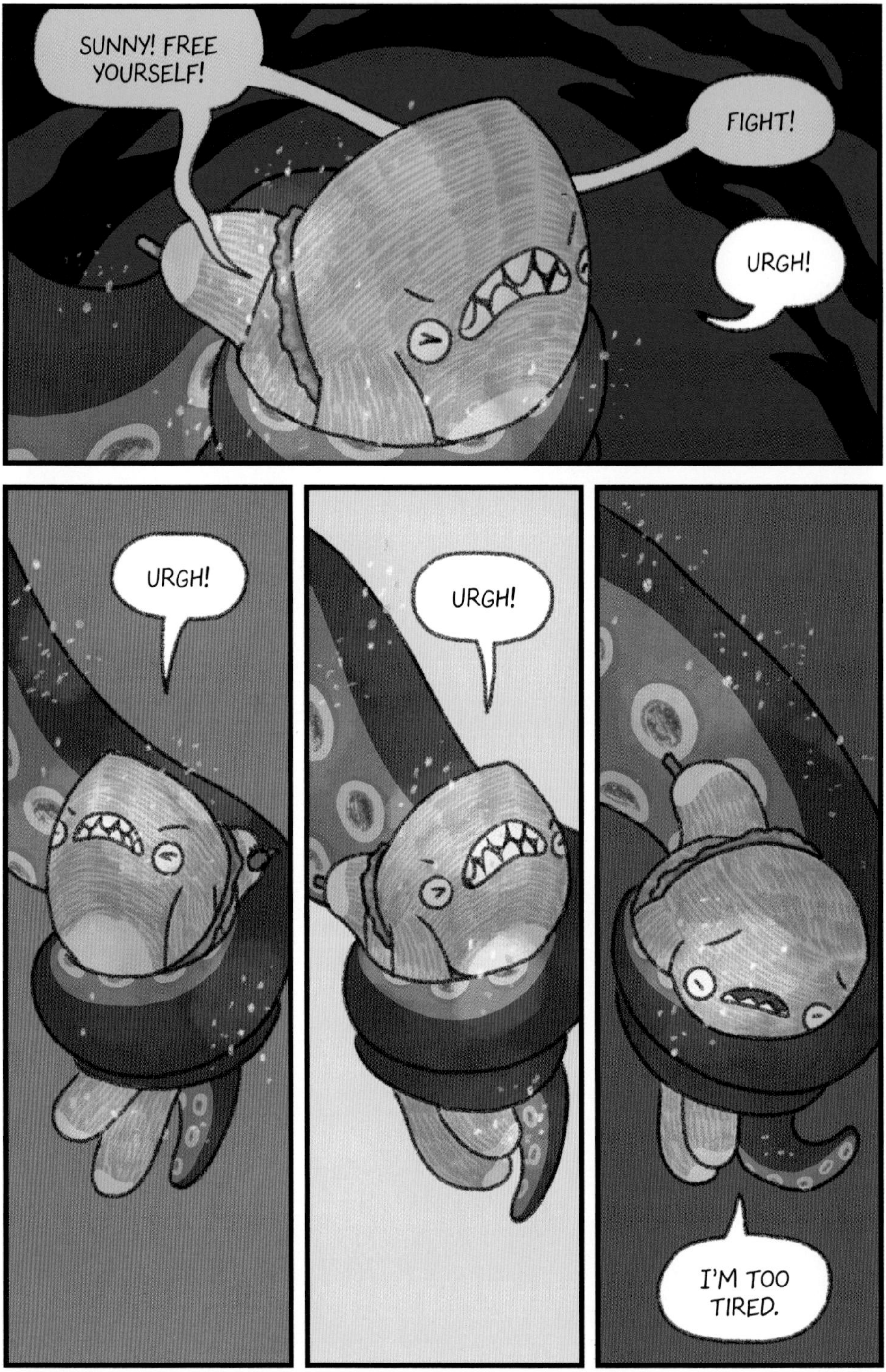
SUNNY! FREE YOURSELF!
FIGHT!
URGH!
URGH!
URGH!
I'M TOO TIRED.

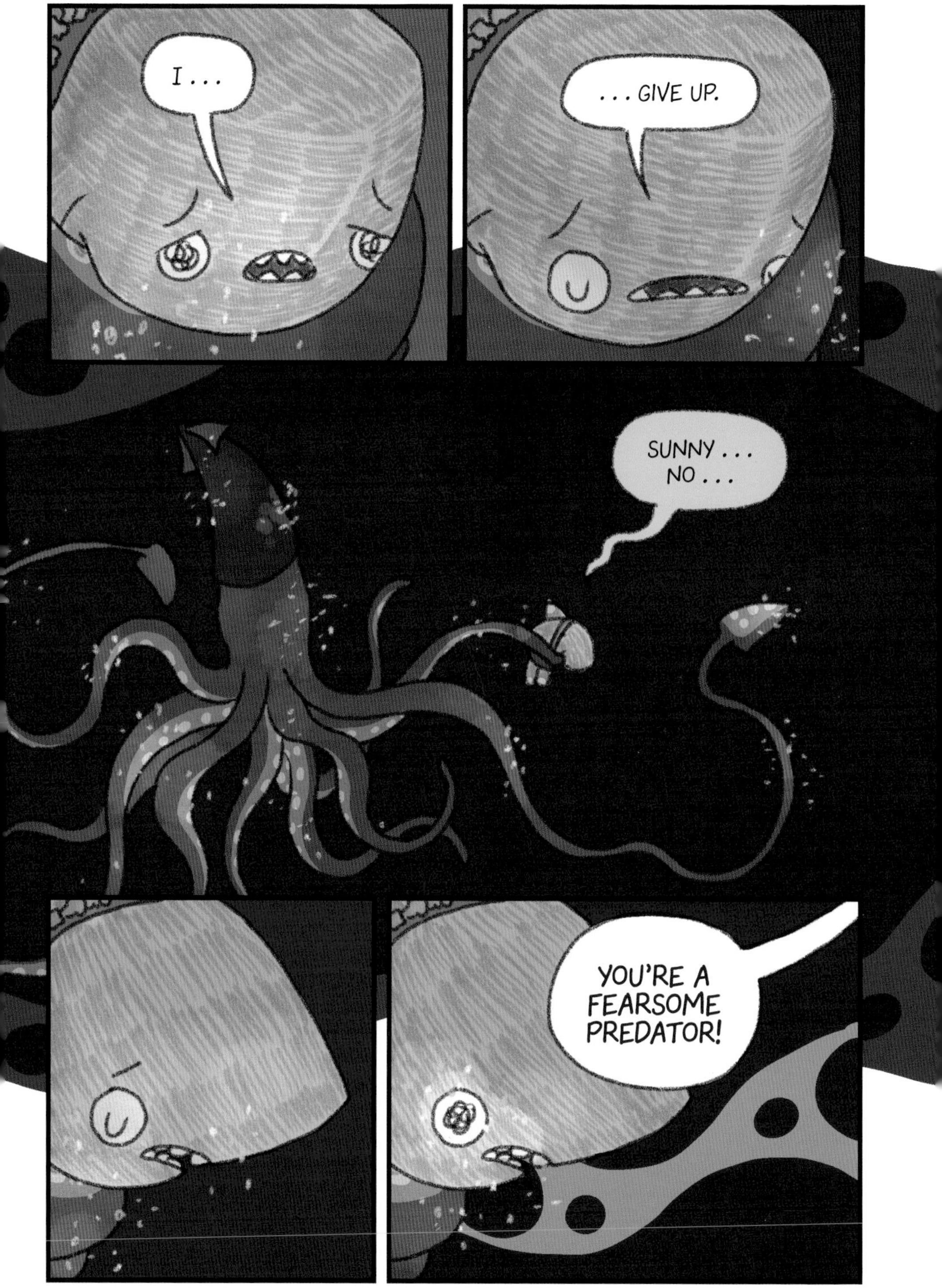
I . . .
. . . GIVE UP.
SUNNY . . . NO . . .
YOU'RE A FEARSOME PREDATOR!

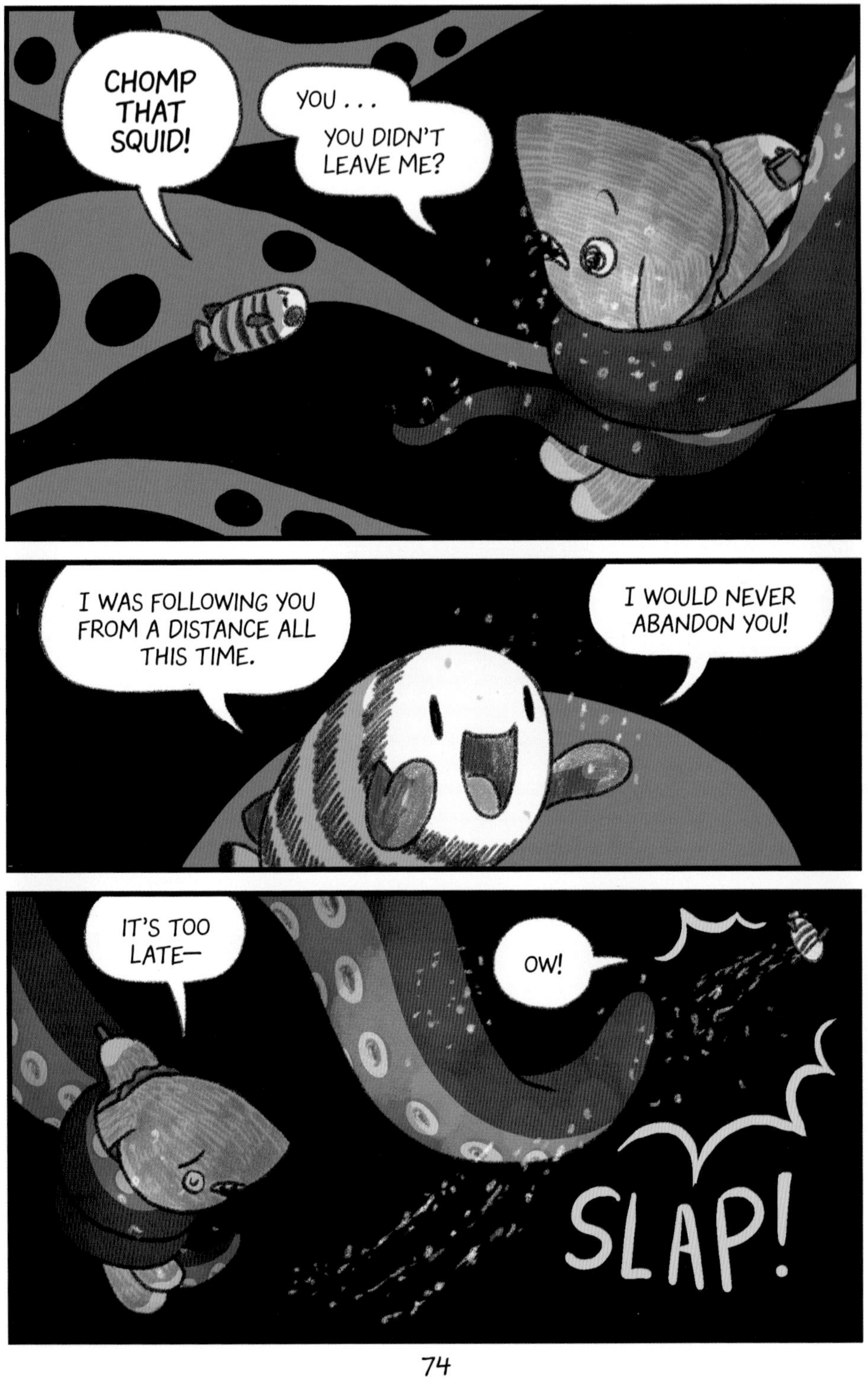
CHOMP THAT SQUID!
YOU . . . YOU DIDN'T LEAVE ME?
I WAS FOLLOWING YOU FROM A DISTANCE ALL THIS TIME.
I WOULD NEVER ABANDON YOU!
IT'S TOO LATE—
OW!
SLAP!

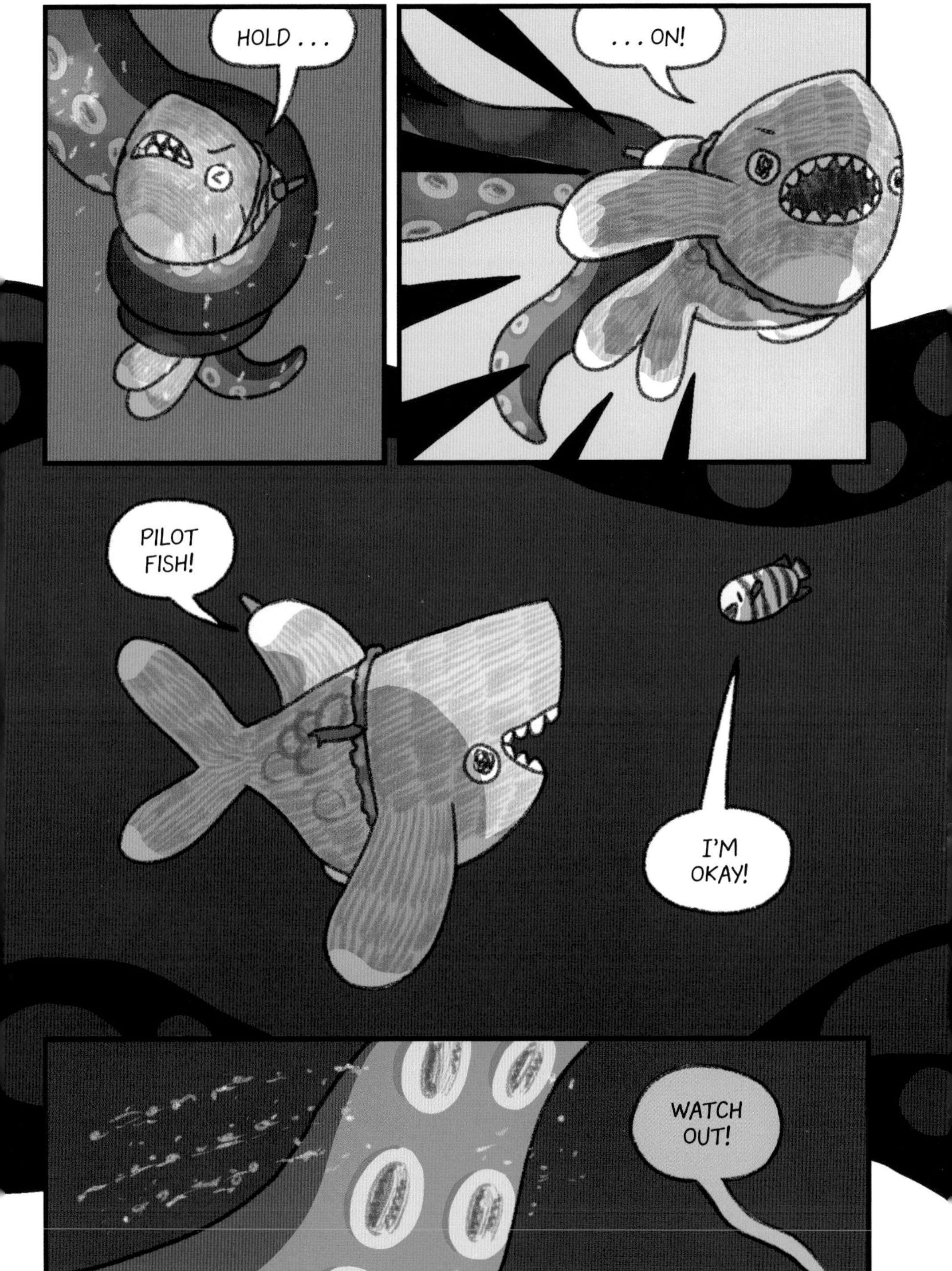
HOLD . . .
. . . ON!
PILOT FISH!
I'M OKAY!
WATCH OUT!

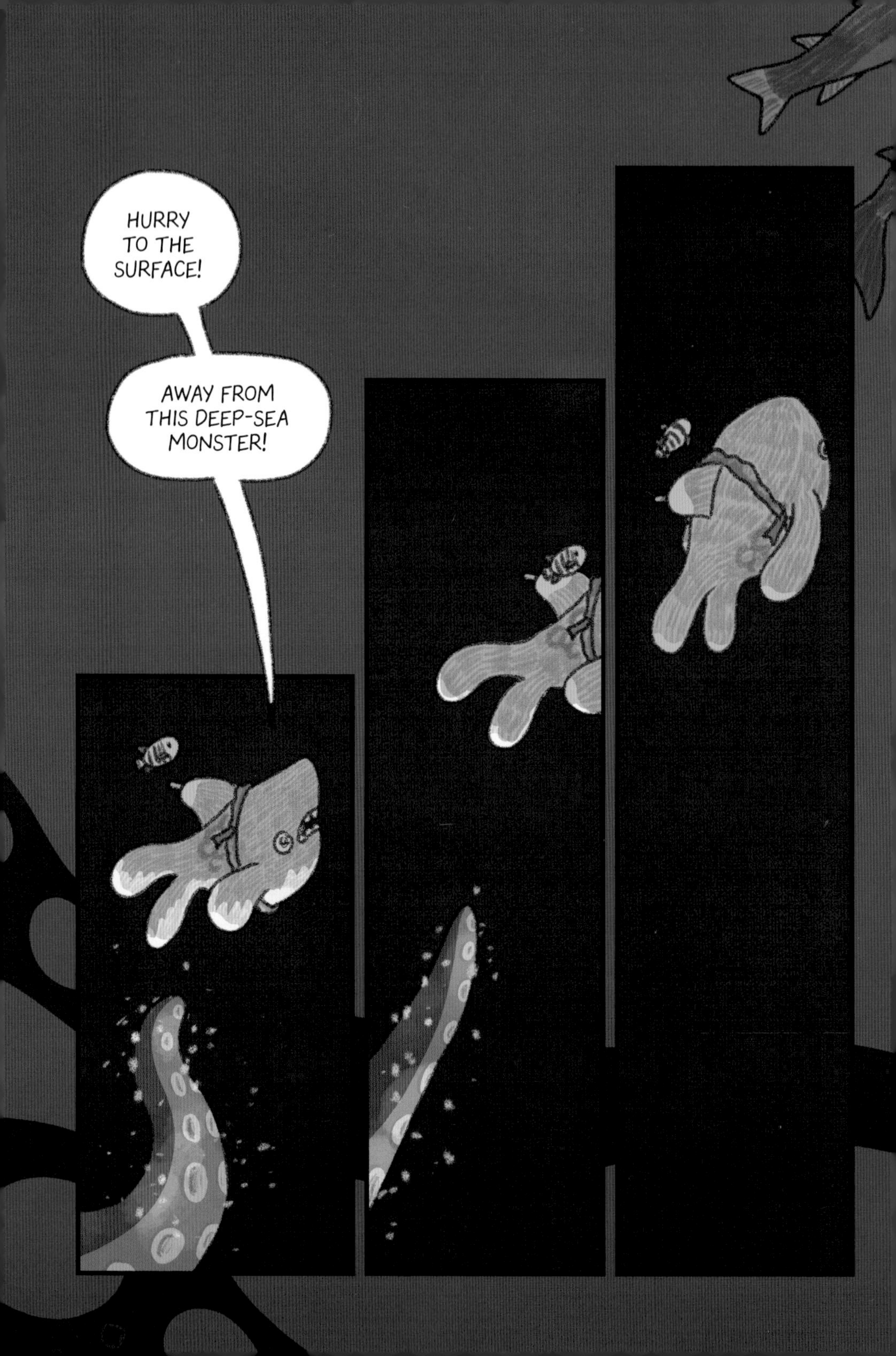
HURRY TO THE SURFACE!
AWAY FROM THIS DEEP-SEA MONSTER!

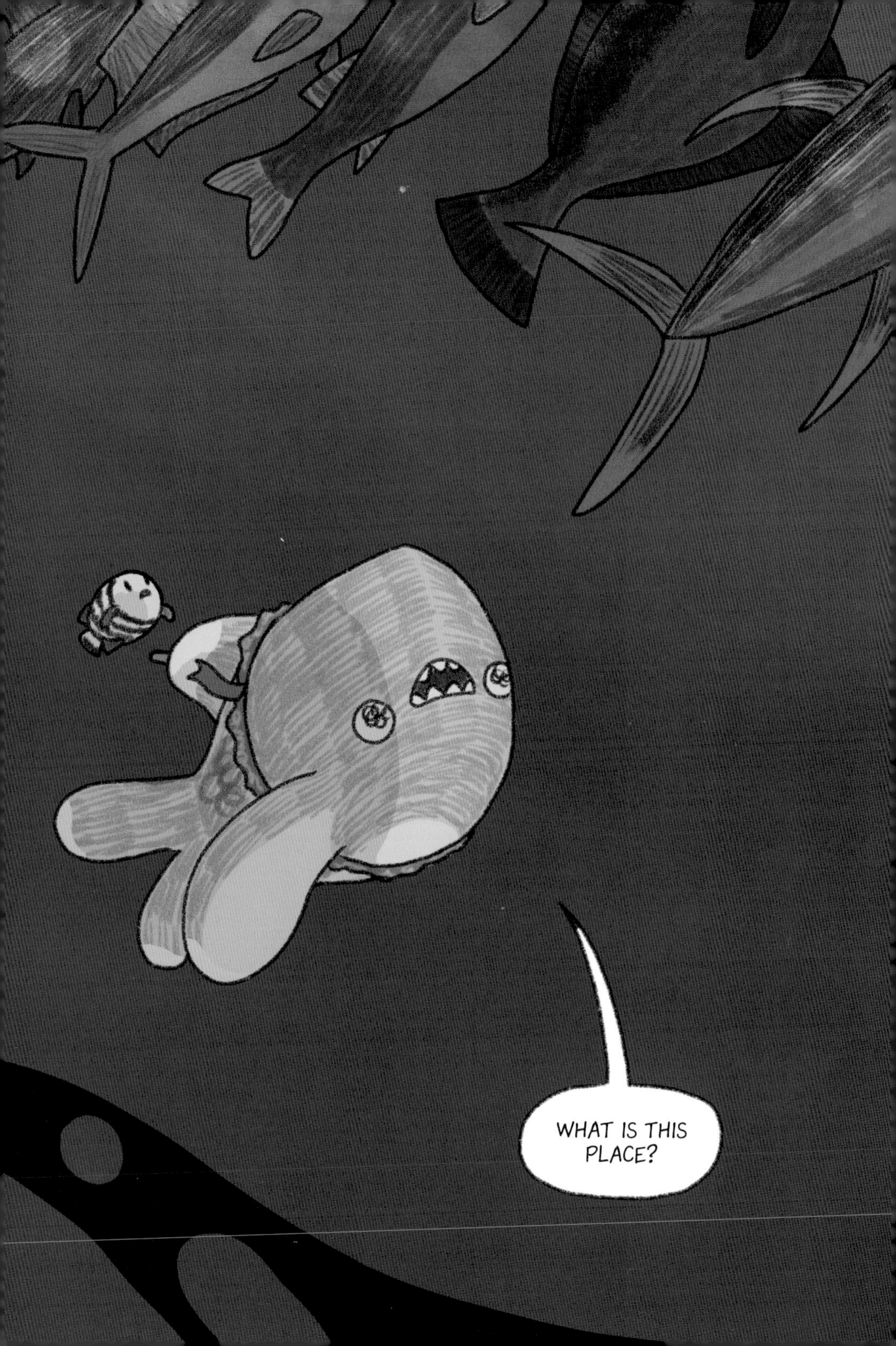
WHAT IS THIS PLACE?

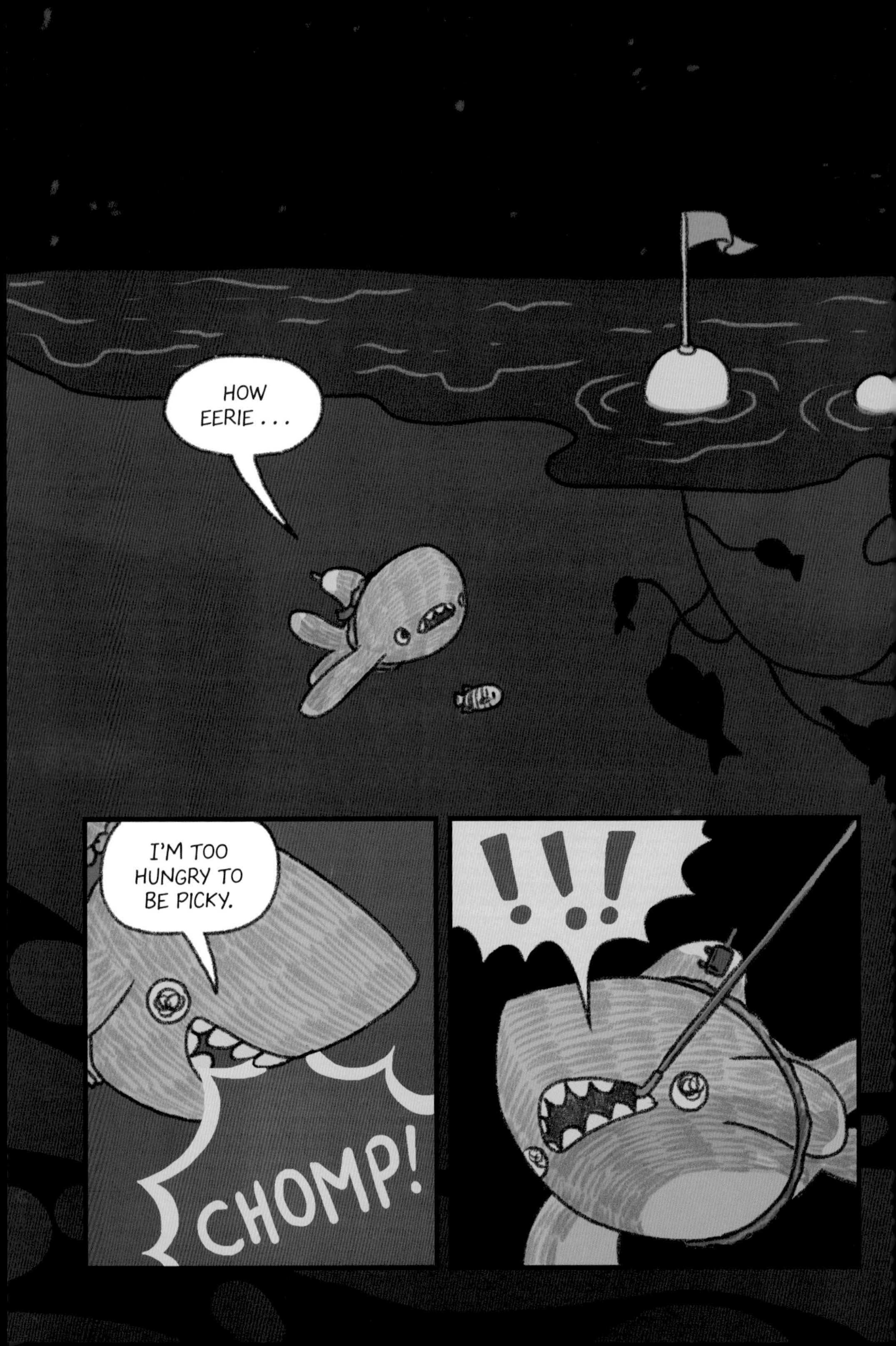
HOW EERIE . . .
I'M TOO HUNGRY TO BE PICKY.
CHOMP!
!!!

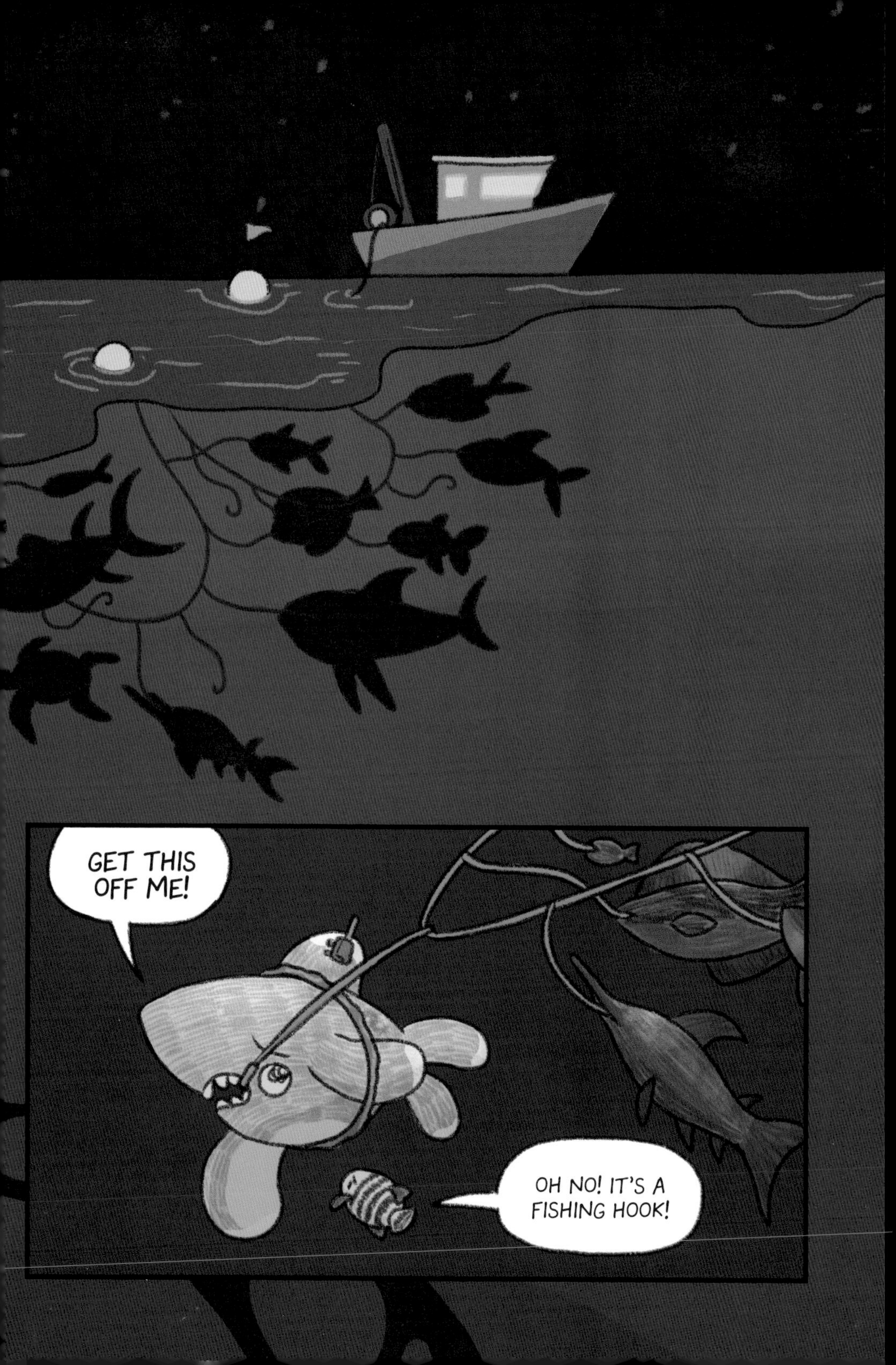
GET THIS OFF ME!
OH NO! IT'S A FISHING HOOK!

SNAP!

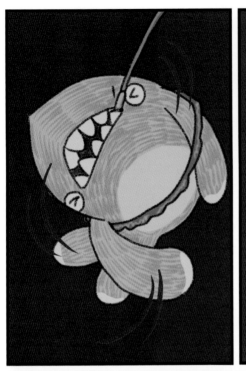

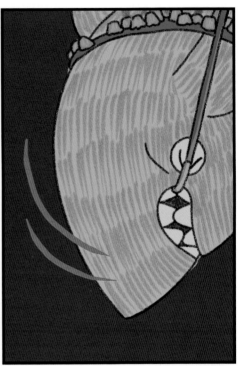

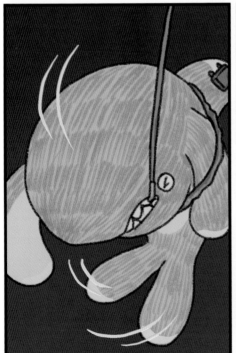

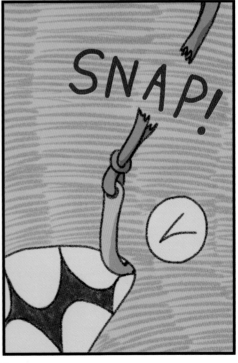

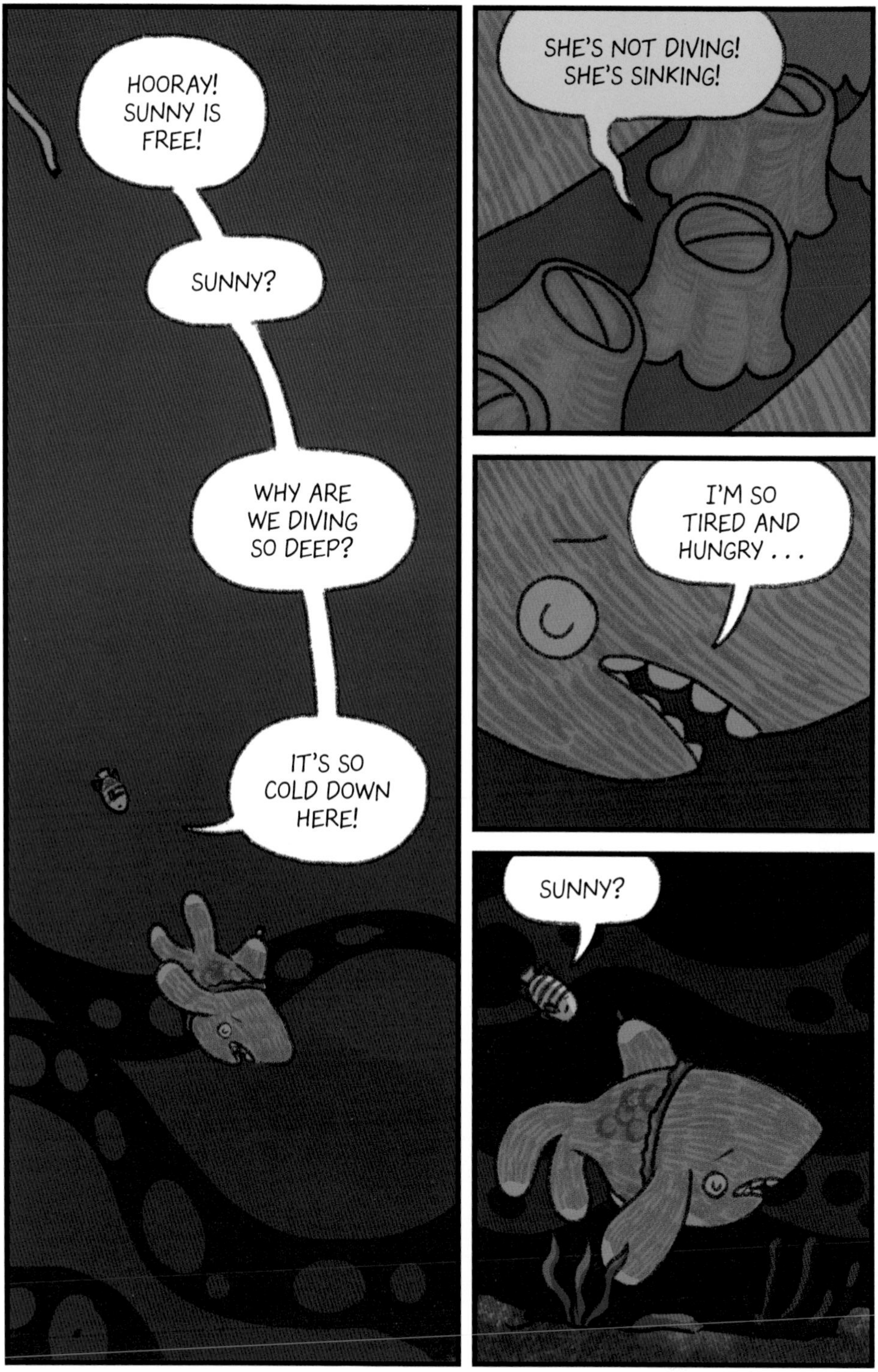
HOORAY! SUNNY IS FREE!
SUNNY?
WHY ARE WE DIVING SO DEEP?
IT'S SO COLD DOWN HERE!
SHE'S NOT DIVING! SHE'S SINKING!
I'M SO TIRED AND HUNGRY . . .
SUNNY?

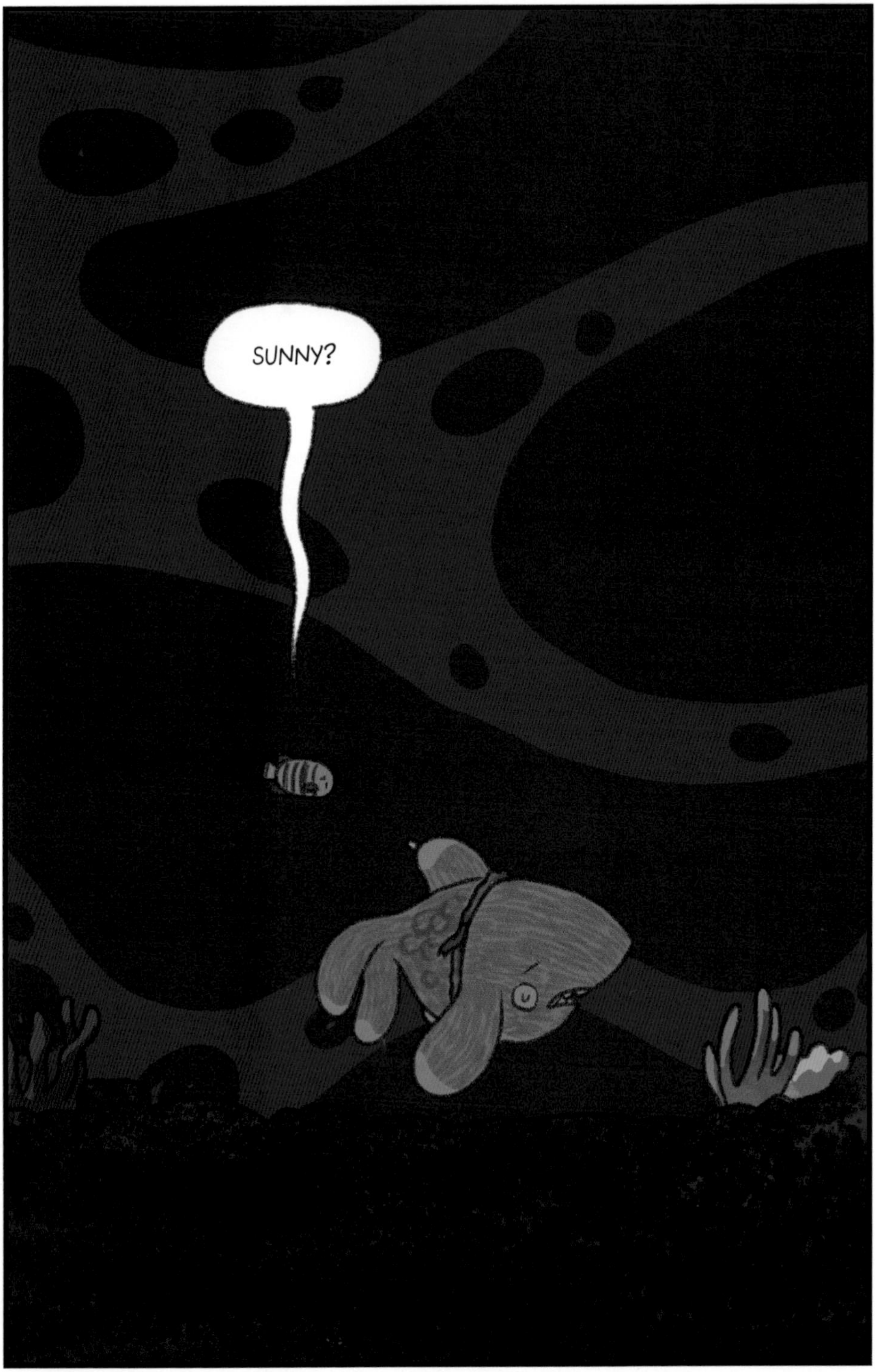
SUNNY?

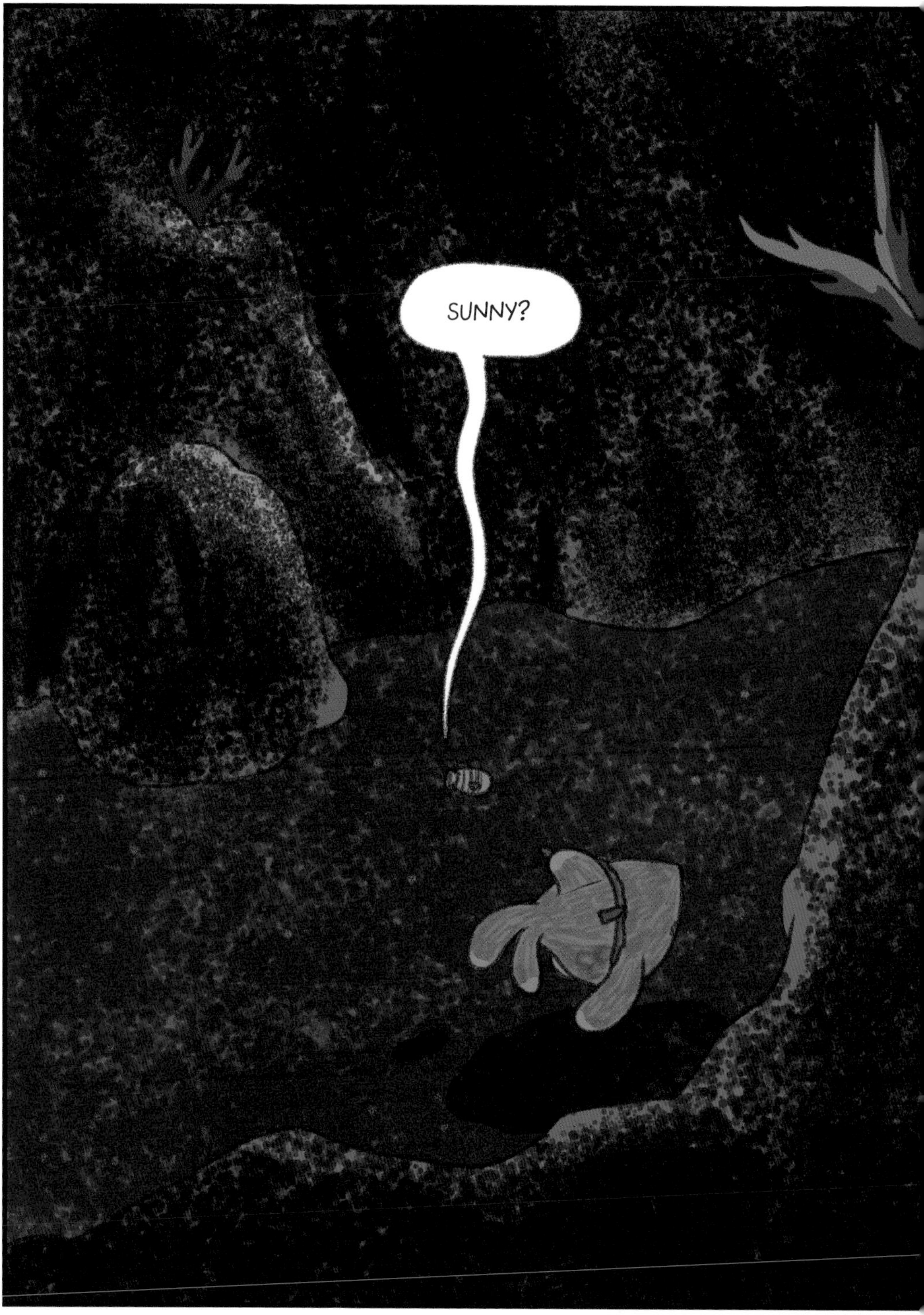
SUNNY?

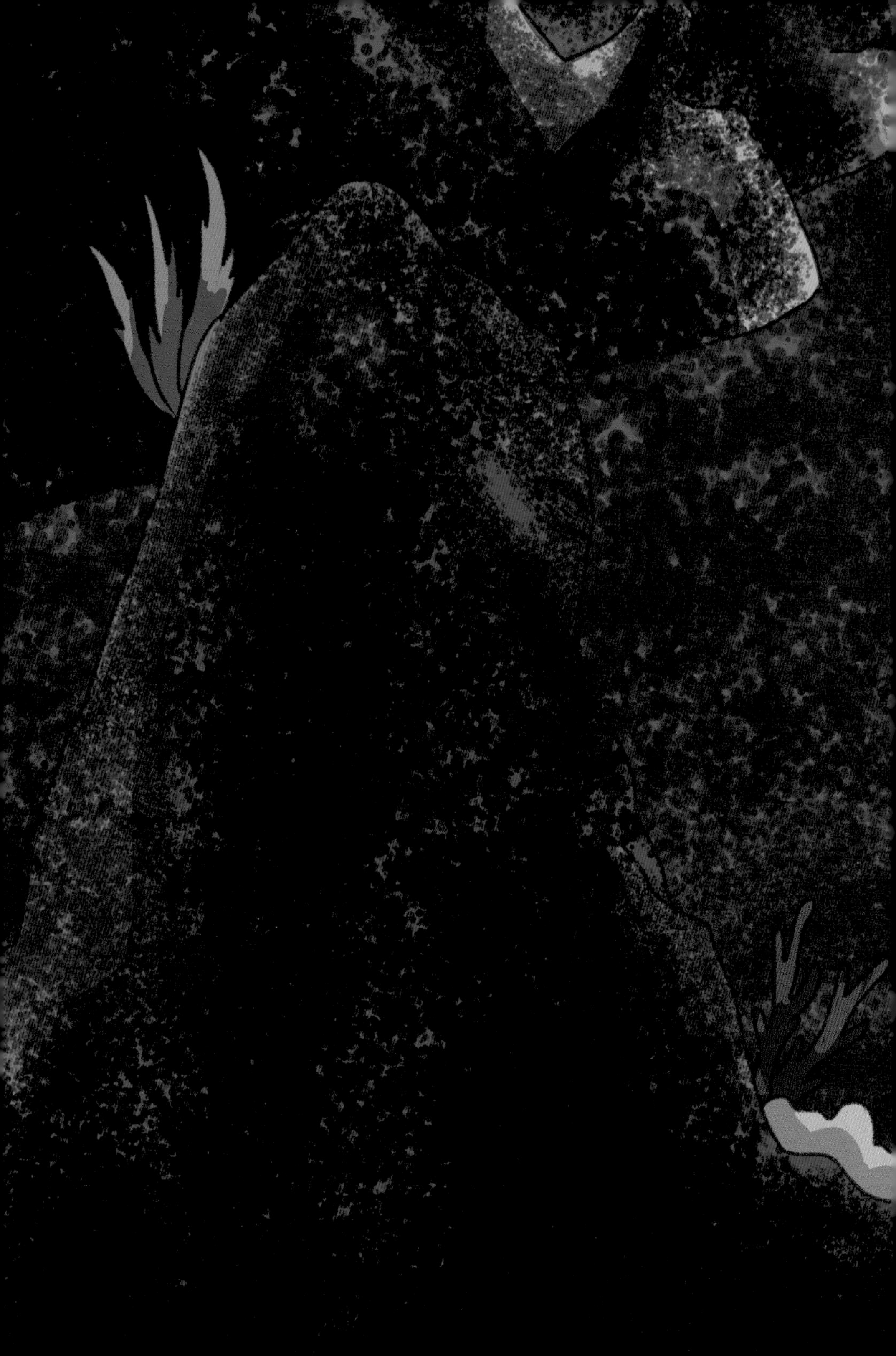

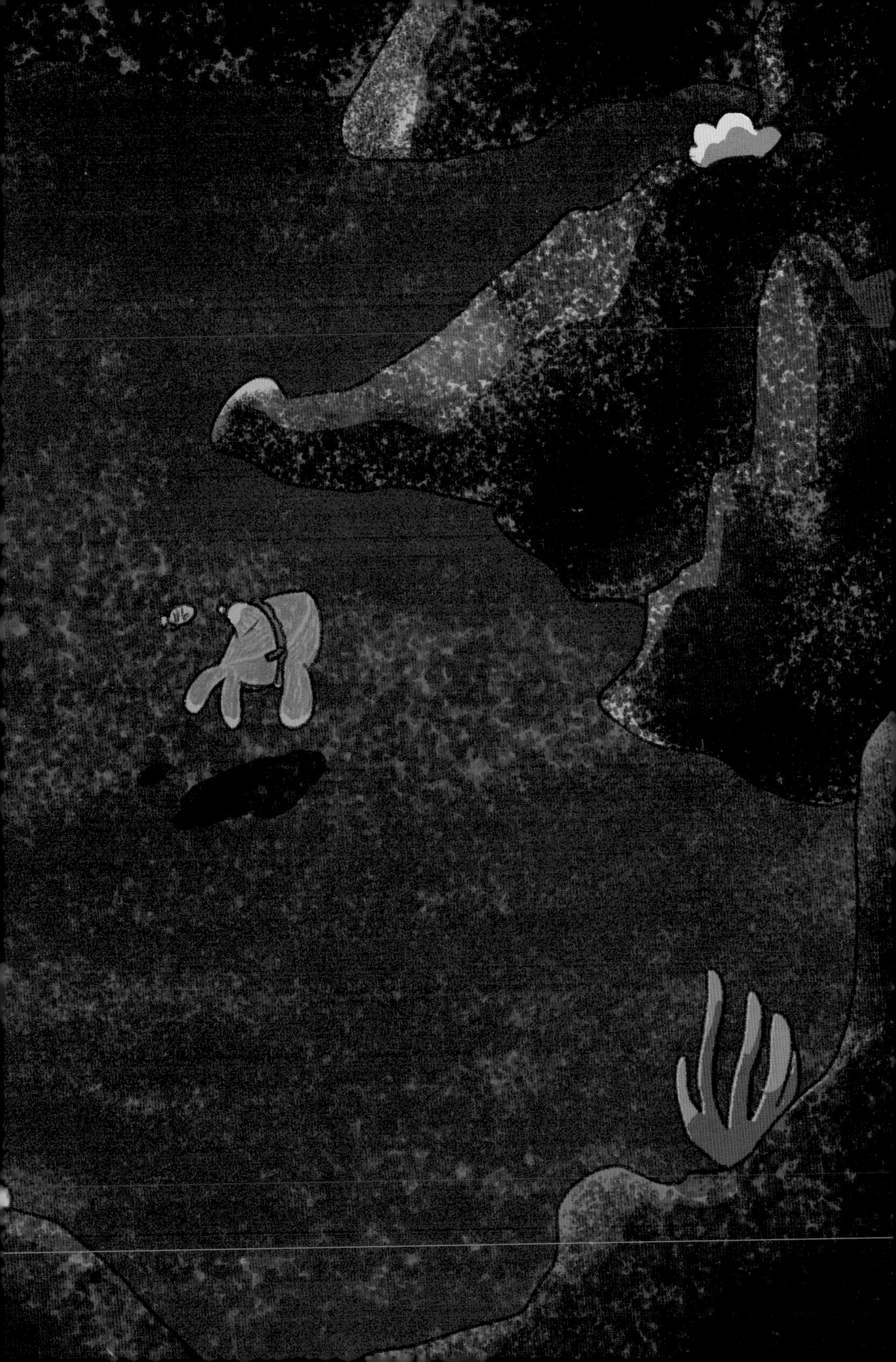

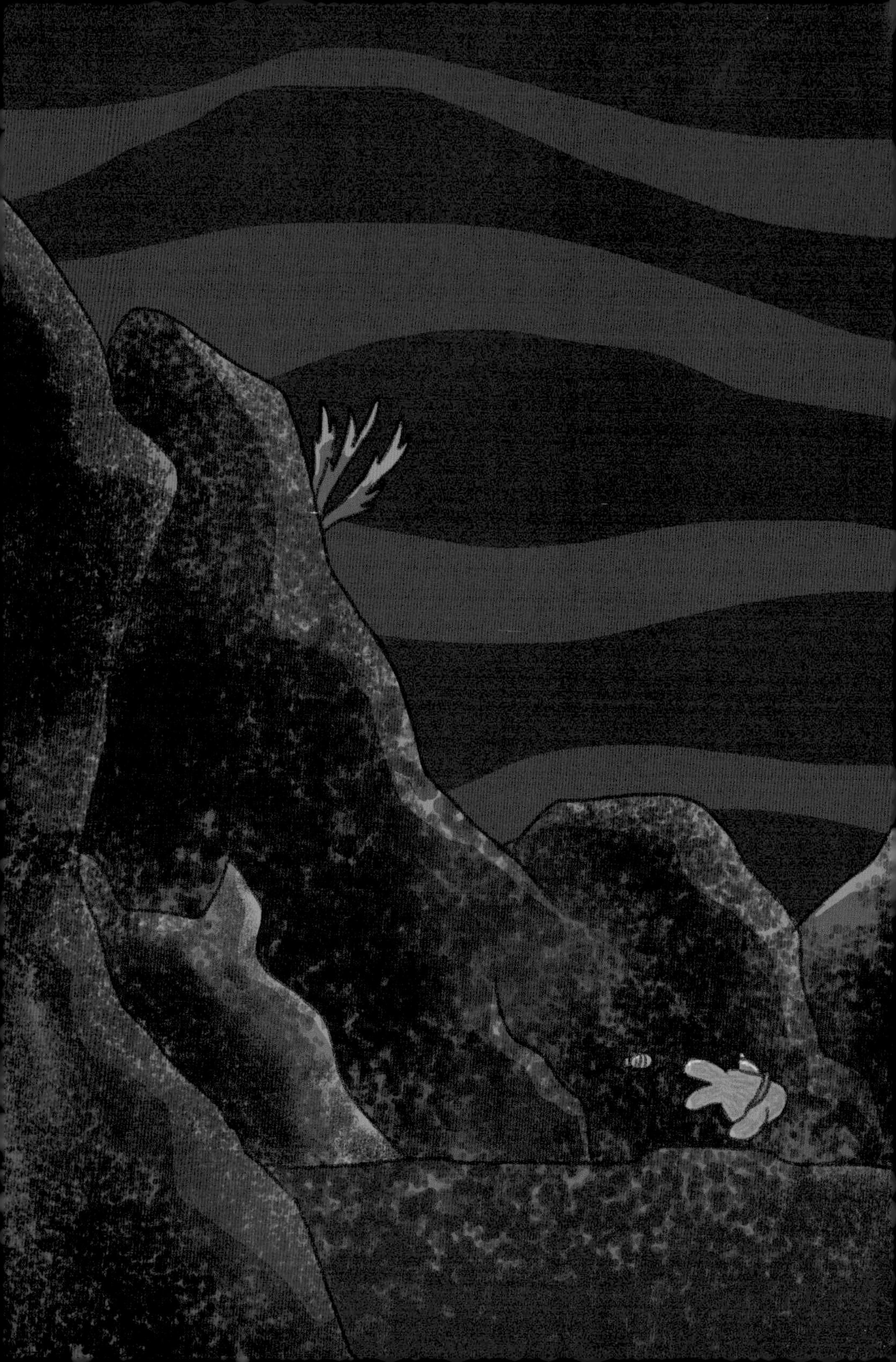

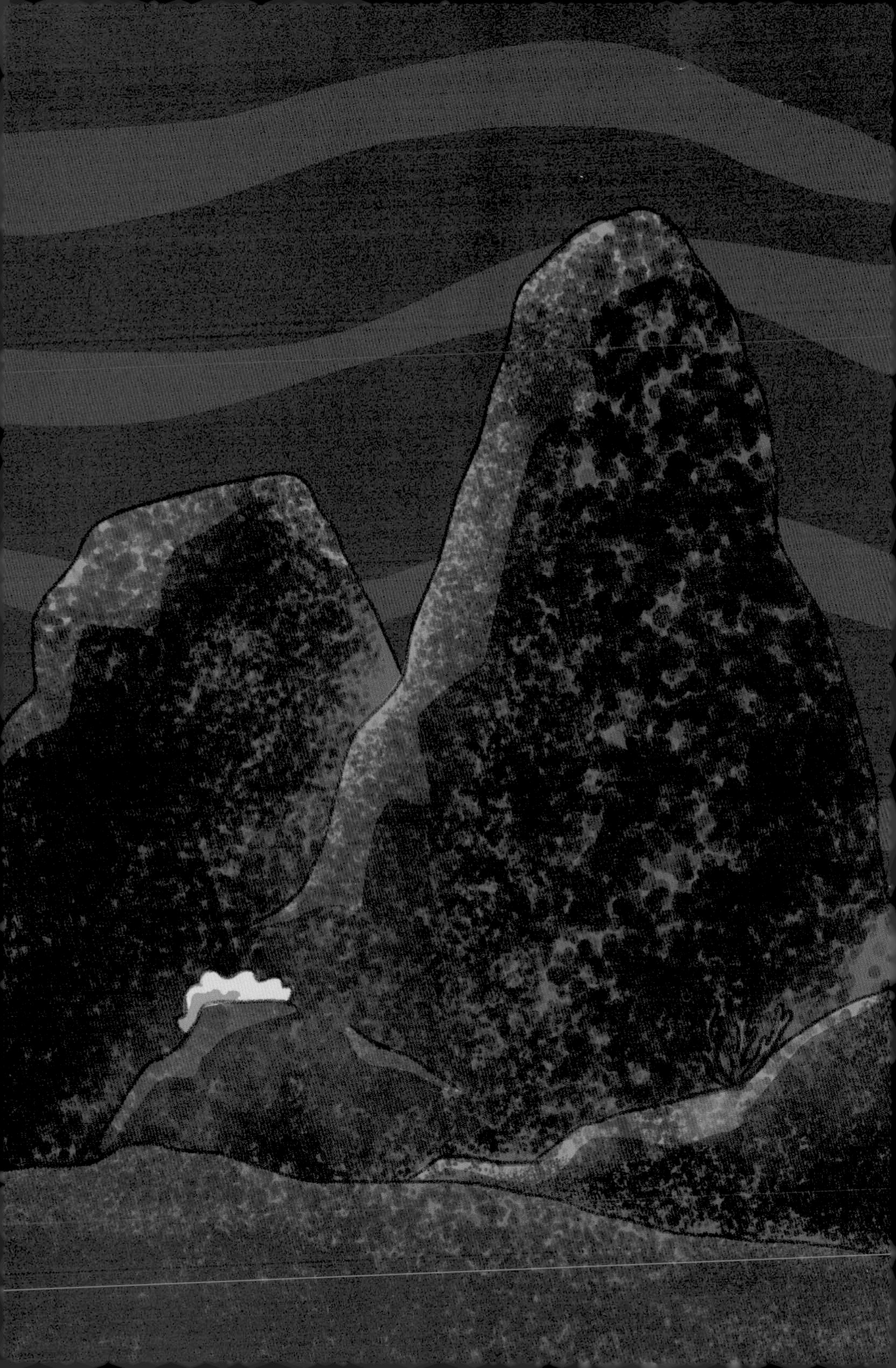

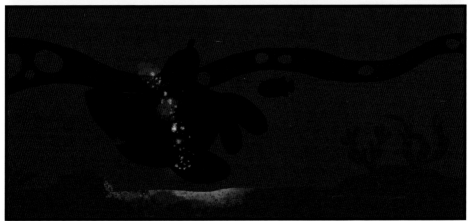

ARE THERE SQUIDS NEARBY?

NO, IT'S US. WE'RE FEEDING ON PLANKTON.

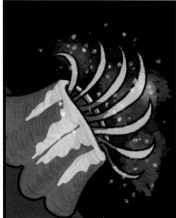

IT'S BRIGHT, LIKE THE SUN.

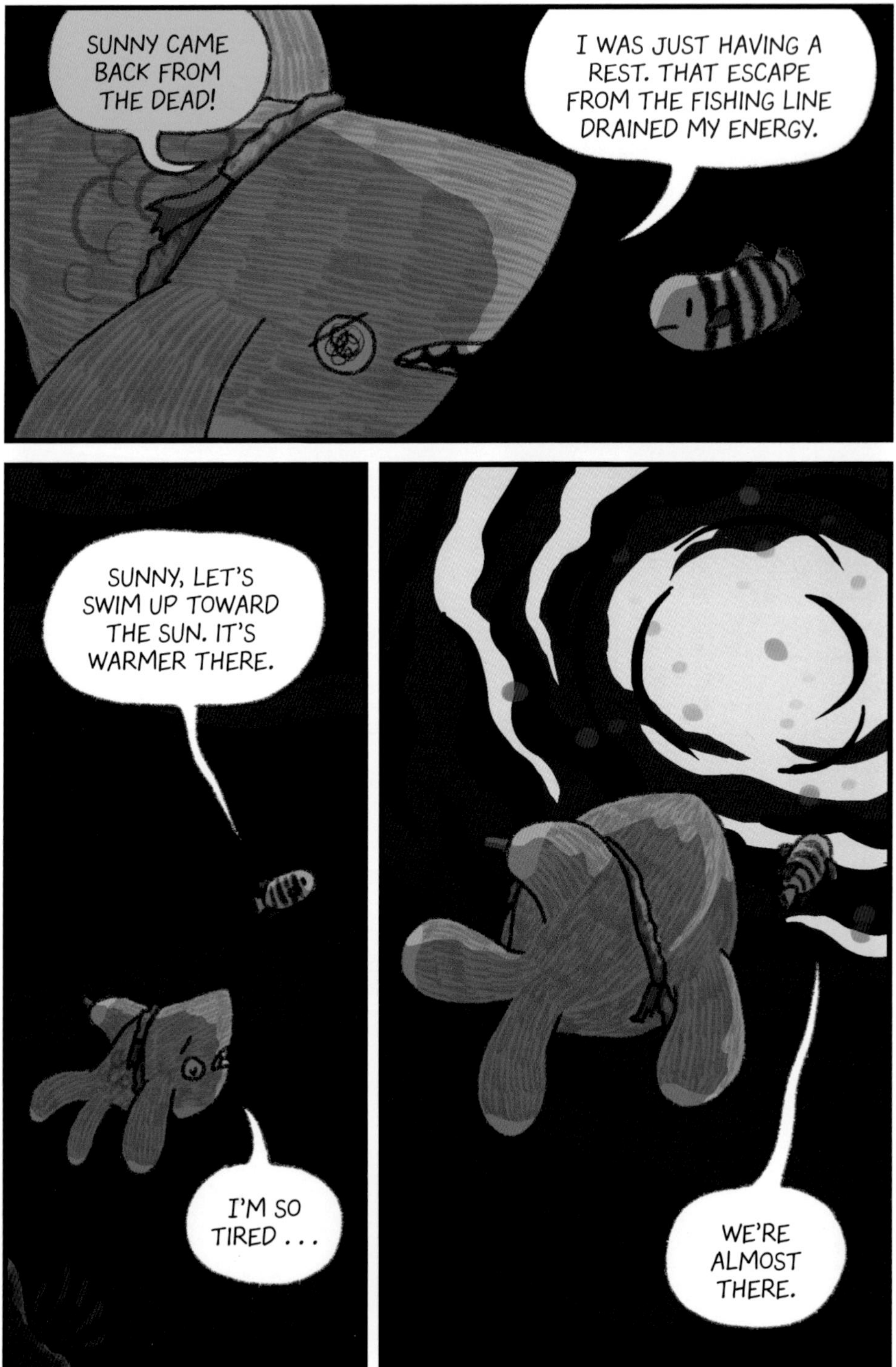
SUNNY CAME BACK FROM THE DEAD!
I WAS JUST HAVING A REST. THAT ESCAPE FROM THE FISHING LINE DRAINED MY ENERGY.
SUNNY, LET'S SWIM UP TOWARD THE SUN. IT'S WARMER THERE.
I'M SO TIRED . . .
WE'RE ALMOST THERE.

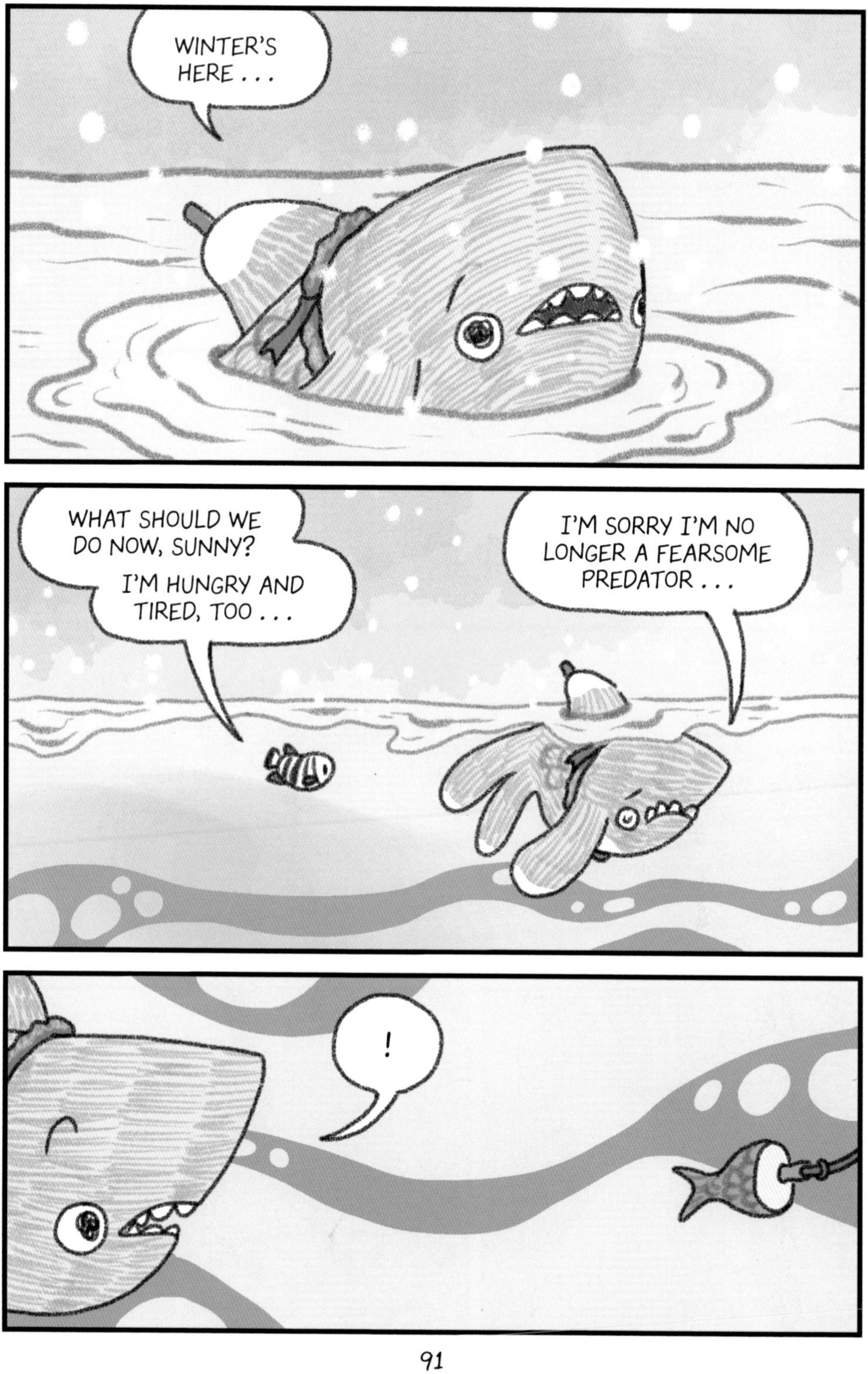
WINTER'S HERE . . .
WHAT SHOULD WE DO NOW, SUNNY?
I'M HUNGRY AND TIRED, TOO . . .
I'M SORRY I'M NO LONGER A FEARSOME PREDATOR . . .
!

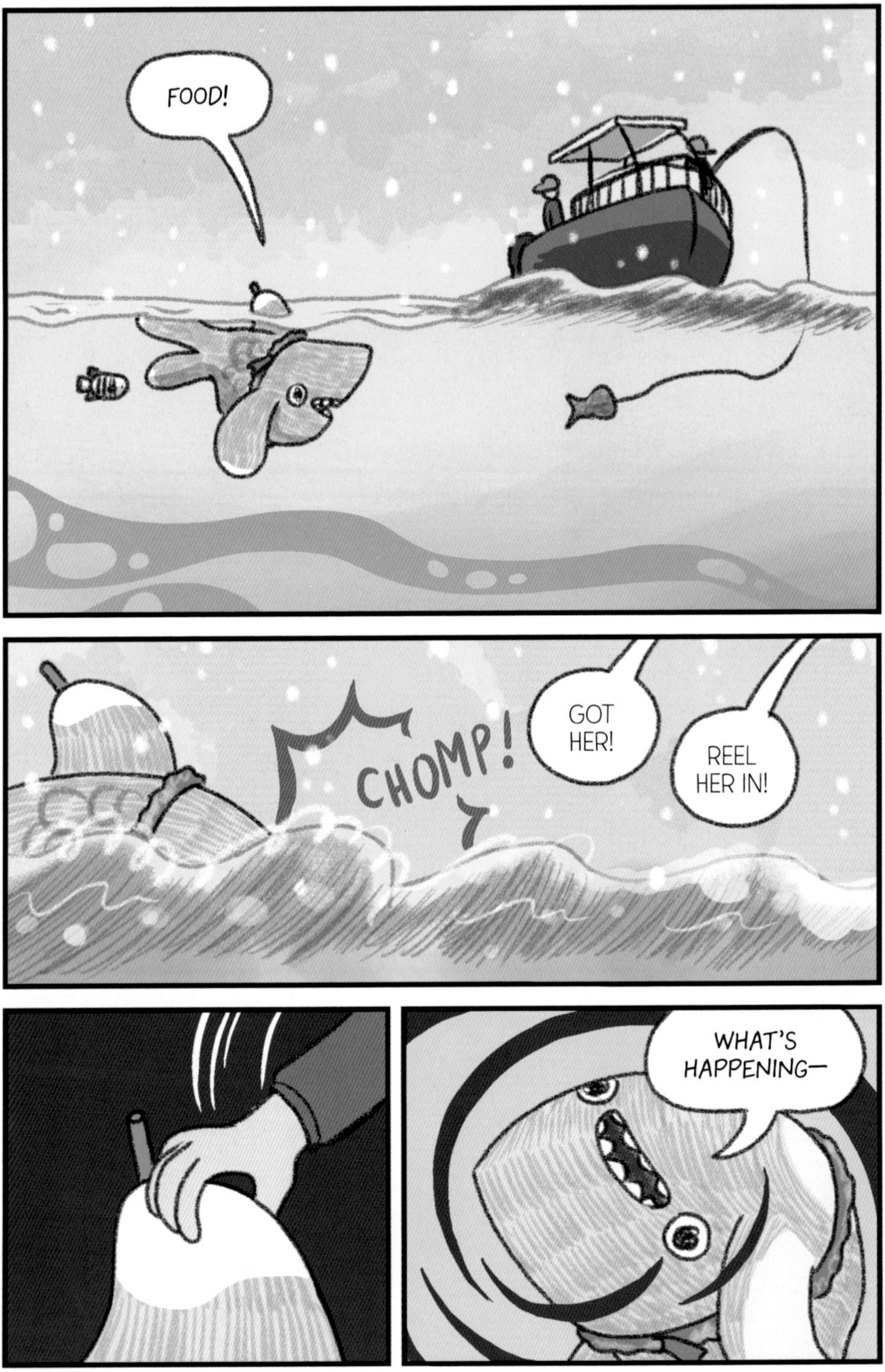
FOOD!
CHOMP!
GOT HER!
REEL HER IN!
WHAT'S HAPPENING—

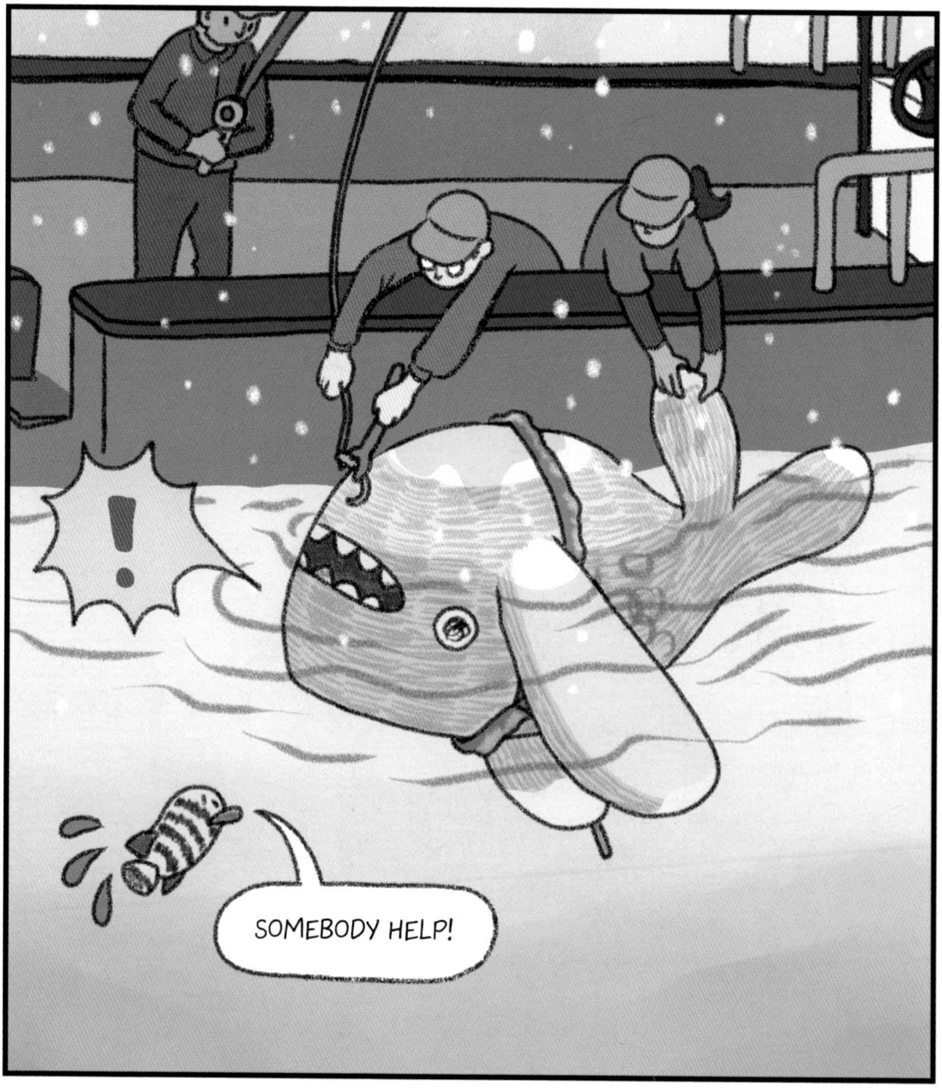
!
SOMEBODY HELP!

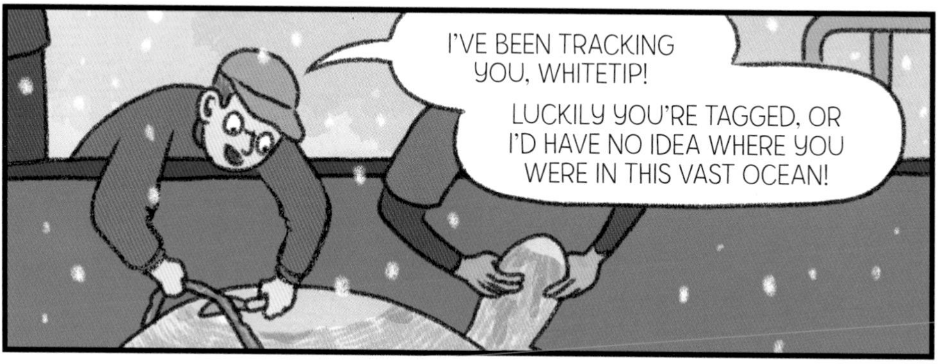
I'VE BEEN TRACKING YOU, WHITETIP!
LUCKILY YOU'RE TAGGED, OR I'D HAVE NO IDEA WHERE YOU WERE IN THIS VAST OCEAN!

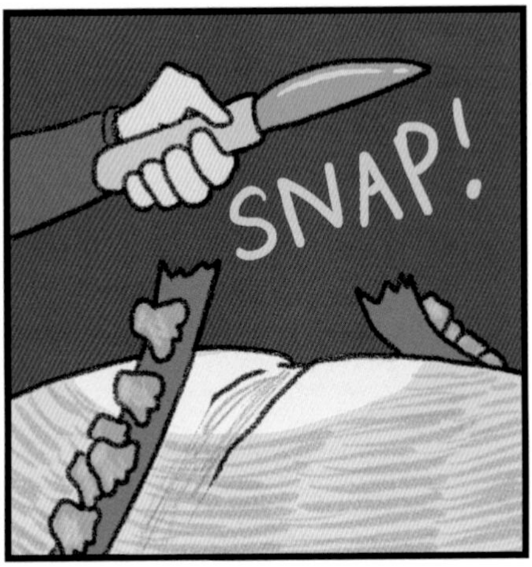
SNAP!

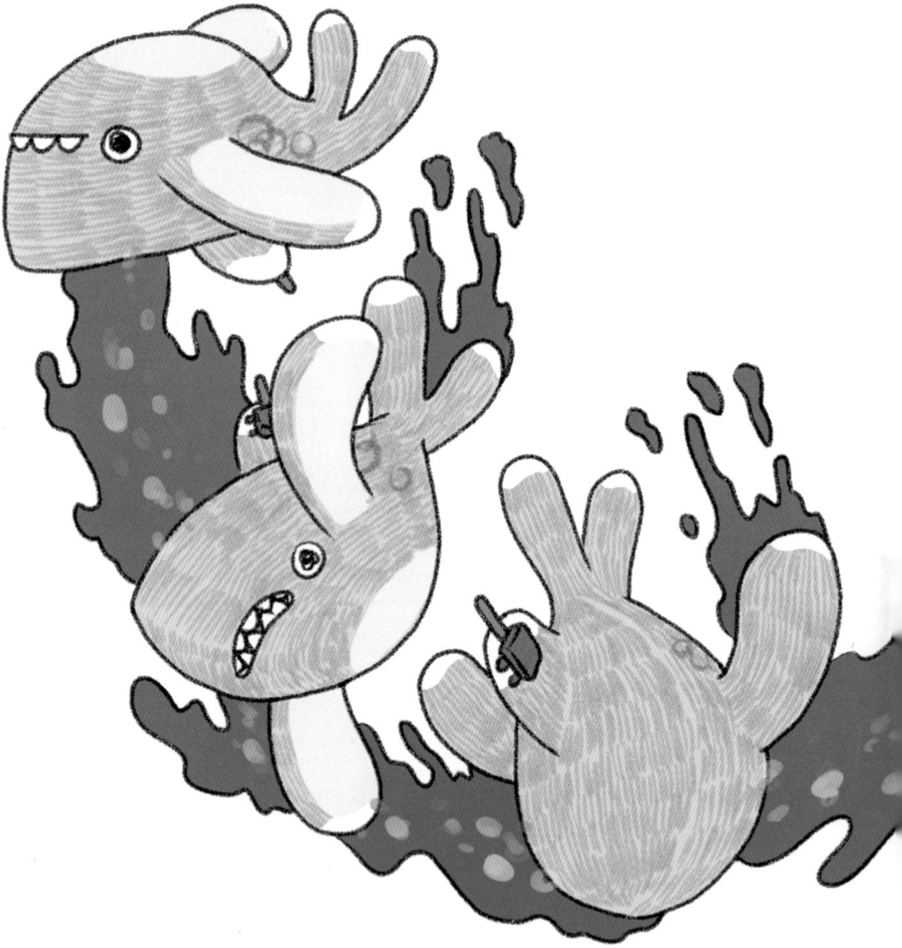

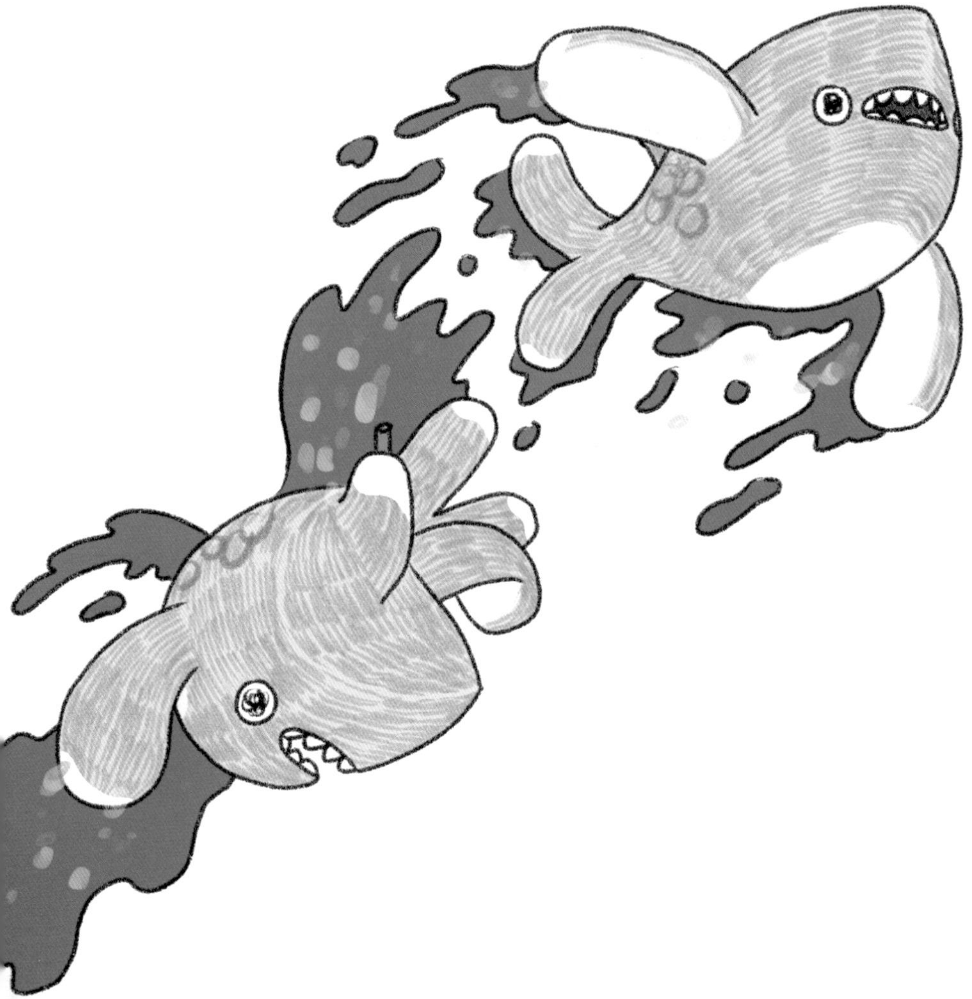

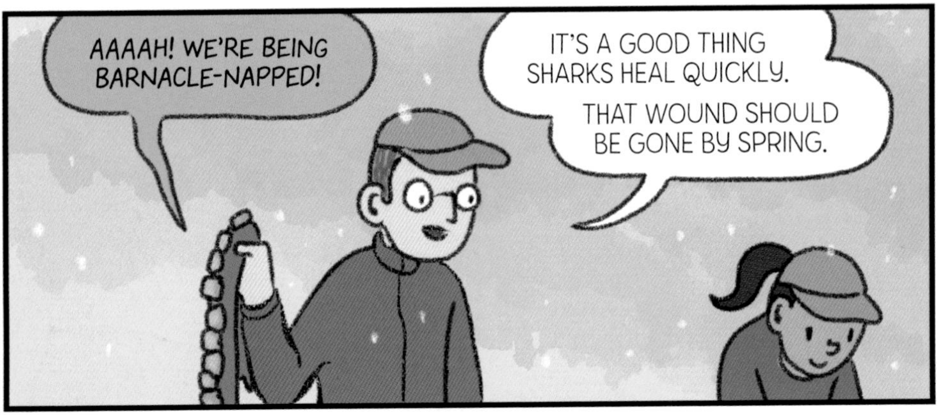
AAAAH! WE'RE BEING BARNACLE-NAPPED!
IT'S A GOOD THING SHARKS HEAL QUICKLY.
THAT WOUND SHOULD BE GONE BY SPRING.

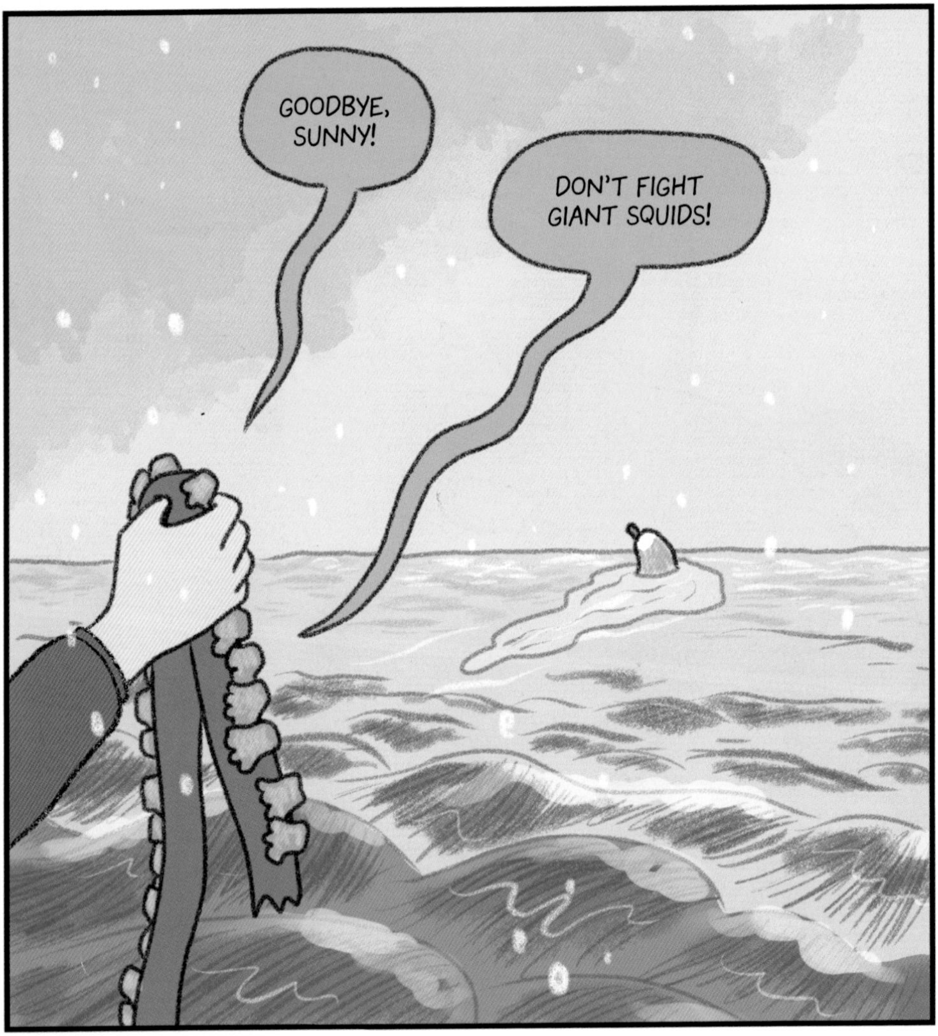
GOODBYE, SUNNY!
DON'T FIGHT GIANT SQUIDS!

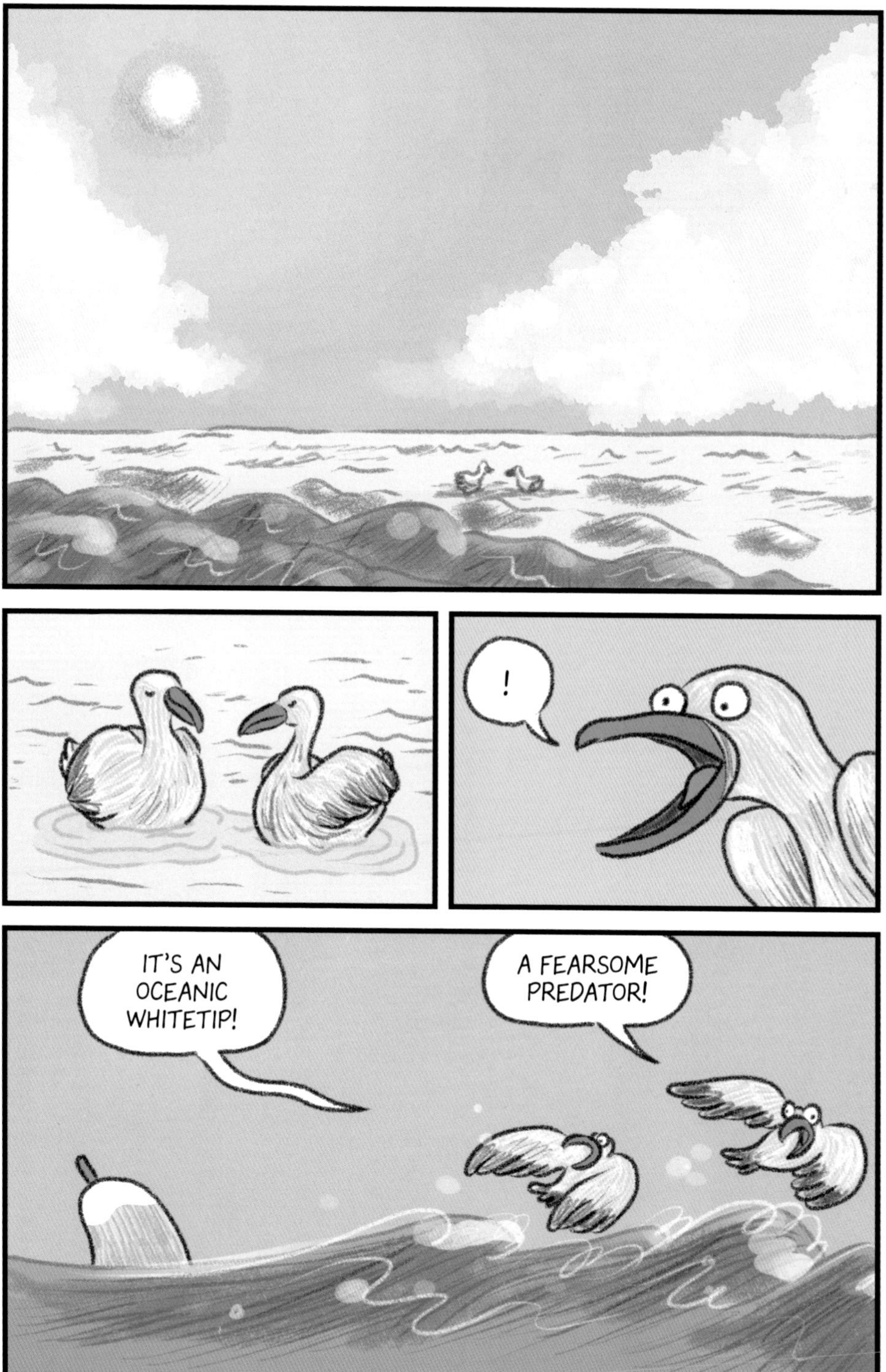
!
IT'S AN OCEANIC WHITETIP!
A FEARSOME PREDATOR!

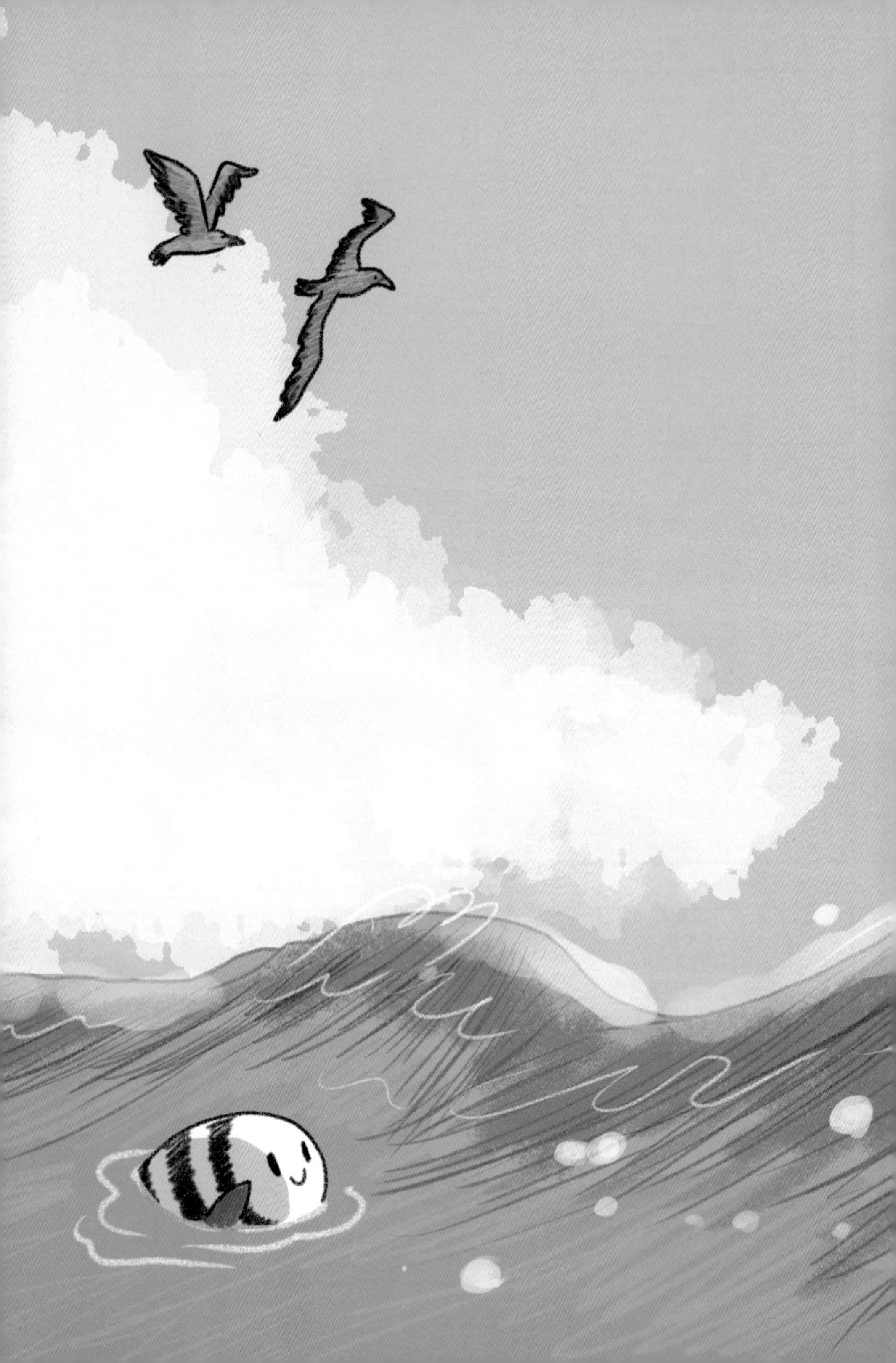

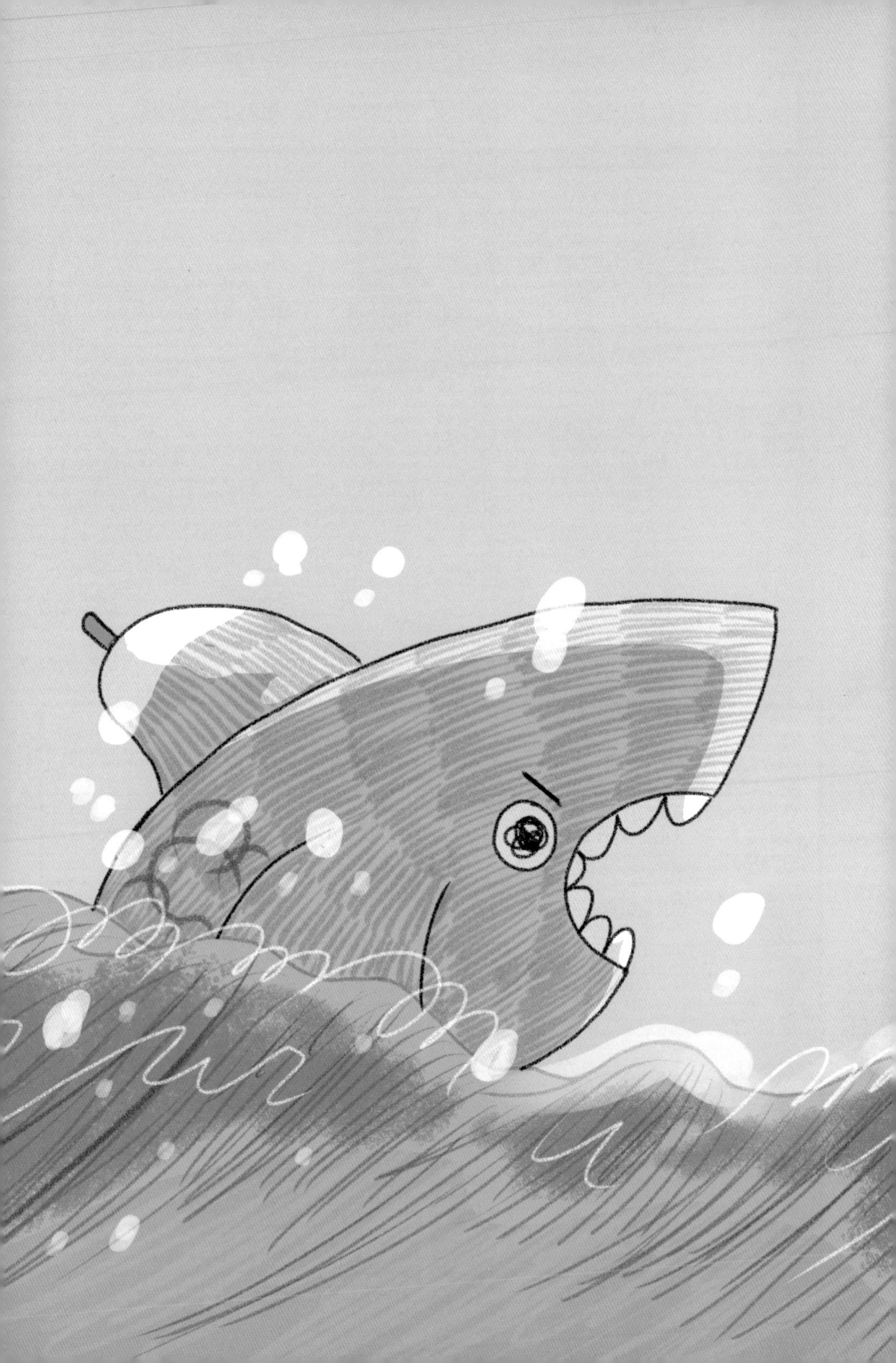

THE TRUE STORY BEHIND SUNNY'S ADVENTURE

IN 2019, DR. JAMES SULIKOWSKI, A PROFESSOR, WAS DOING RESEARCH ON SHARKS OFF THE COAST OF MAINE.

HE REELED IN A SHARK THAT HAD A PLASTIC RING AROUND HER NECK.

HE REMOVED THE PLASTIC, WHICH HAD LEFT HER WOUNDED. HE THEN ATTACHED A SATELLITE TAG—A TRACKING DEVICE—TO HER DORSAL FIN BEFORE RELEASING HER. HE NAMED HER DESTINY.

HIS TEAM WAS ABLE TO TRACK HER MOVEMENTS, AND SHE SEEMED TO BE RECOVERING WELL. SADLY, TWO MONTHS LATER, SHE WAS CAUGHT BY A COMMERCIAL FISHERMAN.

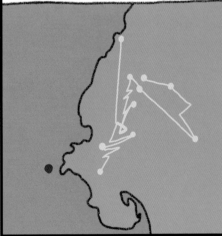

100

WHILE THE PLASTIC ON DESTINY DID NOT REACH HER PECTORAL FIN, AS IT DID FOR SUNNY, IT STILL CUT INTO DESTINY AS SHE GREW.
SHE WOULD NOT HAVE SURVIVED WITHOUT THE PROFESSOR'S HELP.

THE AUTHOR CHOSE TO HAVE THE RIBBON RING FROM THE BALLOON PIN SUNNY'S PECTORAL FIN BACK AS THIS MADE THE DANGERS POSED BY THE PLASTIC MORE OBVIOUS TO READERS.

DESTINY WAS ALSO A PORBEAGLE SHARK, NOT AN OCEANIC WHITETIP LIKE SUNNY. THE AUTHOR MADE THIS CHANGE BECAUSE SHE WANTED SUNNY TO HAVE A FRIEND TO TALK TO DURING HER JOURNEY.

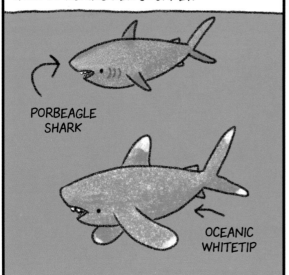

PORBEAGLE SHARK

OCEANIC WHITETIP

IN REAL LIFE, MOST SHARKS ARE SOLITARY. HOWEVER, SOME SHARKS ARE FOLLOWED BY PILOT FISH.

THAT'S US!

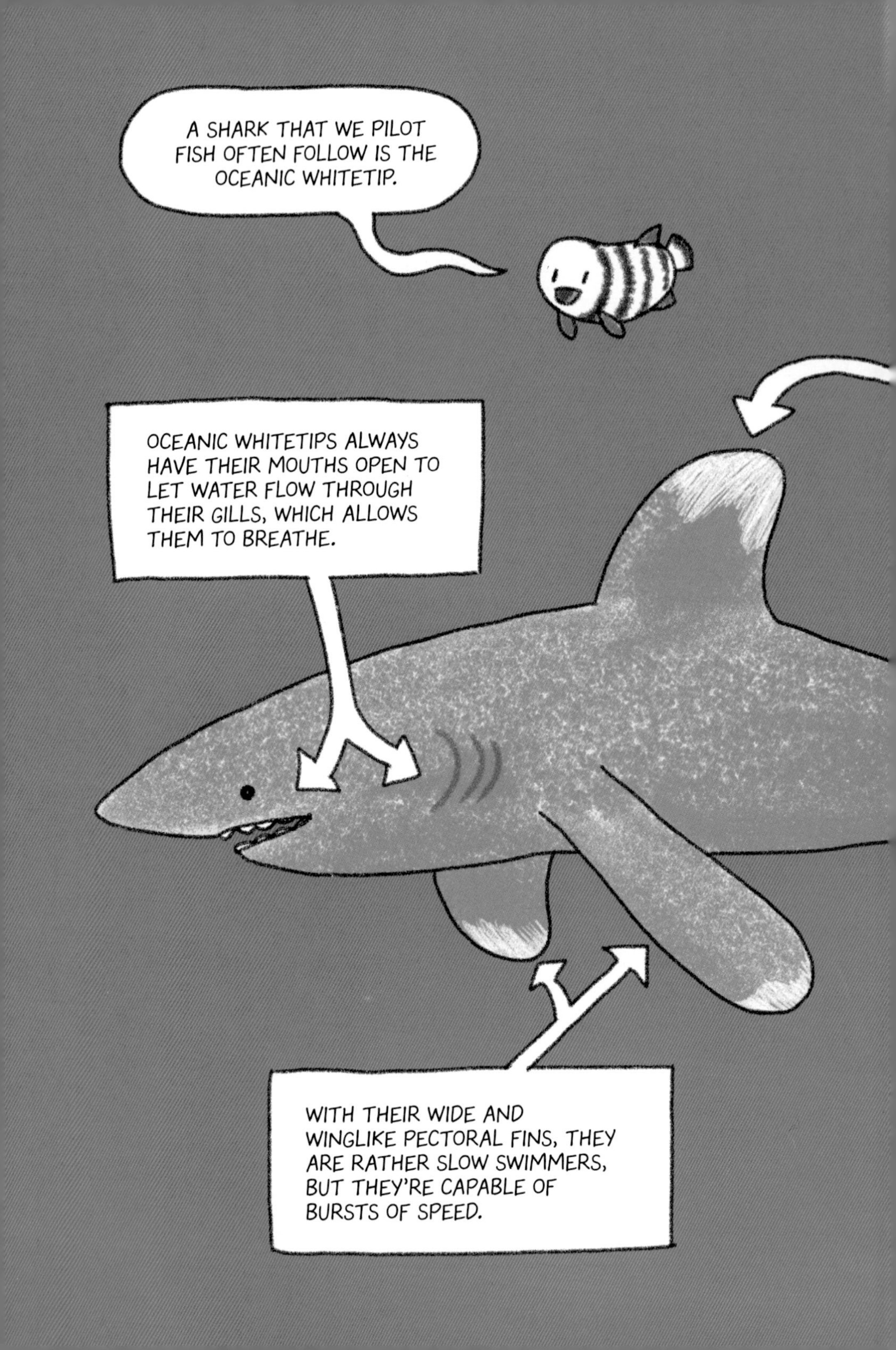
A SHARK THAT WE PILOT FISH OFTEN FOLLOW IS THE OCEANIC WHITETIP.
OCEANIC WHITETIPS ALWAYS HAVE THEIR MOUTHS OPEN TO LET WATER FLOW THROUGH THEIR GILLS, WHICH ALLOWS THEM TO BREATHE.
WITH THEIR WIDE AND WINGLIKE PECTORAL FINS, THEY ARE RATHER SLOW SWIMMERS, BUT THEY'RE CAPABLE OF BURSTS OF SPEED.

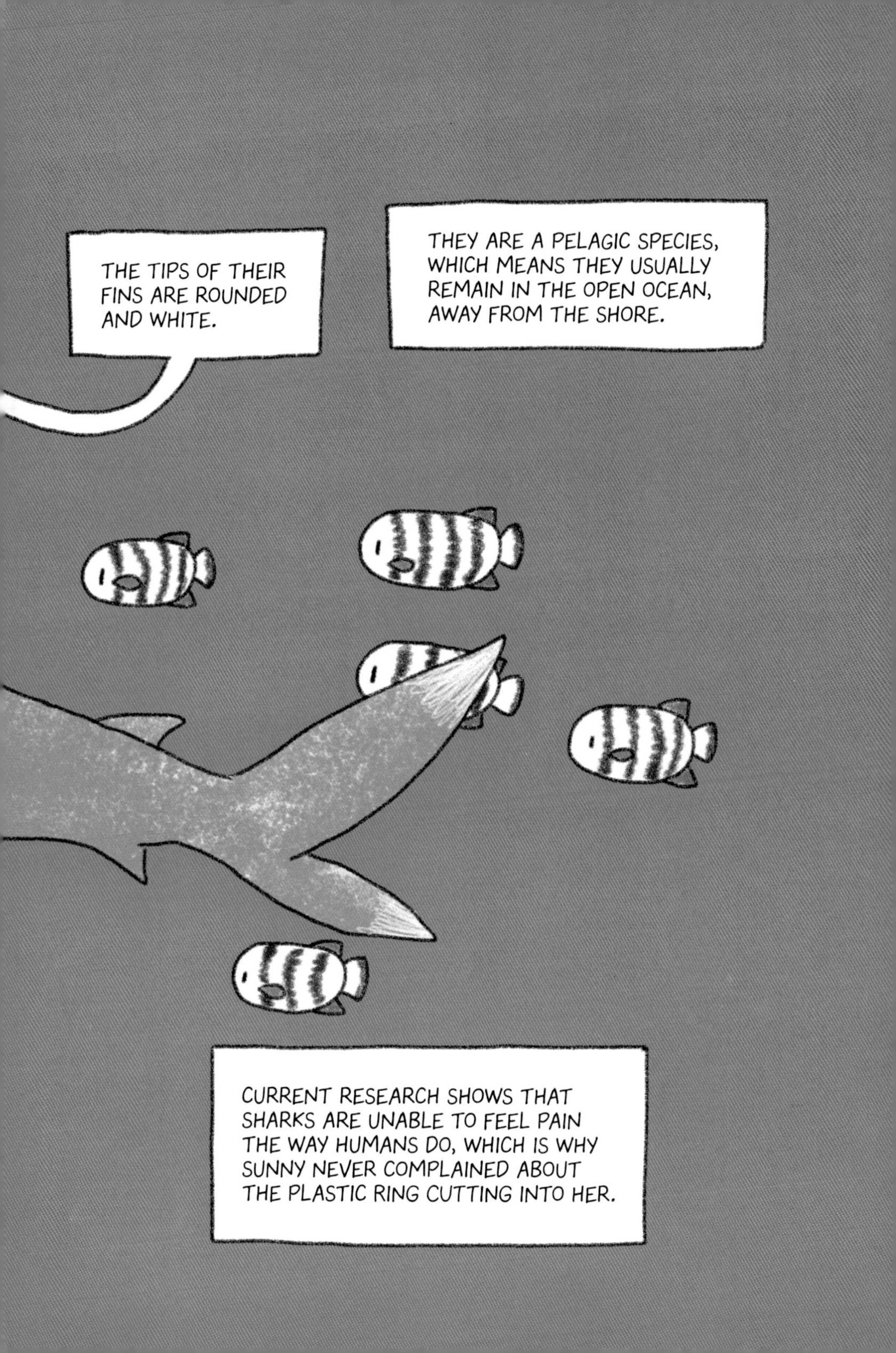
THE TIPS OF THEIR FINS ARE ROUNDED AND WHITE.
THEY ARE A PELAGIC SPECIES, WHICH MEANS THEY USUALLY REMAIN IN THE OPEN OCEAN, AWAY FROM THE SHORE.
CURRENT RESEARCH SHOWS THAT SHARKS ARE UNABLE TO FEEL PAIN THE WAY HUMANS DO, WHICH IS WHY SUNNY NEVER COMPLAINED ABOUT THE PLASTIC RING CUTTING INTO HER.

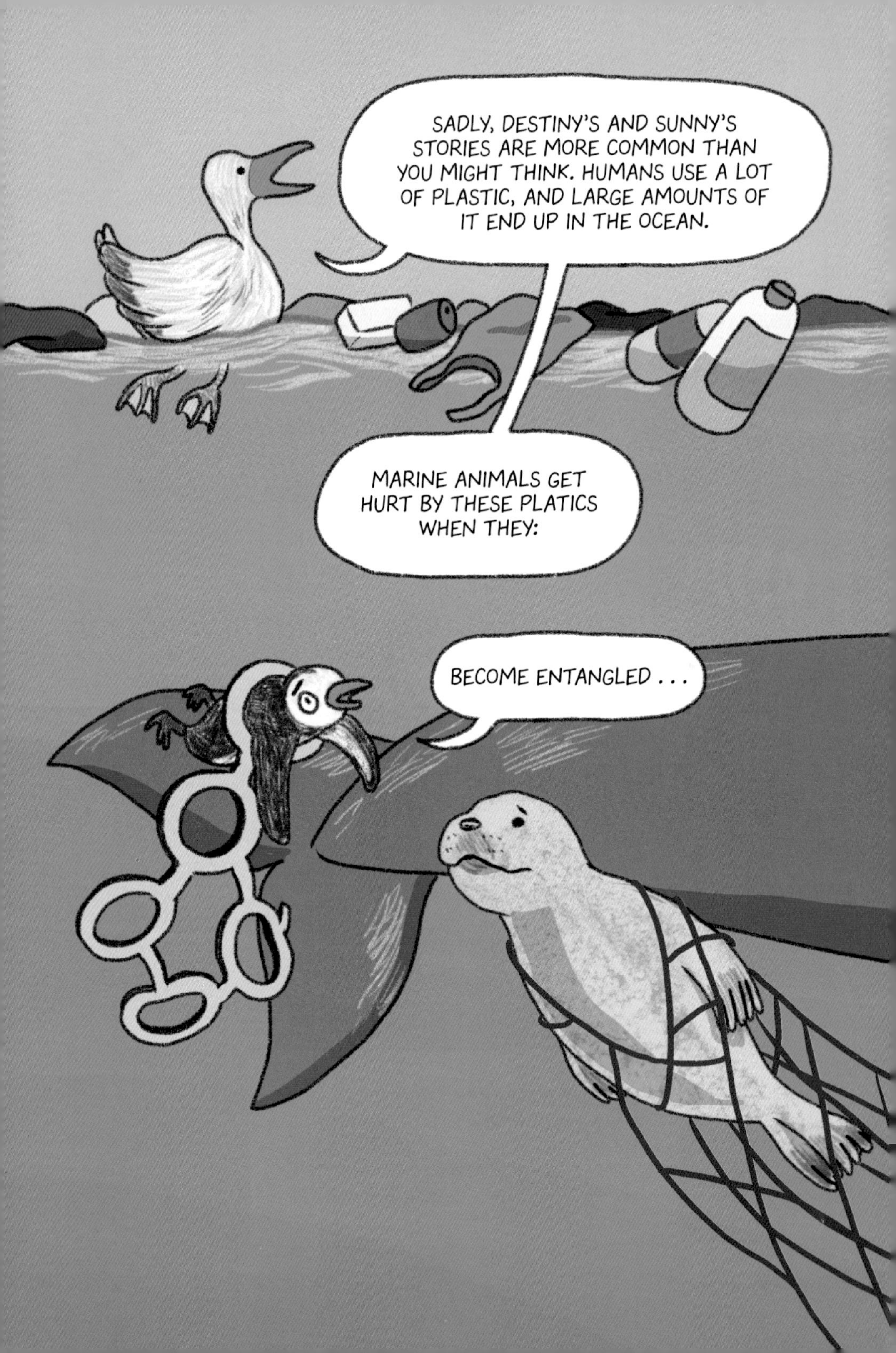
SADLY, DESTINY'S AND SUNNY'S STORIES ARE MORE COMMON THAN YOU MIGHT THINK. HUMANS USE A LOT OF PLASTIC, AND LARGE AMOUNTS OF IT END UP IN THE OCEAN.
MARINE ANIMALS GET HURT BY THESE PLATICS WHEN THEY:
BECOME ENTANGLED . . .

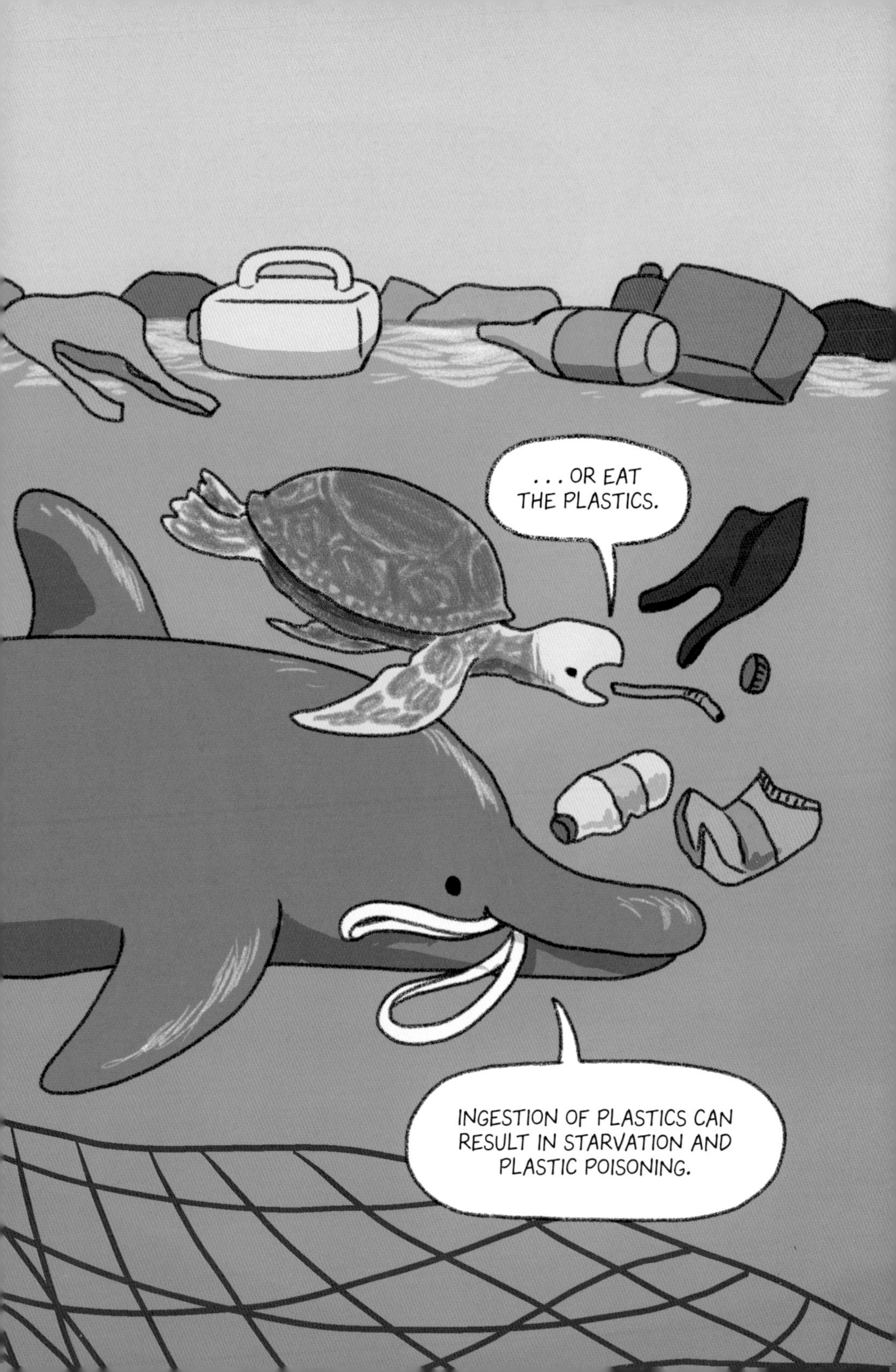
. . . OR EAT
THE PLASTICS.
INGESTION OF PLASTICS CAN
RESULT IN STARVATION AND
PLASTIC POISONING.

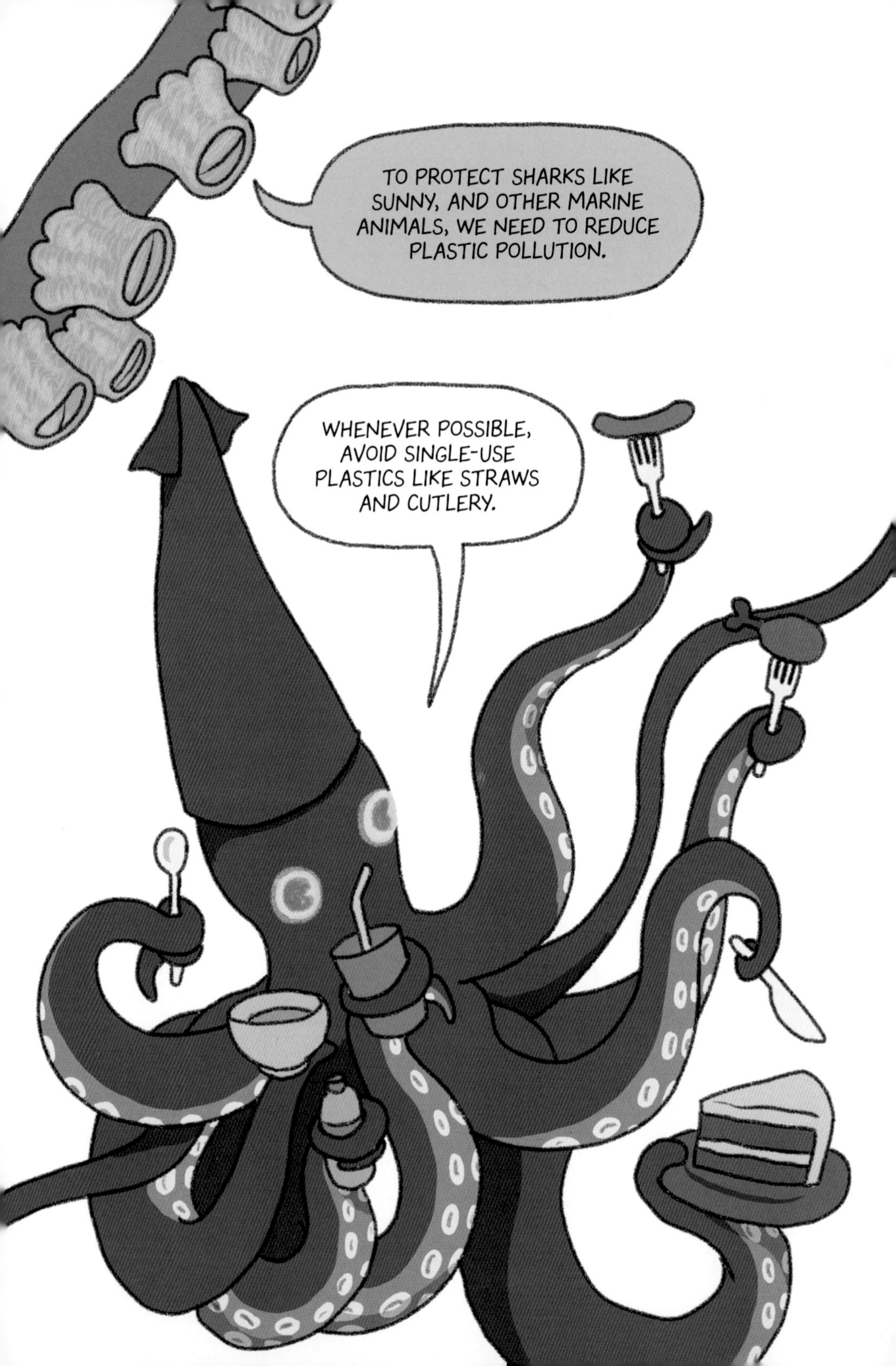
TO PROTECT SHARKS LIKE SUNNY, AND OTHER MARINE ANIMALS, WE NEED TO REDUCE PLASTIC POLLUTION.
WHENEVER POSSIBLE, AVOID SINGLE-USE PLASTICS LIKE STRAWS AND CUTLERY.

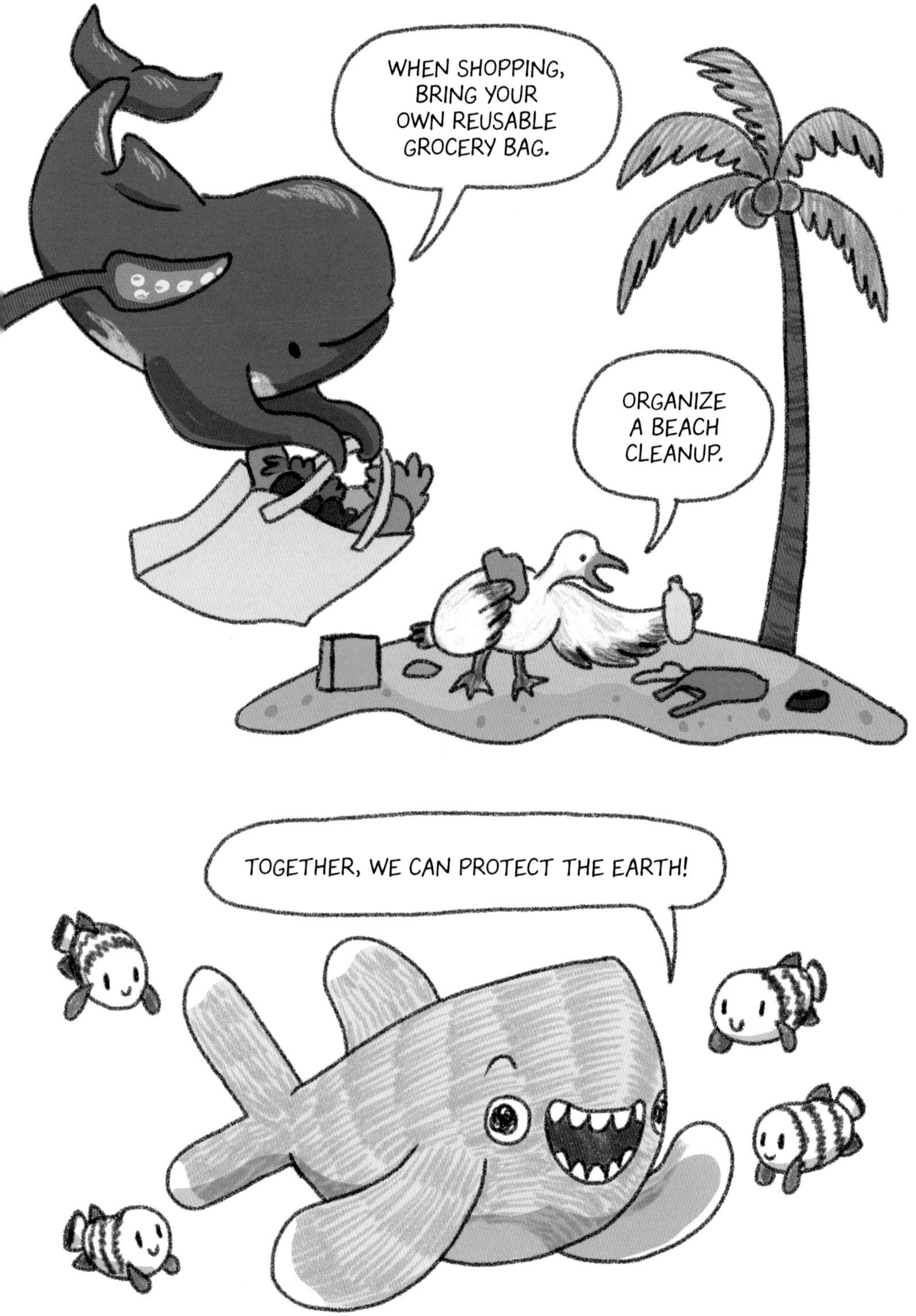
WHEN SHOPPING, BRING YOUR OWN REUSABLE GROCERY BAG.
ORGANIZE A BEACH CLEANUP.
TOGETHER, WE CAN PROTECT THE EARTH!

ARE YOU READY TO EMBARK ON MORE EXCITING ADVENTURES? THE WILDERNESS AWAITS IN:

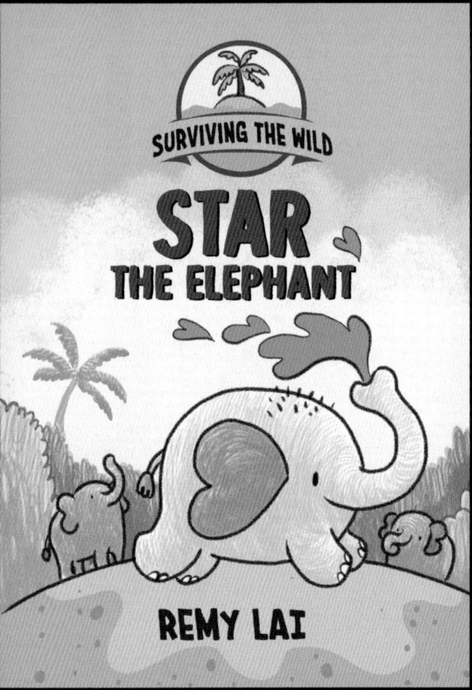
SURVIVING THE WILD
STAR
THE ELEPHANT
REMY LAI

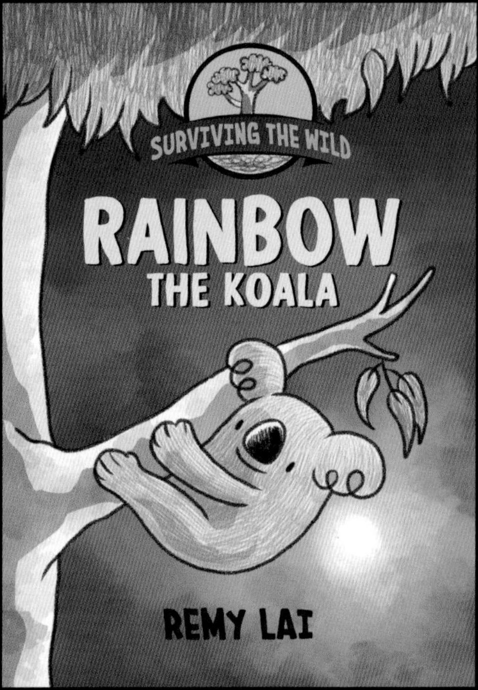
SURVIVING THE WILD
RAINBOW
THE KOALA
REMY LAI

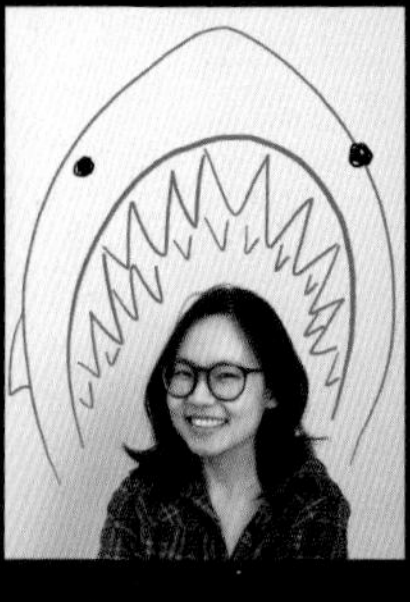

REMY LAI was born in Indonesia, grew up in Singapore, and currently lives in Brisbane, Australia, where she writes and draws stories for kids with her two dogs by her side. She is also the author of the critically acclaimed *Pie in the Sky*, *Fly on the Wall*, and *Pawcasso*. **remylai.com**